S0-AKB-657

• CUBE KID •

DIARY OF AN 8-BIT WARRIOR
GRAPHIC NOVEL

AN OMINOUS THREAT

STORY ADAPTED BY
PIRATE SOURCIL

ILLUSTRATED BY
JEZ

COLORED BY
ODONE

Andrews McMeel
PUBLISHING®

Here we go with another comic! Thanks again to the team. What an adventure! Special thanks to Marion as well for her continued support. And, of course, thank you, reader!

THOMAS

My thanks to the team, Joël, Thomas, and Anne-Charlotte; Cyrine; and everyone who has worked on this comic. Thanks again to Cube Kid for letting us play with his characters. Thanks to my family and friends for their support. Love to my darling Maite and my children, Meryl and Eliot. Thanks to our readers. The next one will be even better!

JEZ

Translated and based on the series of novels originally created by Cube Kid © 404 éditions, a department of Édi8. Text by Pirate Sourcil, illustrations by Jez, and colors by Odone © 2019 Editions Jungle/Édi8.

Minecraft is a Notch Development AB registered trademark. This book is a work of fiction and not an official Minecraft product, nor approved by or associated with Mojang. The other names, characters, places, and plots are either imagined by the author or used fictitiously.

Andrews McMeel Publishing
a division of Andrews McMeel Universal
1130 Walnut Street, Kansas City, Missouri 64106
www.andrewsmcmeel.com

21 22 23 24 25 SDB 10 9 8 7 6 5 4 3 2 1

ISBN: 978-1-5248-6317-3 (Paperback)
ISBN: 978-1-5248-6809-3 (Hardback)

Library of Congress Control Number: 2021930968

Made by:
King Yip (Dongguan) Printing & Packaging Factory Ltd.
Address and location of manufacturer:
Daning Administrative District, Humen Town
Dongguan Guangdong, China 523930
1st printing—5/31/21

ATTENTION: SCHOOLS AND BUSINESSES
Andrews McMeel books are available at quantity discounts with bulk purchase for educational, business, or sales promotional use. For information, please e-mail the Andrews McMeel Publishing Special Sales Department: specialsales@amuniversal.com.

PART ONE

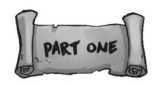

CROSSING THE DESERT

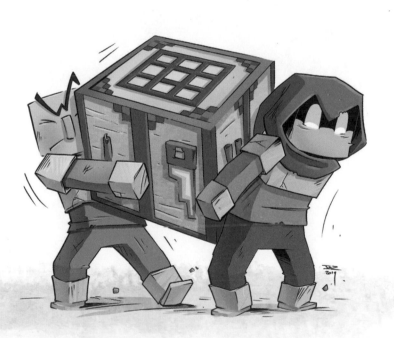

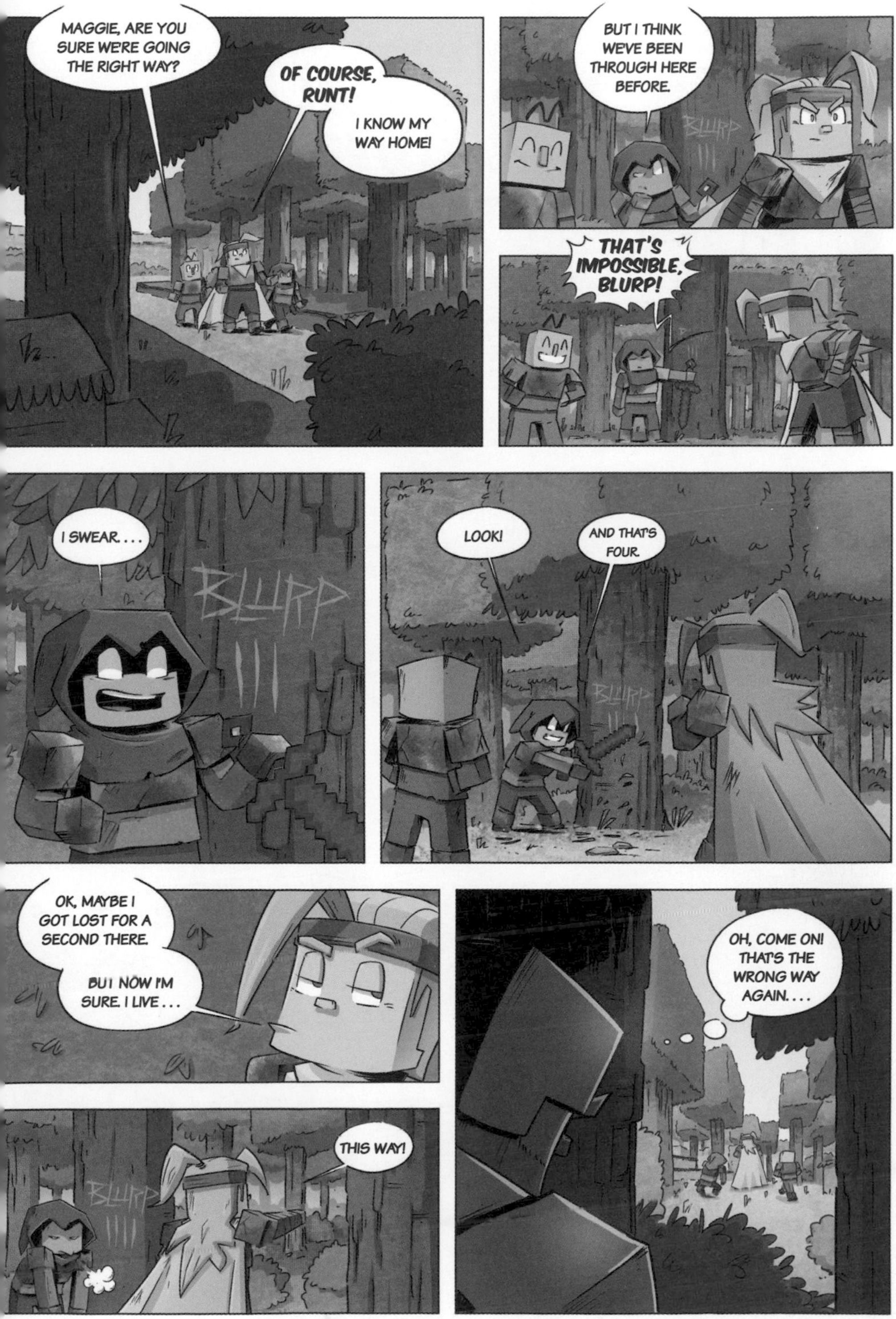
MAGGIE, ARE YOU SURE WE'RE GOING THE RIGHT WAY?
OF COURSE, RUNT!
I KNOW MY WAY HOME!
BUT I THINK WE'VE BEEN THROUGH HERE BEFORE.
BLURP
THAT'S IMPOSSIBLE, BLURP!
I SWEAR . . .
BLURP
LOOK!
AND THAT'S FOUR.
BLURP
OK, MAYBE I GOT LOST FOR A SECOND THERE.
BUT NOW I'M SURE. I LIVE . . .
THIS WAY!
BLURP
OH, COME ON! THAT'S THE WRONG WAY AGAIN. . . .

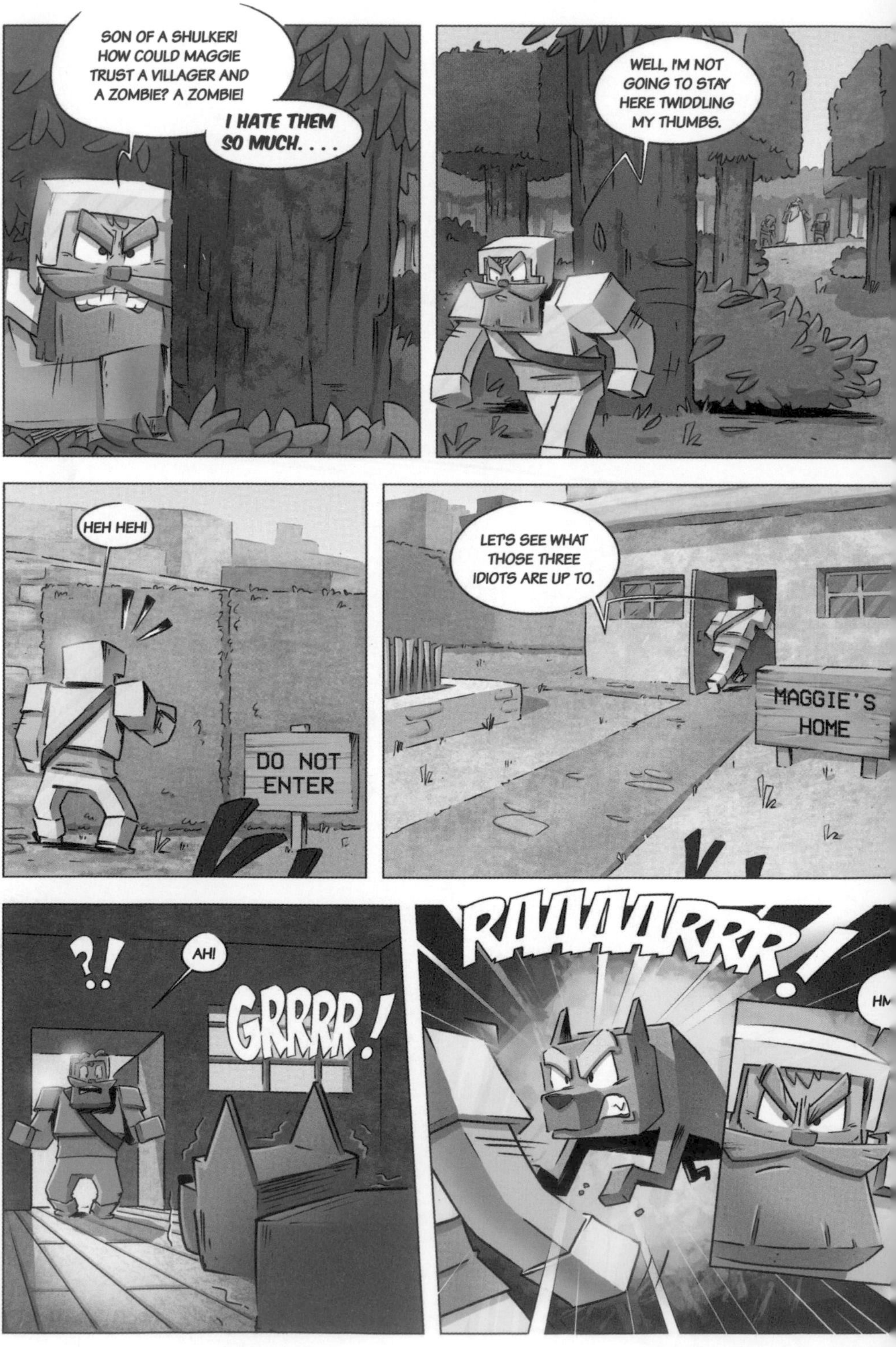
SON OF A SHULKER! HOW COULD MAGGIE TRUST A VILLAGER AND A ZOMBIE? A ZOMBIE!
I HATE THEM SO MUCH. . . .
WELL, I'M NOT GOING TO STAY HERE TWIDDLING MY THUMBS.
HEH HEH!
DO NOT ENTER
LET'S SEE WHAT THOSE THREE IDIOTS ARE UP TO.
MAGGIE'S HOME
?!
AH!
GRRRR!
RAVVVVARRRR!

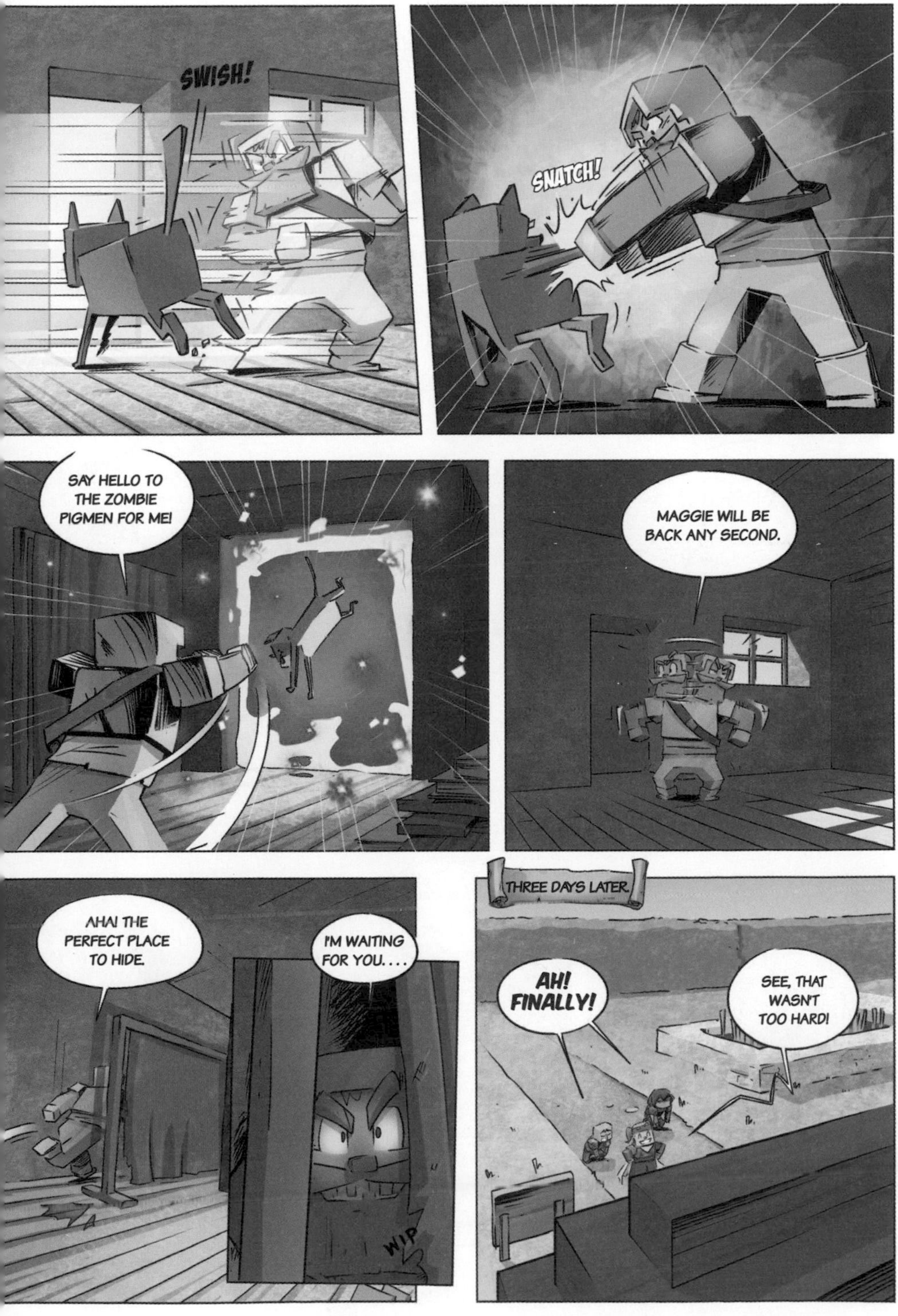
SWISH!
SNATCH!
SAY HELLO TO THE ZOMBIE PIGMEN FOR ME!
MAGGIE WILL BE BACK ANY SECOND.
AHA! THE PERFECT PLACE TO HIDE.
I'M WAITING FOR YOU. . . .
WIP
THREE DAYS LATER.
AH! FINALLY!
SEE, THAT WASN'T TOO HARD!

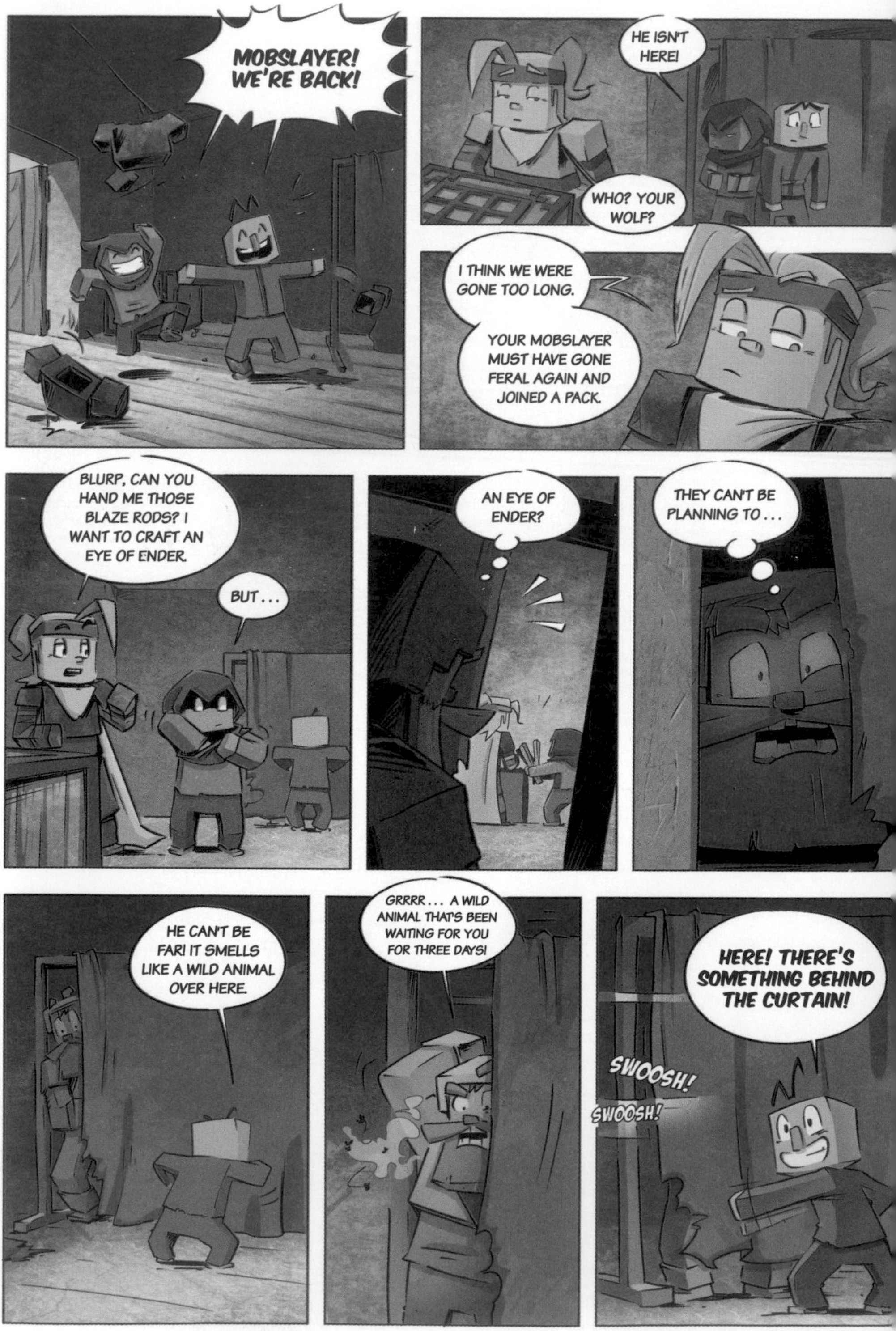
MOBSLAYER! WE'RE BACK!
HE ISN'T HERE!
WHO? YOUR WOLF?
I THINK WE WERE GONE TOO LONG.
YOUR MOBSLAYER MUST HAVE GONE FERAL AGAIN AND JOINED A PACK.
BLURP, CAN YOU HAND ME THOSE BLAZE RODS? I WANT TO CRAFT AN EYE OF ENDER.
BUT . . .
AN EYE OF ENDER?
THEY CAN'T BE PLANNING TO . . .
HE CAN'T BE FAR! IT SMELLS LIKE A WILD ANIMAL OVER HERE.
GRRRR . . . A WILD ANIMAL THAT'S BEEN WAITING FOR YOU FOR THREE DAYS!
HERE! THERE'S SOMETHING BEHIND THE CURTAIN!
SWOOSH!
SWOOSH!

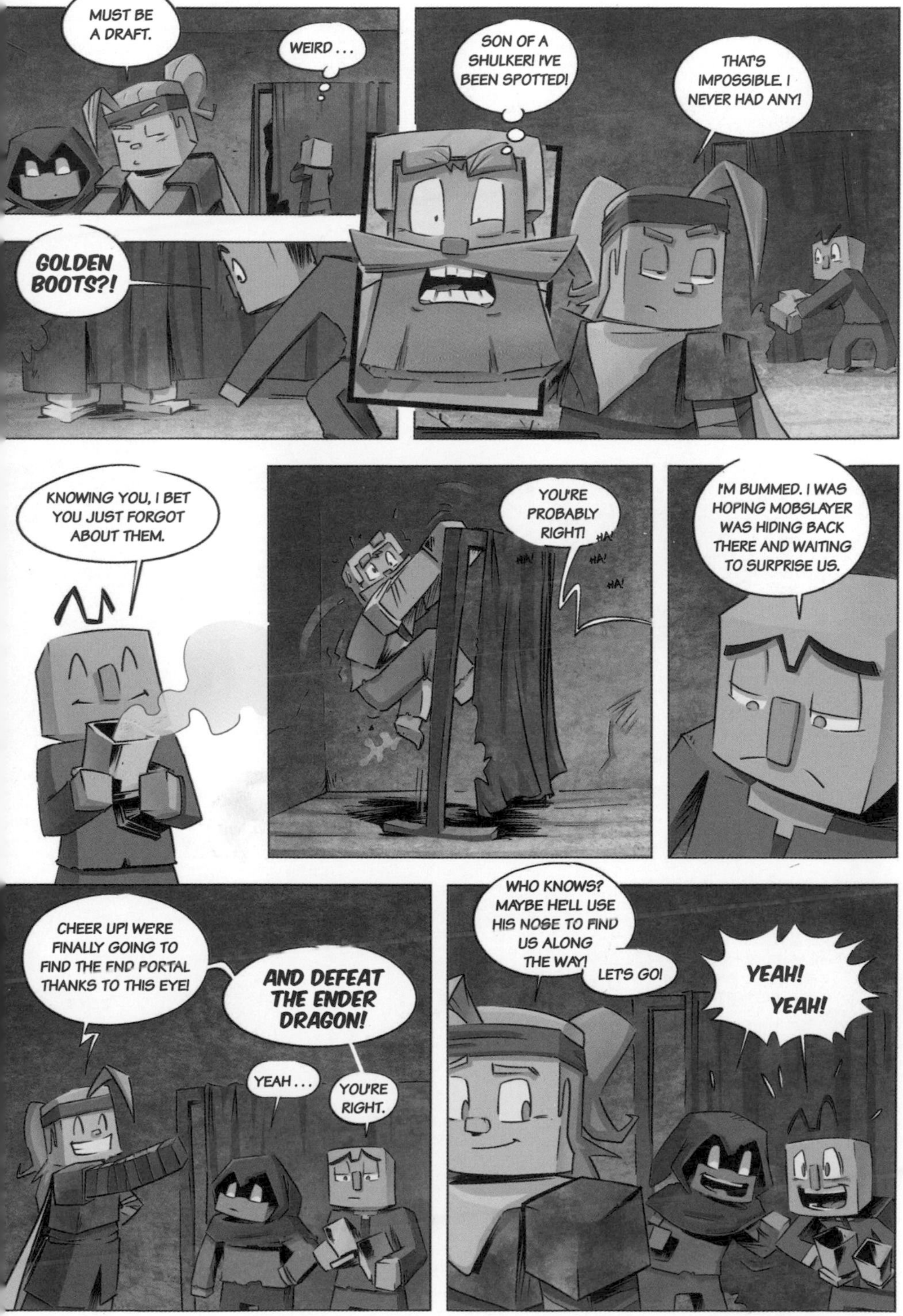
MUST BE A DRAFT.
WEIRD . . .
SON OF A SHULKER! I'VE BEEN SPOTTED!
THAT'S IMPOSSIBLE. I NEVER HAD ANY!
GOLDEN BOOTS?!
KNOWING YOU, I BET YOU JUST FORGOT ABOUT THEM.
YOU'RE PROBABLY RIGHT!
HA! HA! HA! HA!
I'M BUMMED. I WAS HOPING MOBSLAYER WAS HIDING BACK THERE AND WAITING TO SURPRISE US.
CHEER UP! WE'RE FINALLY GOING TO FIND THE END PORTAL THANKS TO THIS EYE!
AND DEFEAT THE ENDER DRAGON!
YEAH . . .
YOU'RE RIGHT.
WHO KNOWS? MAYBE HE'LL USE HIS NOSE TO FIND US ALONG THE WAY!
LET'S GO!
YEAH!
YEAH!

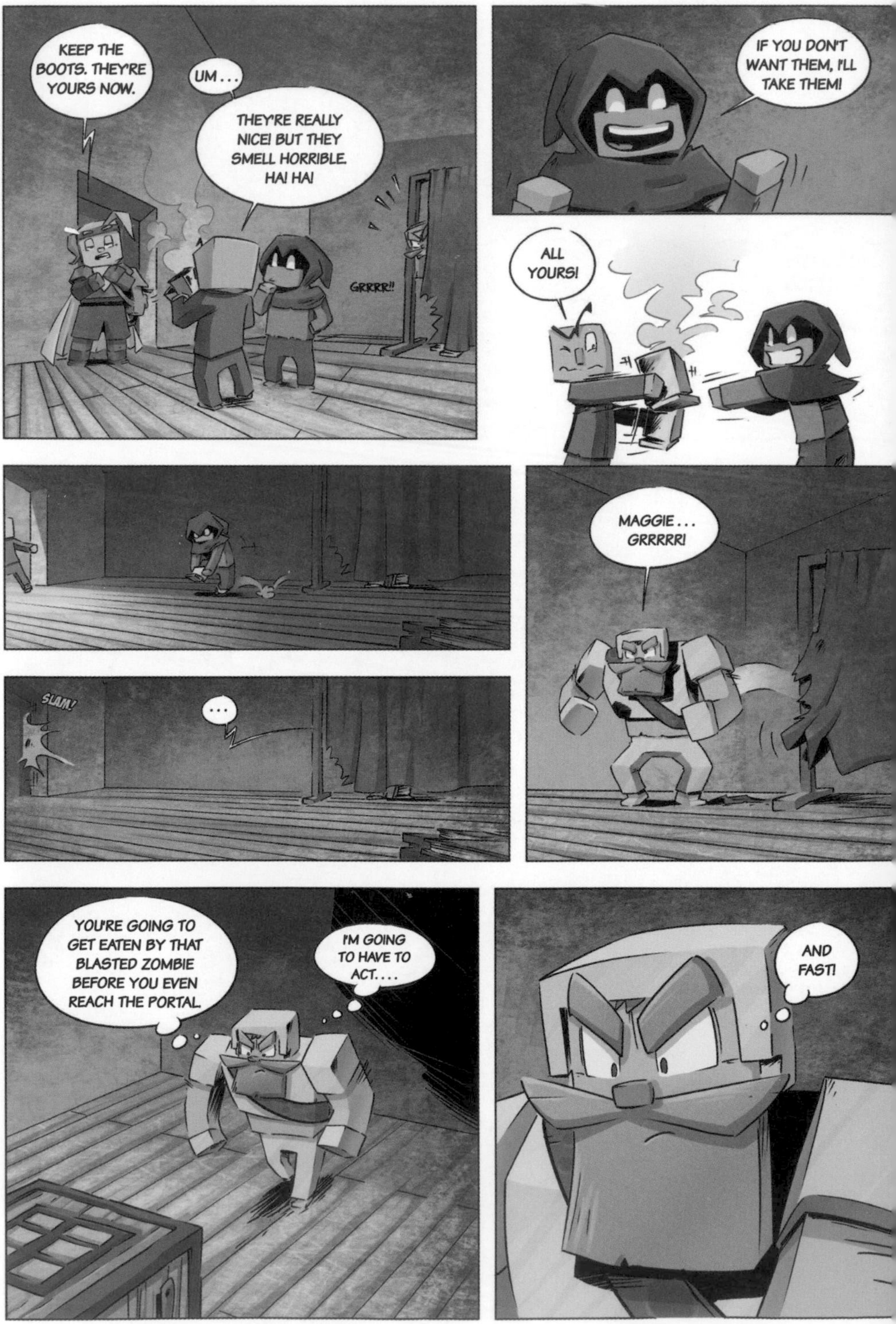
KEEP THE BOOTS. THEY'RE YOURS NOW.
UM . . .
THEY'RE REALLY NICE! BUT THEY SMELL HORRIBLE. HA! HA!
GRRRR!!
IF YOU DON'T WANT THEM, I'LL TAKE THEM!
ALL YOURS!
SLAM!
. . .
MAGGIE . . . GRRRRR!
YOU'RE GOING TO GET EATEN BY THAT BLASTED ZOMBIE BEFORE YOU EVEN REACH THE PORTAL.
I'M GOING TO HAVE TO ACT. . . .
AND FAST!

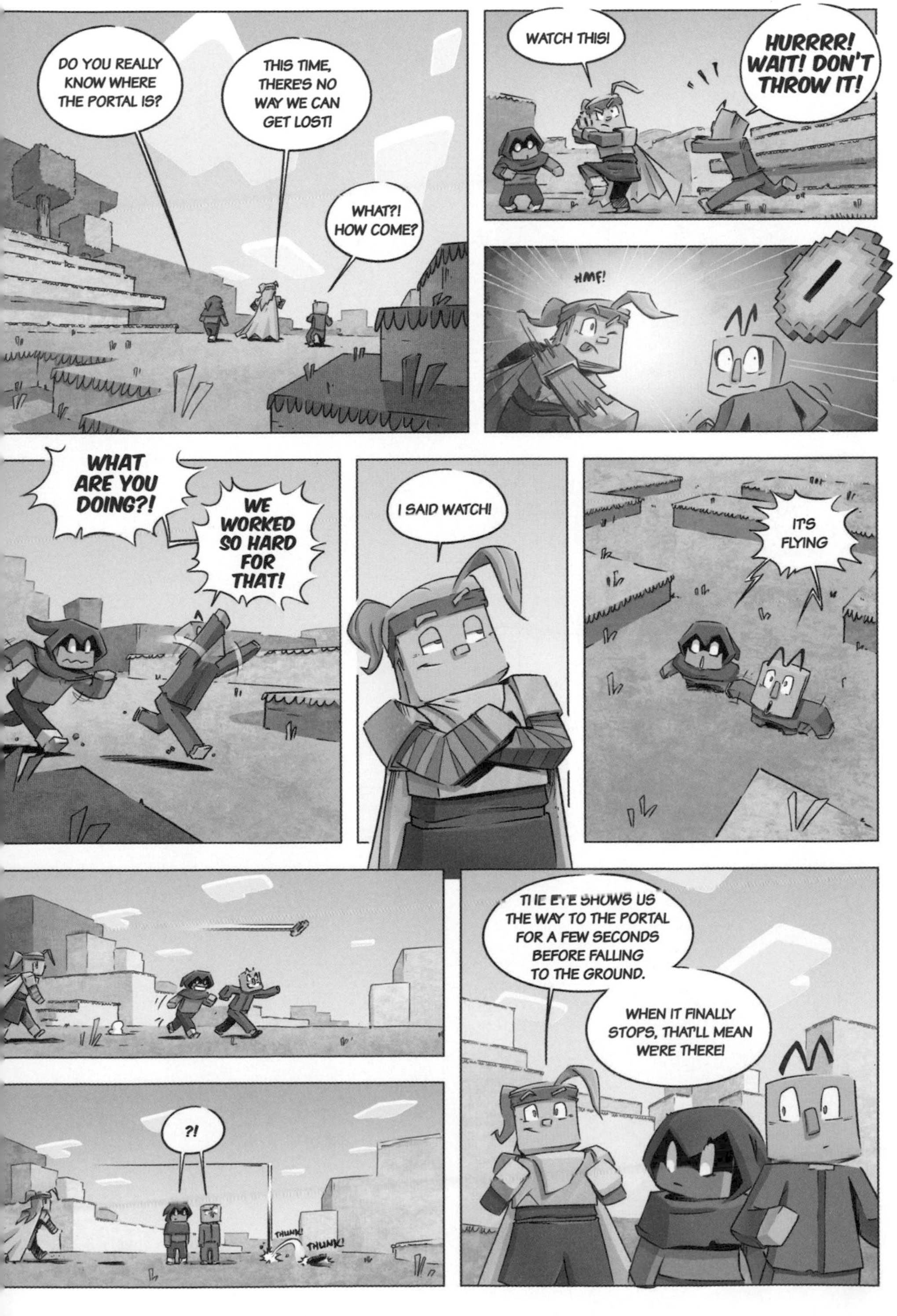
DO YOU REALLY KNOW WHERE THE PORTAL IS?
THIS TIME, THERE'S NO WAY WE CAN GET LOST!
WHAT?! HOW COME?
WATCH THIS!
HURRRR! WAIT! DON'T THROW IT!
HMF!
WHAT ARE YOU DOING?!
WE WORKED SO HARD FOR THAT!
I SAID WATCH!
IT'S FLYING
?!
THUNK!
THUNK!
THE EYE SHOWS US THE WAY TO THE PORTAL FOR A FEW SECONDS BEFORE FALLING TO THE GROUND.
WHEN IT FINALLY STOPS, THAT'LL MEAN WE'RE THERE!

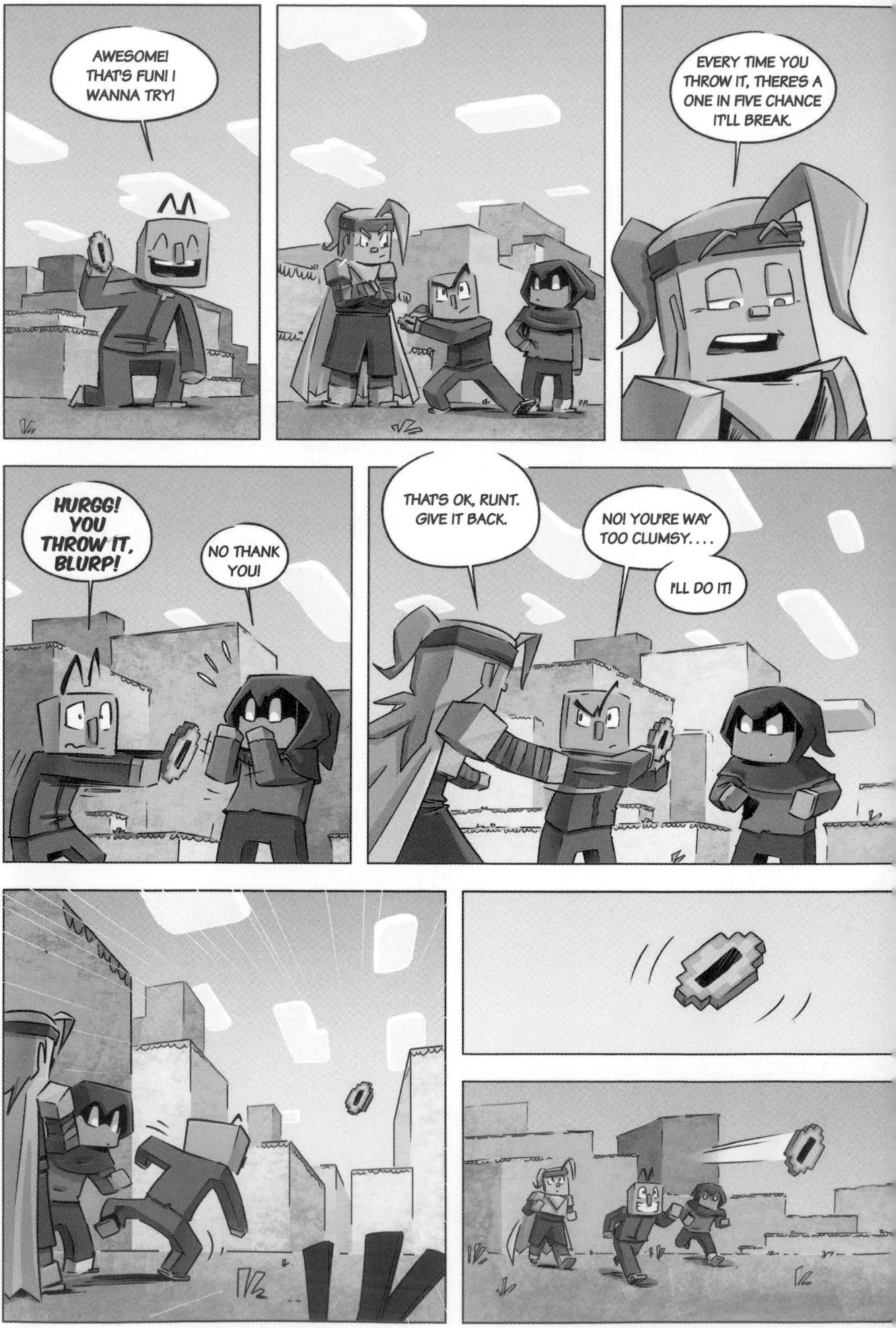
AWESOME! THAT'S FUN! I WANNA TRY!
EVERY TIME YOU THROW IT, THERE'S A ONE IN FIVE CHANCE IT'LL BREAK.
HURGG! YOU THROW IT, BLURP!
NO THANK YOU!
THAT'S OK, RUNT. GIVE IT BACK.
NO! YOU'RE WAY TOO CLUMSY....
I'LL DO IT!

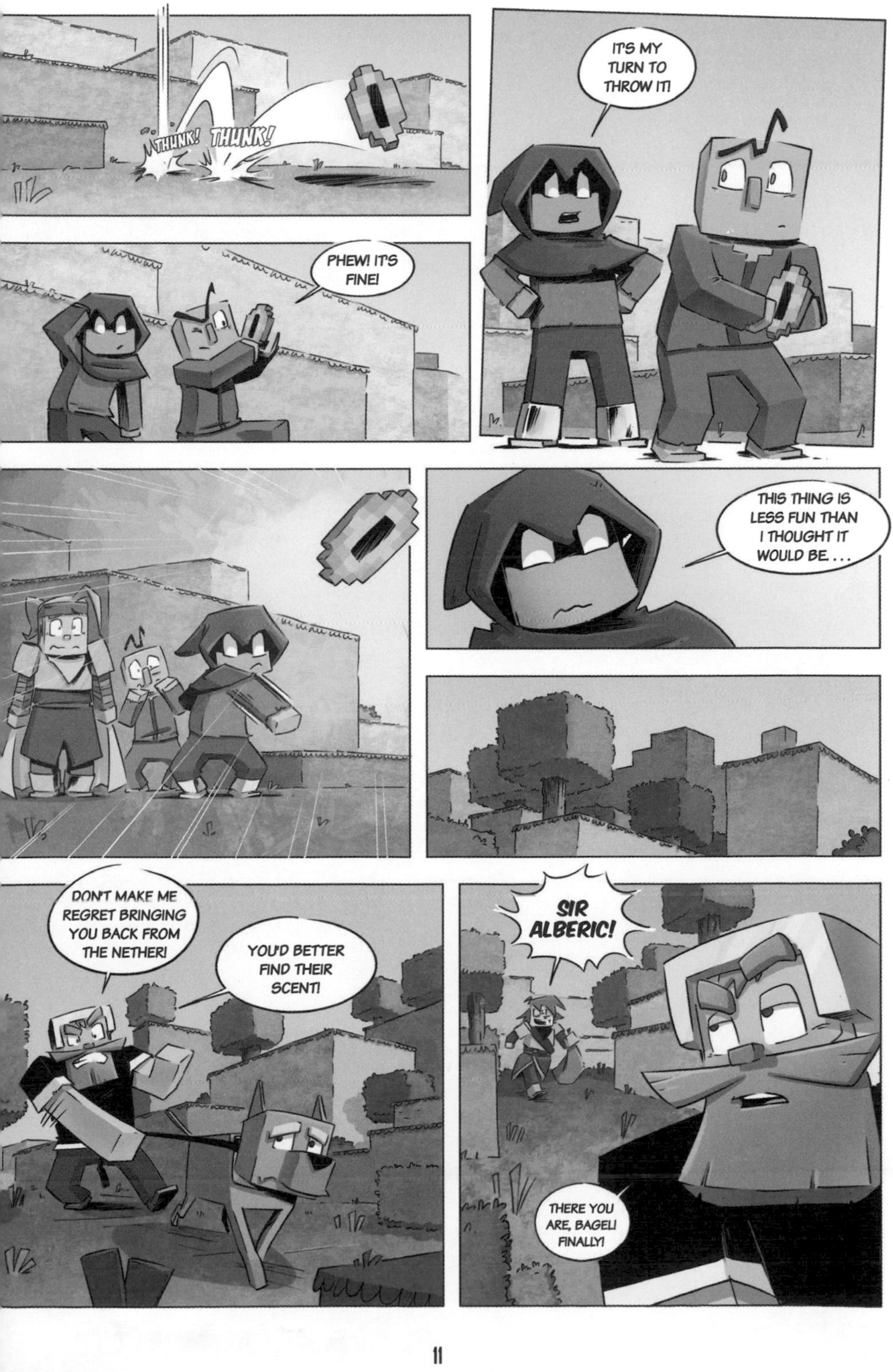
THUNK! THUNK!
IT'S MY TURN TO THROW IT!
PHEW! IT'S FINE!
THIS THING IS LESS FUN THAN I THOUGHT IT WOULD BE . . .
DON'T MAKE ME REGRET BRINGING YOU BACK FROM THE NETHER!
YOU'D BETTER FIND THEIR SCENT!
SIR ALBERIC!
THERE YOU ARE, BAGEL! FINALLY!

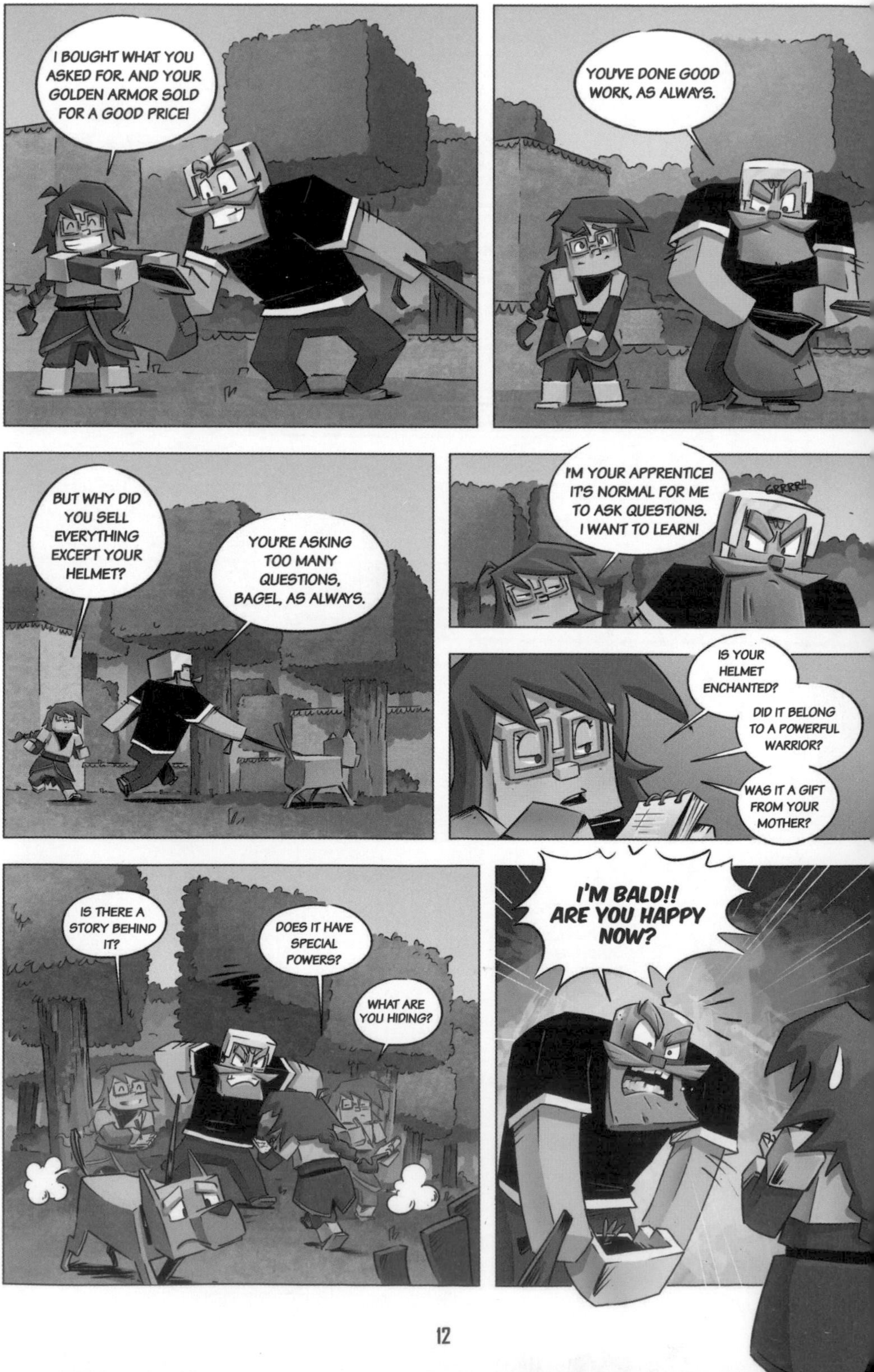
I BOUGHT WHAT YOU ASKED FOR. AND YOUR GOLDEN ARMOR SOLD FOR A GOOD PRICE!
YOU'VE DONE GOOD WORK, AS ALWAYS.
BUT WHY DID YOU SELL EVERYTHING EXCEPT YOUR HELMET?
YOU'RE ASKING TOO MANY QUESTIONS, BAGEL, AS ALWAYS.
I'M YOUR APPRENTICE! IT'S NORMAL FOR ME TO ASK QUESTIONS. I WANT TO LEARN!
GRRRR!!
IS YOUR HELMET ENCHANTED?
DID IT BELONG TO A POWERFUL WARRIOR?
WAS IT A GIFT FROM YOUR MOTHER?
IS THERE A STORY BEHIND IT?
DOES IT HAVE SPECIAL POWERS?
WHAT ARE YOU HIDING?
I'M BALD!! ARE YOU HAPPY NOW?

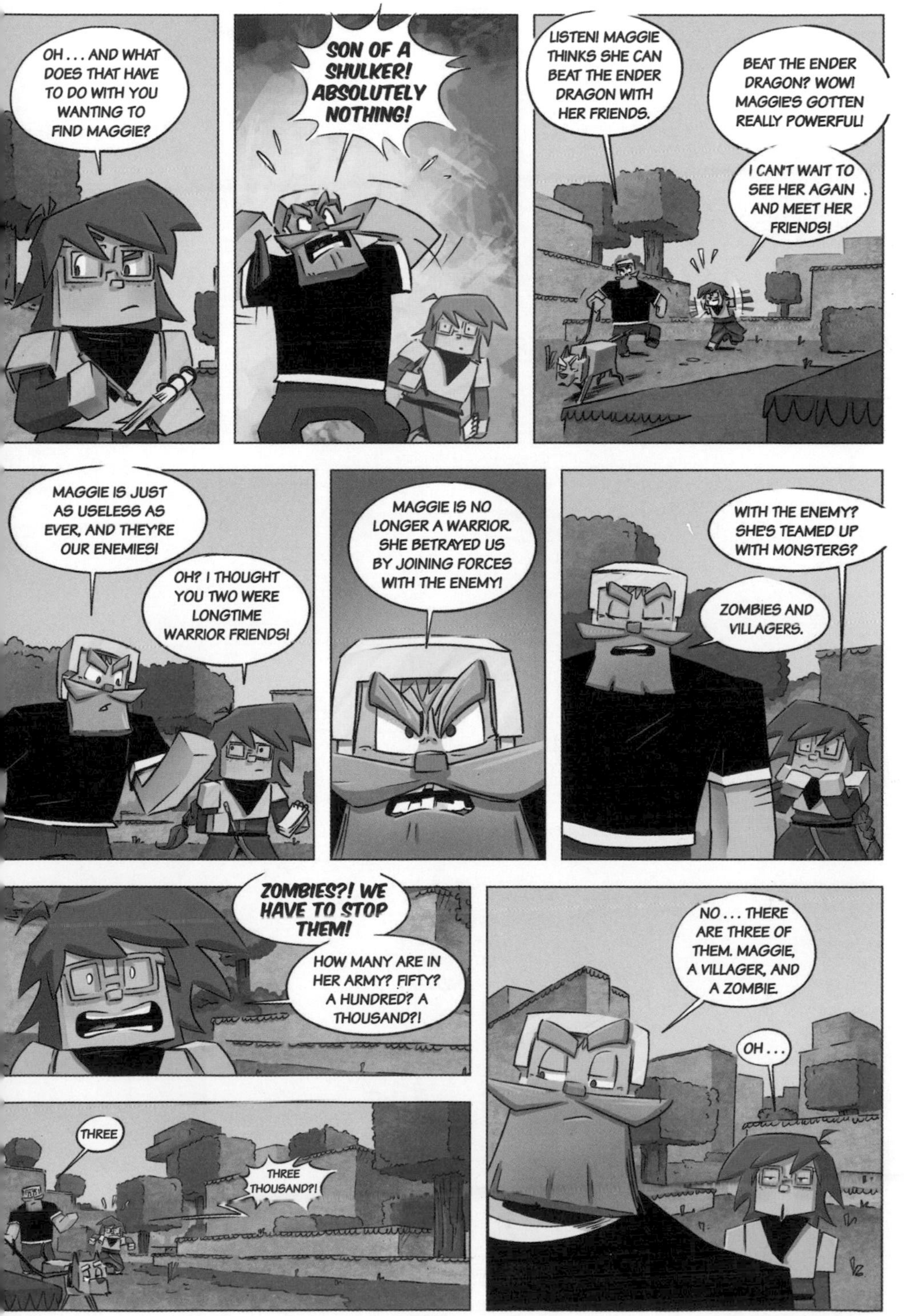
OH . . . AND WHAT DOES THAT HAVE TO DO WITH YOU WANTING TO FIND MAGGIE?
SON OF A SHULKER! ABSOLUTELY NOTHING!
LISTEN! MAGGIE THINKS SHE CAN BEAT THE ENDER DRAGON WITH HER FRIENDS.
BEAT THE ENDER DRAGON? WOW! MAGGIE'S GOTTEN REALLY POWERFUL!
I CAN'T WAIT TO SEE HER AGAIN AND MEET HER FRIENDS!
MAGGIE IS JUST AS USELESS AS EVER, AND THEY'RE OUR ENEMIES!
OH? I THOUGHT YOU TWO WERE LONGTIME WARRIOR FRIENDS!
MAGGIE IS NO LONGER A WARRIOR. SHE BETRAYED US BY JOINING FORCES WITH THE ENEMY!
WITH THE ENEMY? SHE'S TEAMED UP WITH MONSTERS?
ZOMBIES AND VILLAGERS.
ZOMBIES?! WE HAVE TO STOP THEM!
HOW MANY ARE IN HER ARMY? FIFTY? A HUNDRED? A THOUSAND?!
THREE
THREE THOUSAND?!
NO . . . THERE ARE THREE OF THEM. MAGGIE, A VILLAGER, AND A ZOMBIE.
OH . . .

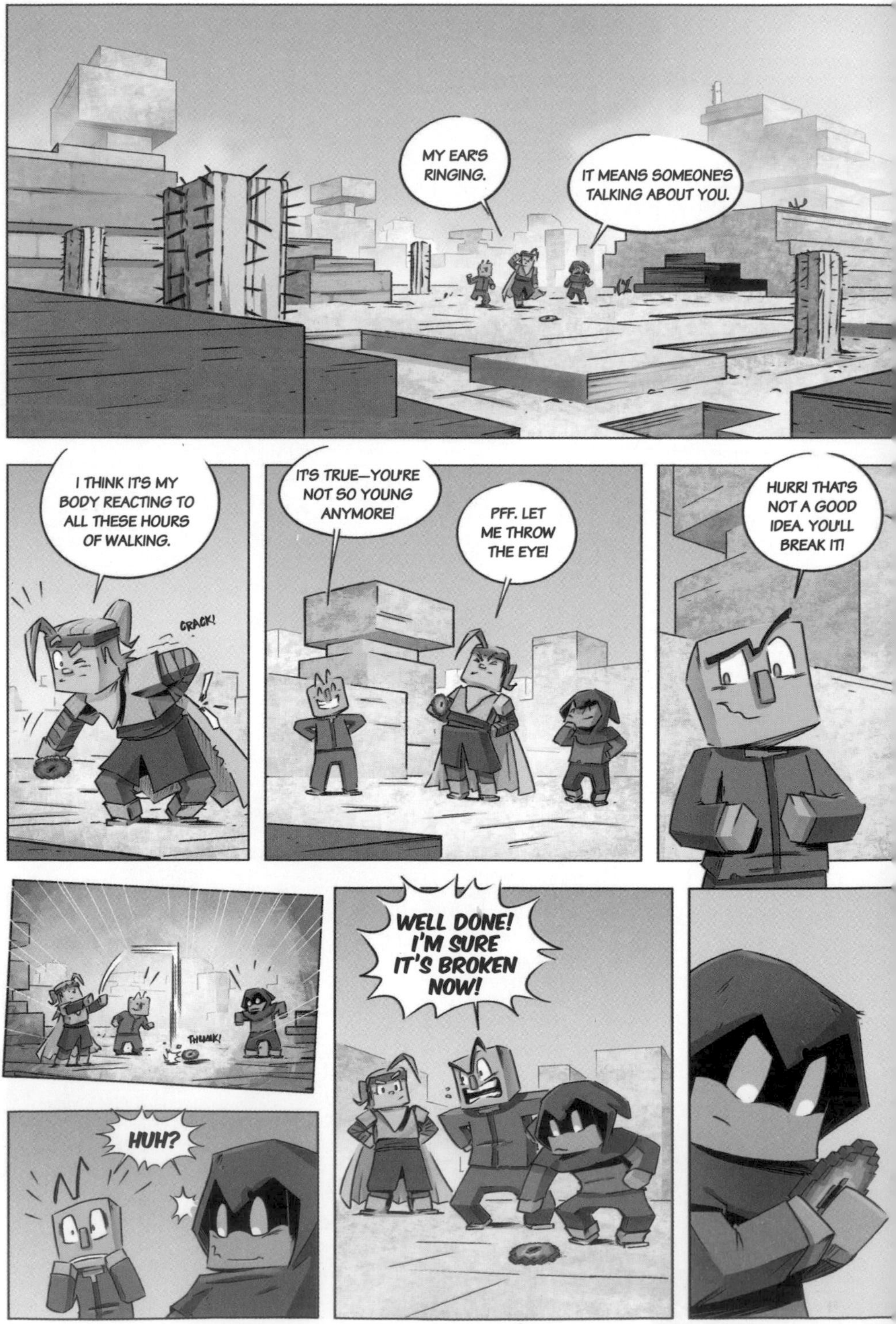

MY EAR'S RINGING.
IT MEANS SOMEONE'S TALKING ABOUT YOU.
I THINK IT'S MY BODY REACTING TO ALL THESE HOURS OF WALKING.
CRACK!
IT'S TRUE—YOU'RE NOT SO YOUNG ANYMORE!
PFF. LET ME THROW THE EYE!
HURR! THAT'S NOT A GOOD IDEA. YOU'LL BREAK IT!
THUNK!
HUH?
WELL DONE! I'M SURE IT'S BROKEN NOW!

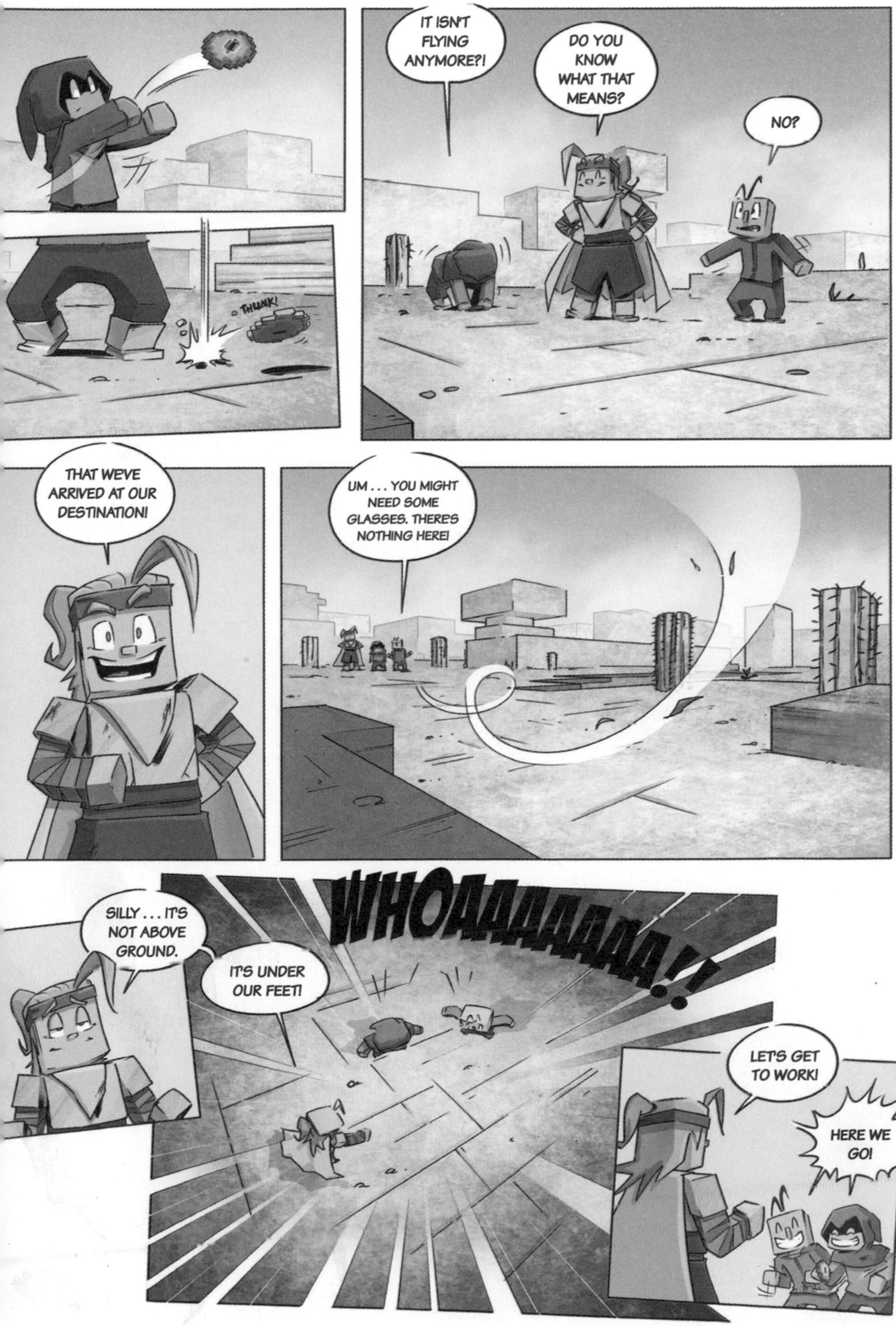
THUNK!
IT ISN'T FLYING ANYMORE?!
DO YOU KNOW WHAT THAT MEANS?
NO?
THAT WE'VE ARRIVED AT OUR DESTINATION!
UM . . . YOU MIGHT NEED SOME GLASSES. THERE'S NOTHING HERE!
SILLY . . . IT'S NOT ABOVE GROUND.
IT'S UNDER OUR FEET!
WHOAAAAAAAA!!
LET'S GET TO WORK!
HERE WE GO!

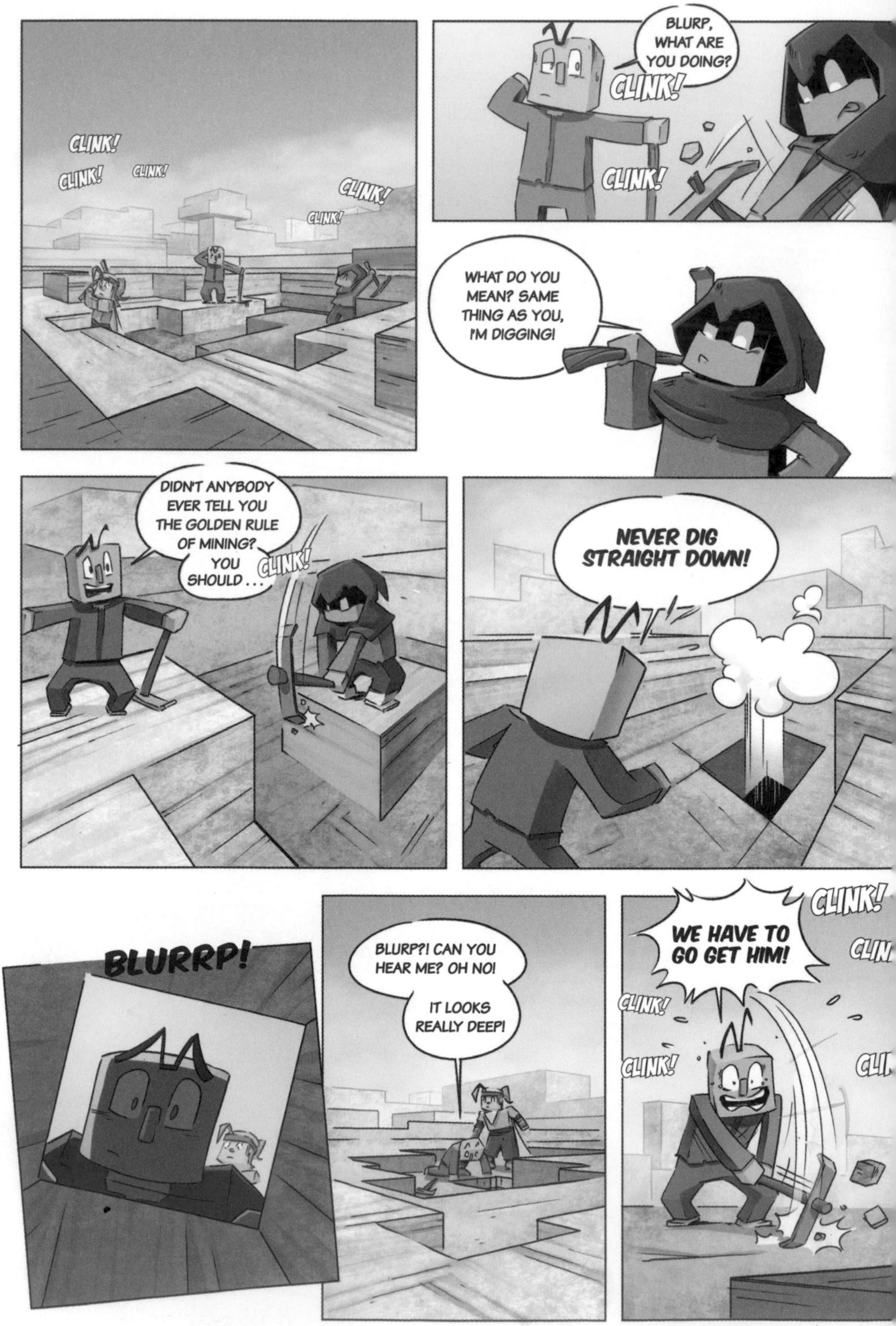
CLINK!
CLINK!
CLINK!
CLINK!
CLINK!
BLURP, WHAT ARE YOU DOING?
CLINK!
CLINK!
WHAT DO YOU MEAN? SAME THING AS YOU, I'M DIGGING!
DIDN'T ANYBODY EVER TELL YOU THE GOLDEN RULE OF MINING? YOU SHOULD . . .
CLINK!
NEVER DIG STRAIGHT DOWN!
BLURRP!
BLURP?! CAN YOU HEAR ME? OH NO!
IT LOOKS REALLY DEEP!
WE HAVE TO GO GET HIM!
CLINK!
CLINK!
CLINK!

WATCH OUT!

PLOP!

I HATE TO SAY THIS, RUNT, BUT THAT WAS QUITE A FALL...

I DON'T KNOW WHAT YOU'RE TALKING ABOUT! WE HAVE TO GO GET HIM!!

I'M GOING TO DIG US A SAFER PATH!

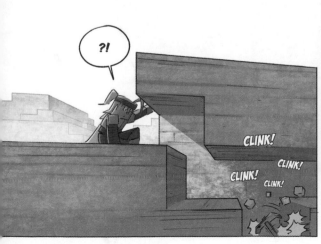

?!

CLINK!

CLINK!

CLINK!

CLINK!

HMPH! IF ONLY YOU'D MADE IT SMALLER!

WE MADE IT!

THERE, WE'RE SAFE NOW!

?!

A CREEPER! GET BACK!

HURRY! HURRY! IT'S GONNA BLOW!

HIIISSSSS!! HIIISSSS... SSSSS! HIIISSSSS!

I'M STUCK!

HIIISSSSSS! SSSSSS!

BOOM!!

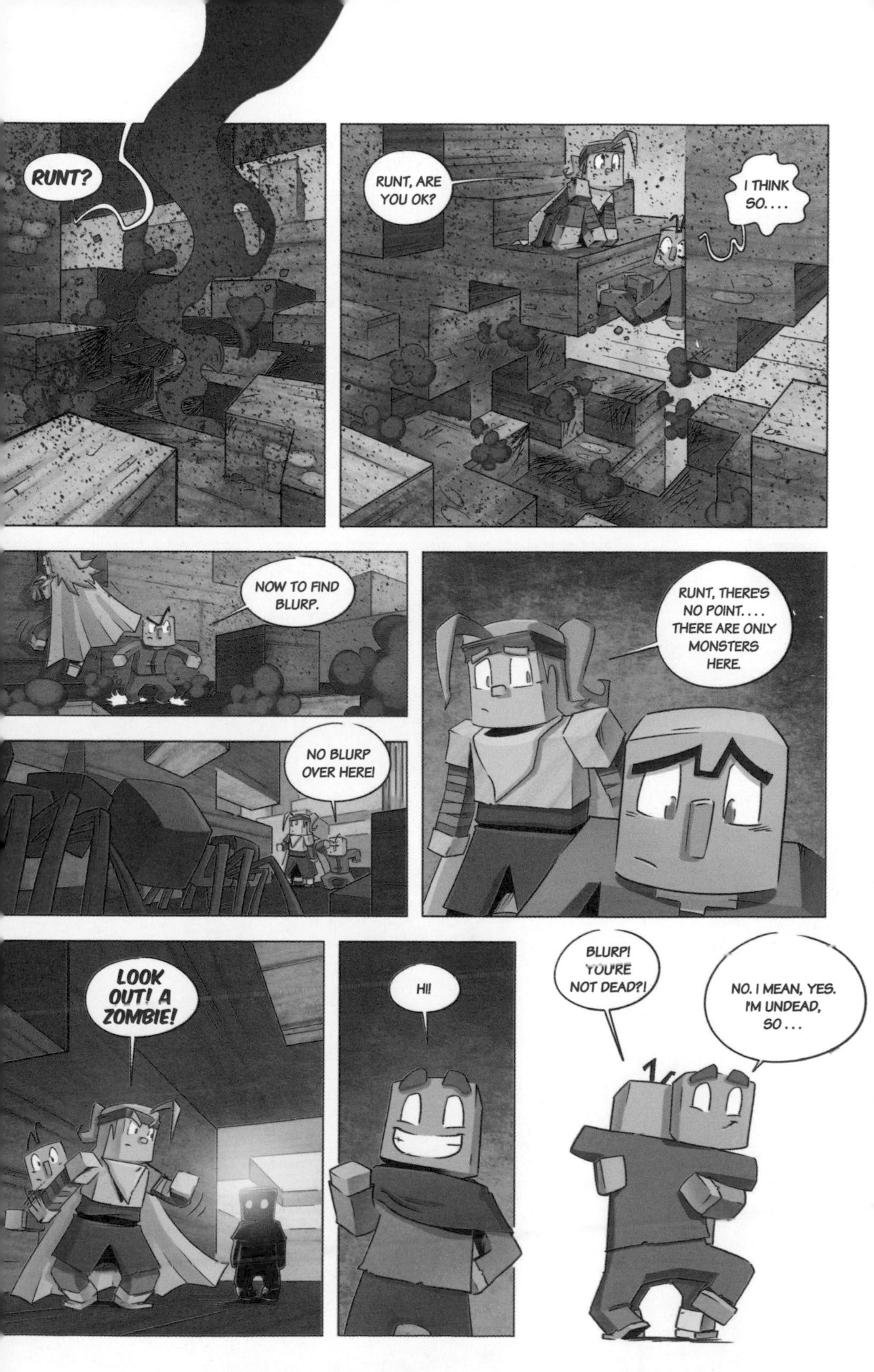
RUNT?
RUNT, ARE YOU OK?
I THINK SO. . . .
NOW TO FIND BLURP.
NO BLURP OVER HERE!
RUNT, THERE'S NO POINT. . . . THERE ARE ONLY MONSTERS HERE.
LOOK OUT! A ZOMBIE!
HI!
BLURP! YOU'RE NOT DEAD?!
NO. I MEAN, YES. I'M UNDEAD, SO . . .

I GUESS I TEND TO FORGET YOU'RE A ZOMBIE.

WHAT'S GREAT IS THAT MONSTERS DON'T ATTACK ME!

SO I'VE BEEN WANDERING AROUND. AND LOOK WHAT I FOUND!

?!

A DOOR! WHAT KIND OF WEIRDO WOULD LIVE DOWN HERE?!

NO! THAT'S THE DOORWAY OF A FORTRESS!

THE PORTAL MUST BE RIGHT BEHIND IT!

AAAAAAH!!

WHOAAAAAAAAAA!!

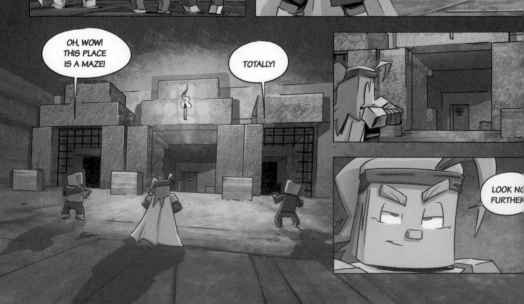

OH, WOW! THIS PLACE IS A MAZE!

TOTALLY!

LOOK NO FURTHER

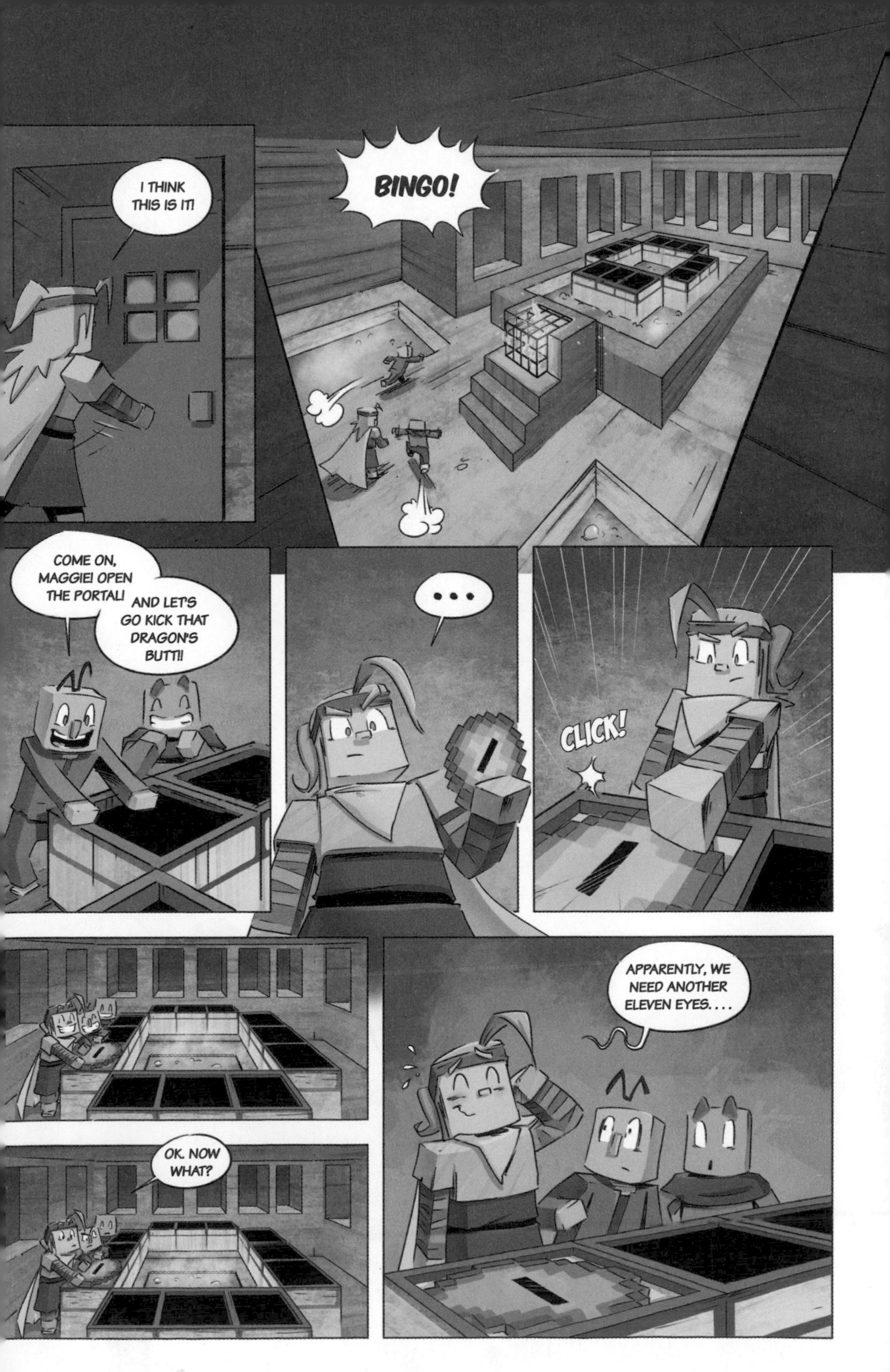
I THINK THIS IS IT!
BINGO!
COME ON, MAGGIE! OPEN THE PORTAL!
AND LET'S GO KICK THAT DRAGON'S BUTT!!
...
CLICK!
OK. NOW WHAT?
APPARENTLY, WE NEED ANOTHER ELEVEN EYES. . . .

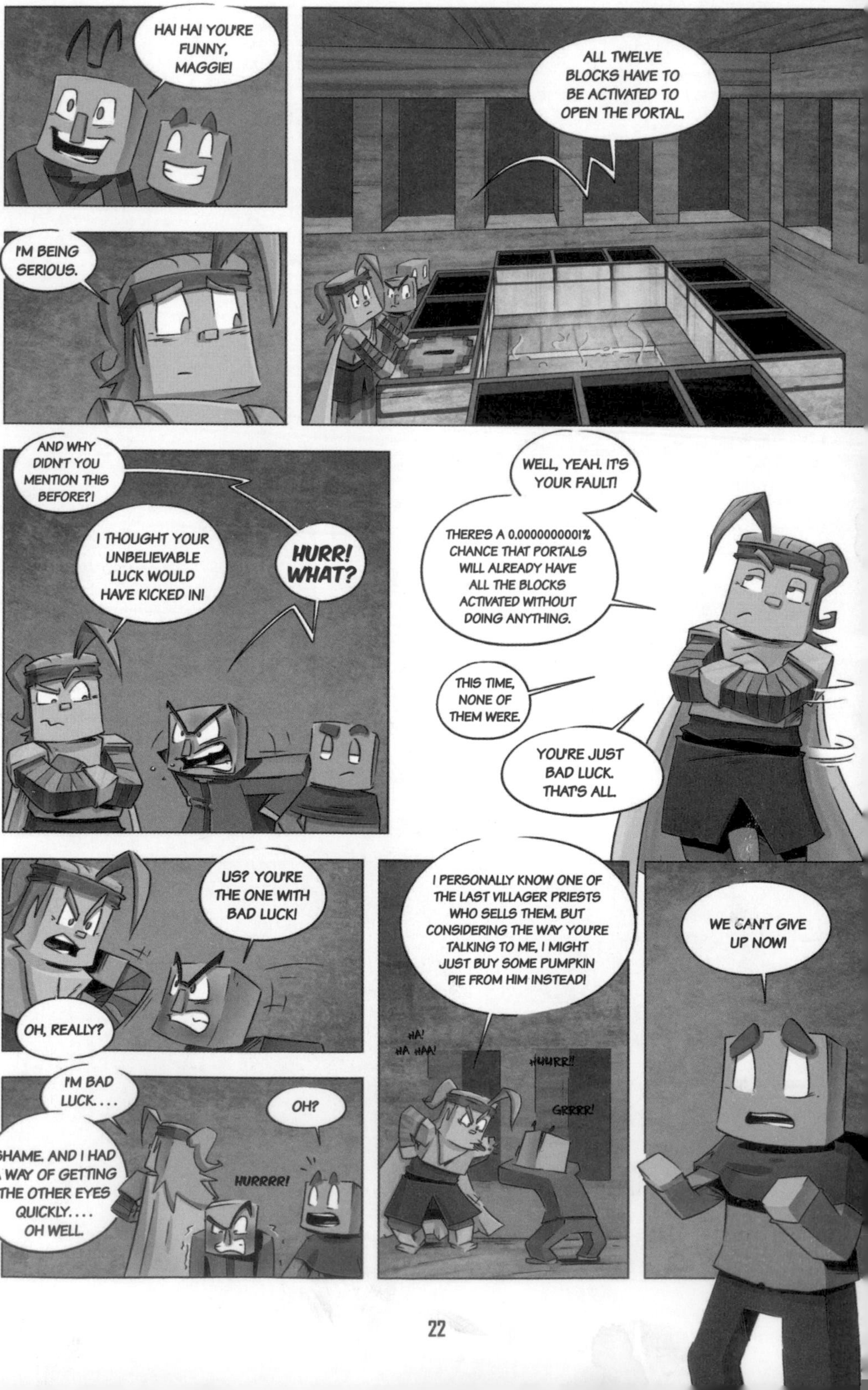
HA! HA! YOU'RE FUNNY, MAGGIE!
I'M BEING SERIOUS.
ALL TWELVE BLOCKS HAVE TO BE ACTIVATED TO OPEN THE PORTAL.
AND WHY DIDN'T YOU MENTION THIS BEFORE?!
I THOUGHT YOUR UNBELIEVABLE LUCK WOULD HAVE KICKED IN!
HURR! WHAT?
WELL, YEAH. IT'S YOUR FAULT!
THERE'S A 0.0000000001% CHANCE THAT PORTALS WILL ALREADY HAVE ALL THE BLOCKS ACTIVATED WITHOUT DOING ANYTHING.
THIS TIME, NONE OF THEM WERE.
YOU'RE JUST BAD LUCK. THAT'S ALL.
US? YOU'RE THE ONE WITH BAD LUCK!
OH, REALLY?
I'M BAD LUCK....
OH?
SHAME. AND I HAD A WAY OF GETTING THE OTHER EYES QUICKLY.... OH WELL.
HURRRR!
I PERSONALLY KNOW ONE OF THE LAST VILLAGER PRIESTS WHO SELLS THEM. BUT CONSIDERING THE WAY YOU'RE TALKING TO ME, I MIGHT JUST BUY SOME PUMPKIN PIE FROM HIM INSTEAD!
HA! HA HAA!
HUURR!!
GRRRR!
WE CAN'T GIVE UP NOW!

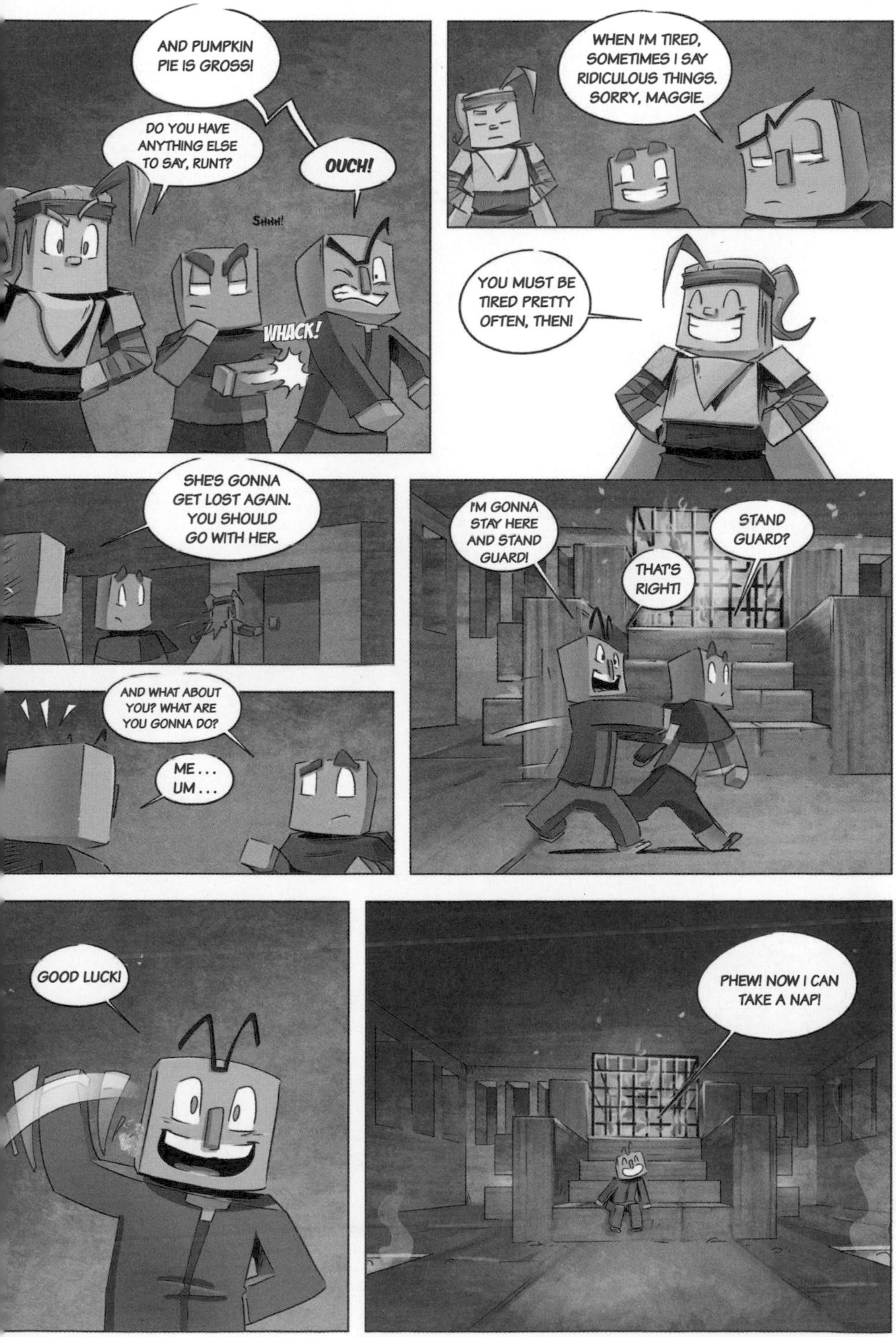
AND PUMPKIN PIE IS GROSS!
DO YOU HAVE ANYTHING ELSE TO SAY, RUNT?
OUCH!
SHHH!
WHACK!
WHEN I'M TIRED, SOMETIMES I SAY RIDICULOUS THINGS. SORRY, MAGGIE.
YOU MUST BE TIRED PRETTY OFTEN, THEN!
SHE'S GONNA GET LOST AGAIN. YOU SHOULD GO WITH HER.
AND WHAT ABOUT YOU? WHAT ARE YOU GONNA DO?
ME . . . UM . . .
I'M GONNA STAY HERE AND STAND GUARD!
THAT'S RIGHT!
STAND GUARD?
GOOD LUCK!
PHEW! NOW I CAN TAKE A NAP!

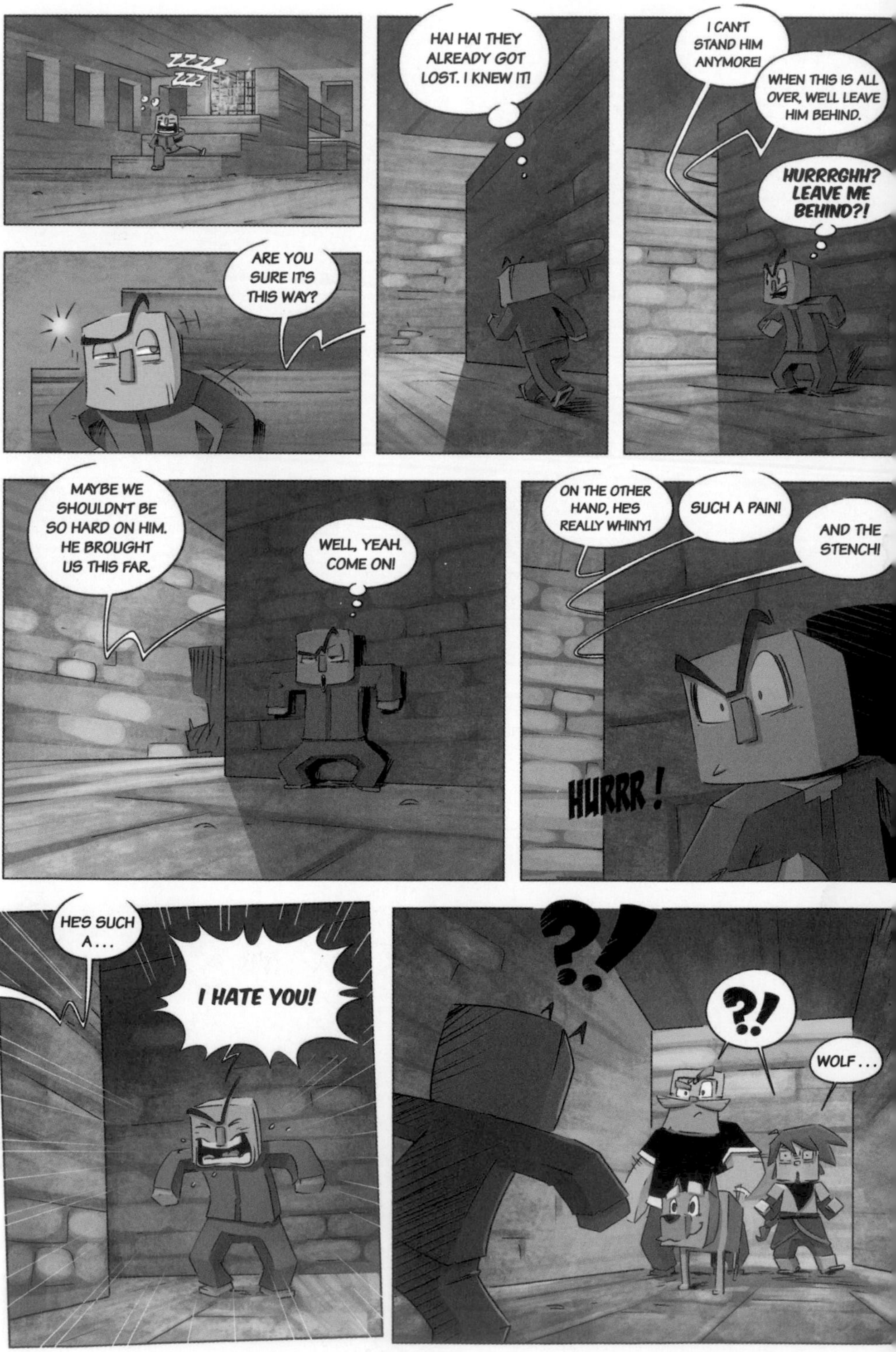
ZZZZ ZZZ
ARE YOU SURE IT'S THIS WAY?
HA! HA! THEY ALREADY GOT LOST. I KNEW IT!
I CAN'T STAND HIM ANYMORE!
WHEN THIS IS ALL OVER, WE'LL LEAVE HIM BEHIND.
HURRRGHH? LEAVE ME BEHIND?!
MAYBE WE SHOULDN'T BE SO HARD ON HIM. HE BROUGHT US THIS FAR.
WELL, YEAH. COME ON!
ON THE OTHER HAND, HE'S REALLY WHINY!
SUCH A PAIN!
AND THE STENCH!
HURRR!
HE'S SUCH A . . .
I HATE YOU!
?!
?!
WOLF . . .

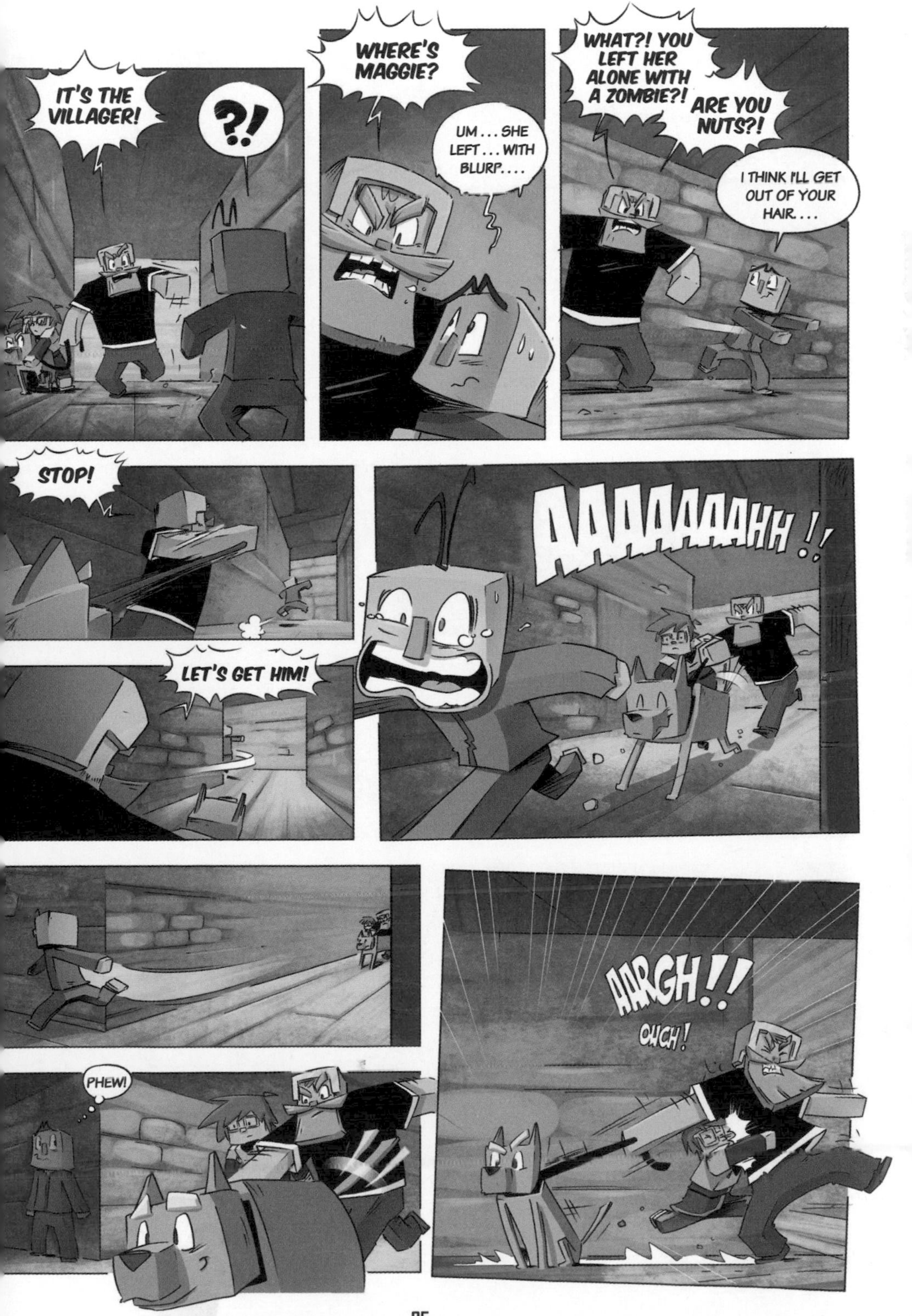
IT'S THE VILLAGER!
?!
WHERE'S MAGGIE?
UM . . . SHE LEFT . . . WITH BLURP. . . .
WHAT?! YOU LEFT HER ALONE WITH A ZOMBIE?!
ARE YOU NUTS?!
I THINK I'LL GET OUT OF YOUR HAIR . . .
STOP!
LET'S GET HIM!
AAAAAAAHH!!
PHEW!
AARGH!!
OUCH!

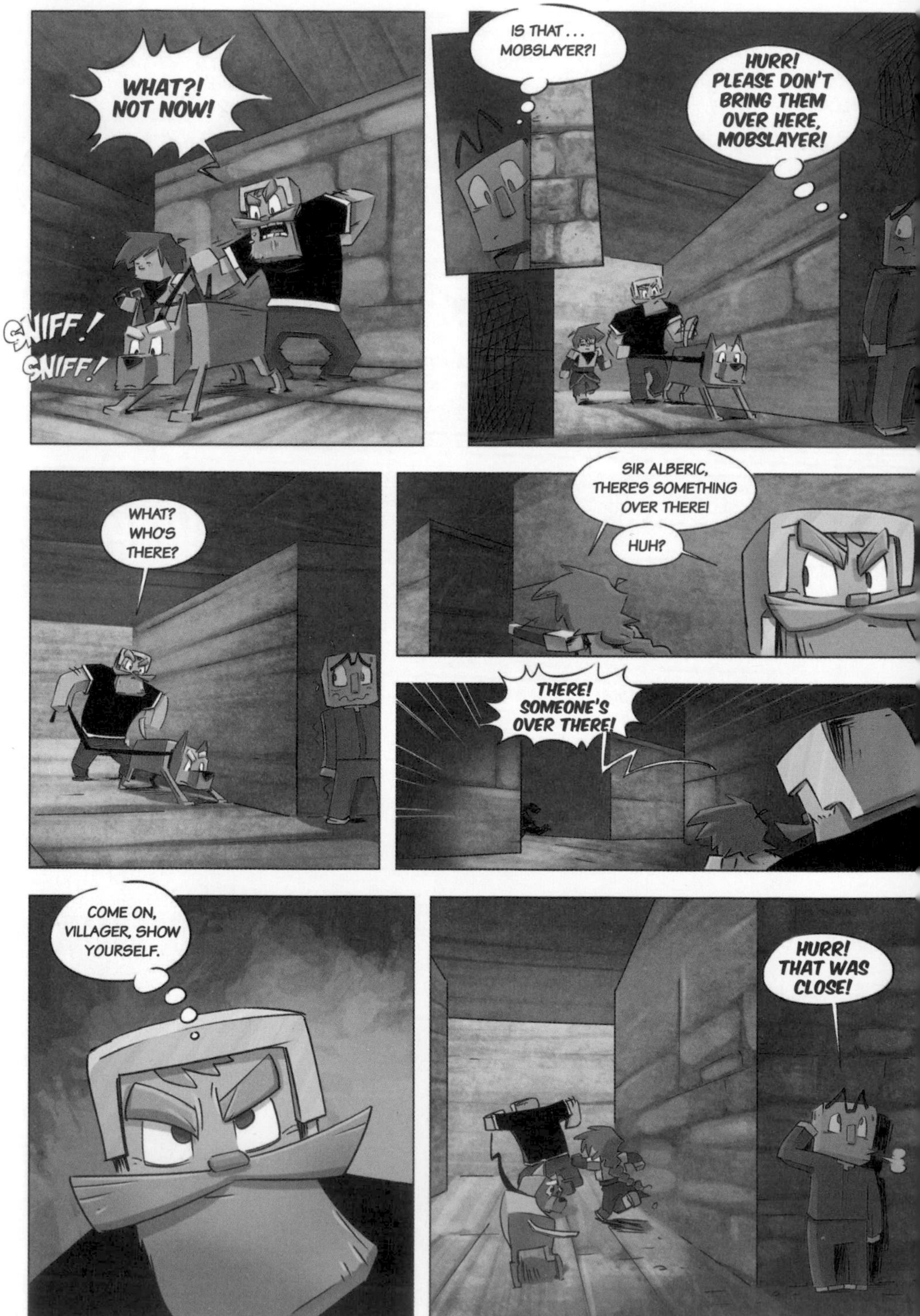
WHAT?!
NOT NOW!
SNIFF! SNIFF!
IS THAT . . .
MOBSLAYER?!
HURR!
PLEASE DON'T
BRING THEM
OVER HERE,
MOBSLAYER!
WHAT?
WHO'S
THERE?
SIR ALBERIC,
THERE'S SOMETHING
OVER THERE!
HUH?
THERE!
SOMEONE'S
OVER THERE!
COME ON,
VILLAGER, SHOW
YOURSELF.
HURR!
THAT WAS
CLOSE!

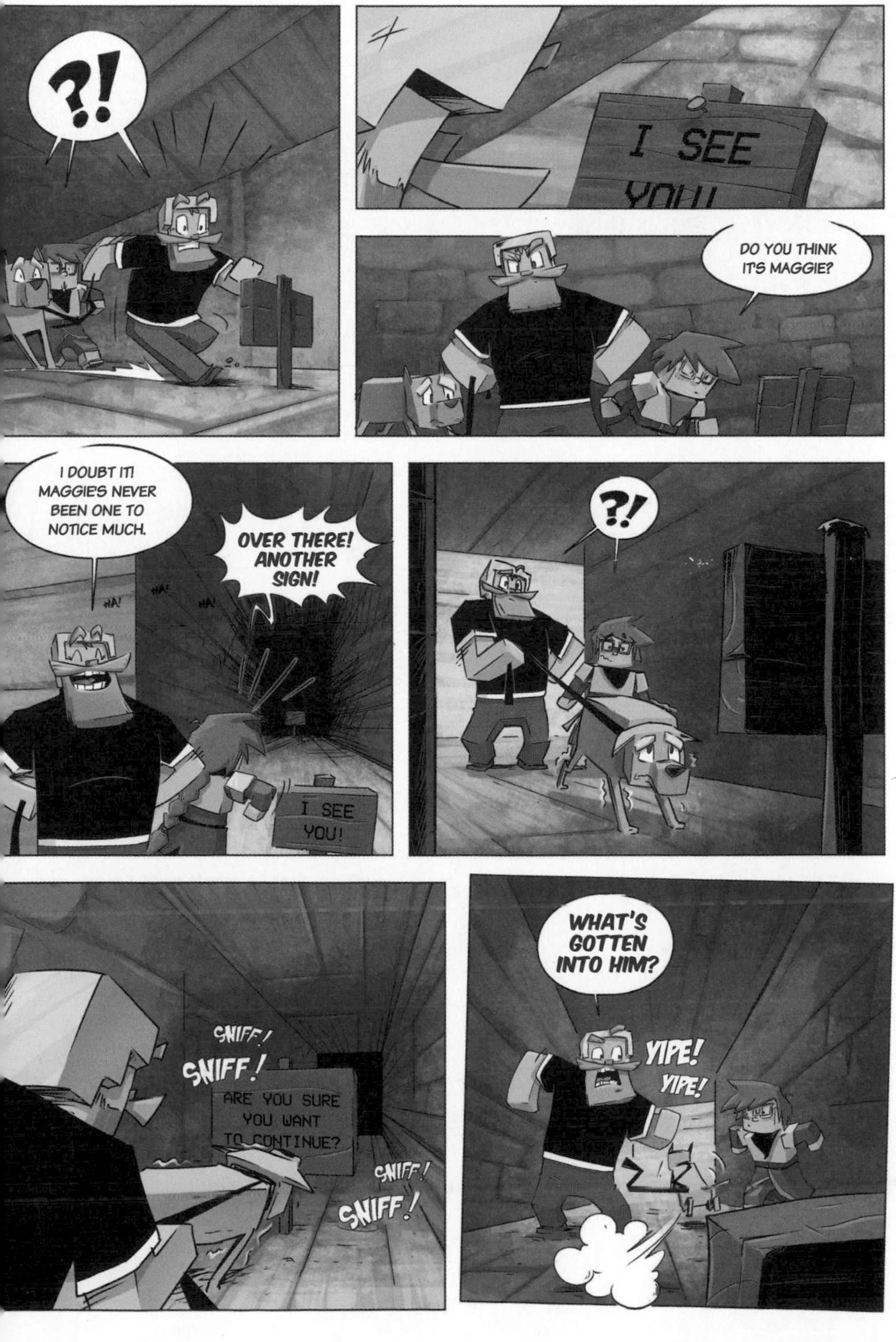
?!
I SEE
DO YOU THINK IT'S MAGGIE?
I DOUBT IT! MAGGIE'S NEVER BEEN ONE TO NOTICE MUCH.
HA!
HA!
HA!
OVER THERE! ANOTHER SIGN!
I SEE YOU!
?!
SNIFF!
SNIFF!
ARE YOU SURE YOU WANT TO CONTINUE?
SNIFF!
SNIFF!
WHAT'S GOTTEN INTO HIM?
YIPE!
YIPE!

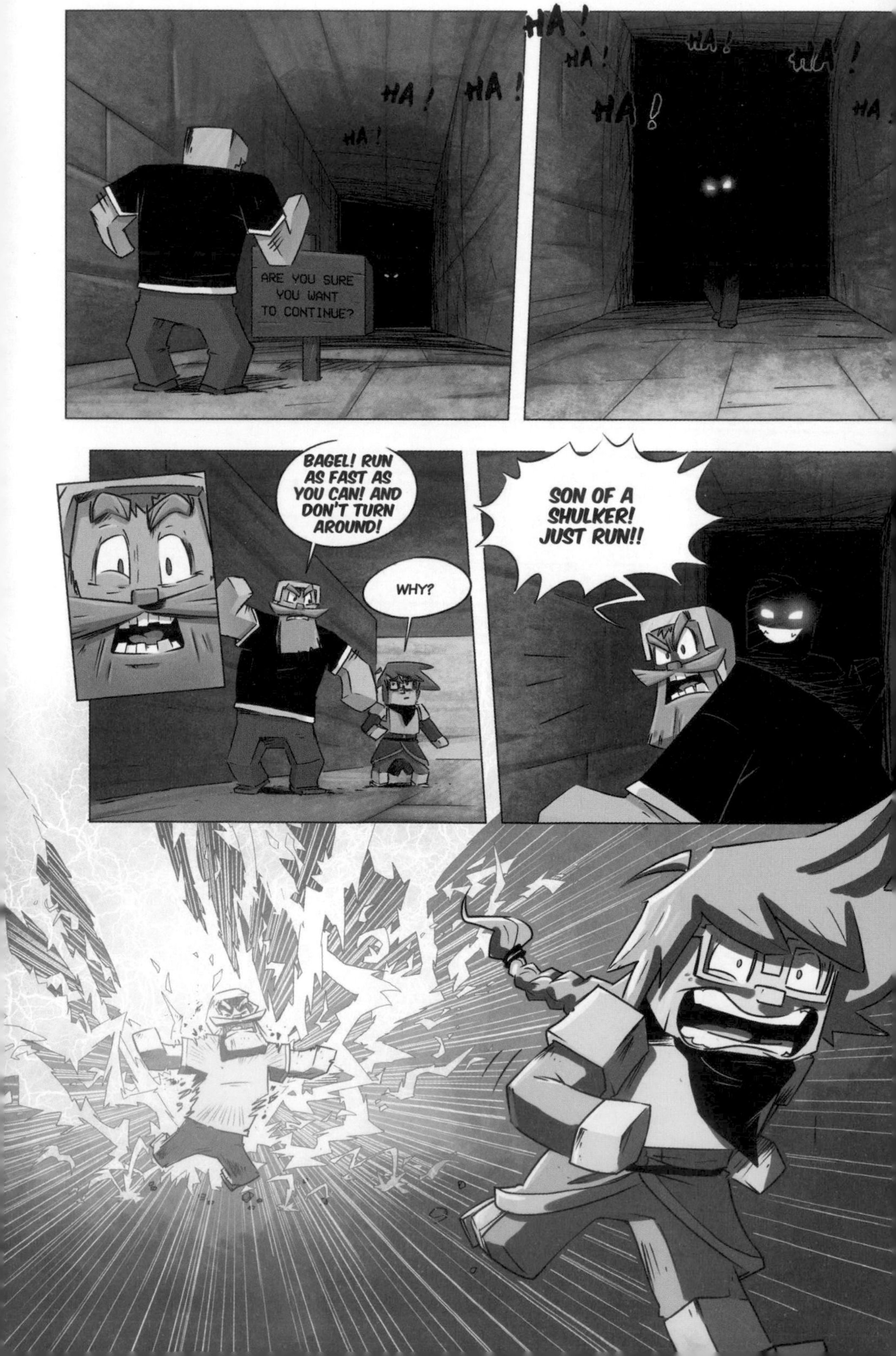
HA!
HA!
HA!
ARE YOU SURE YOU WANT TO CONTINUE?
HA!
HA!
HA!
HA!
HA!
HA
BAGEL! RUN AS FAST AS YOU CAN! AND DON'T TURN AROUND!
WHY?
SON OF A SHULKER! JUST RUN!!

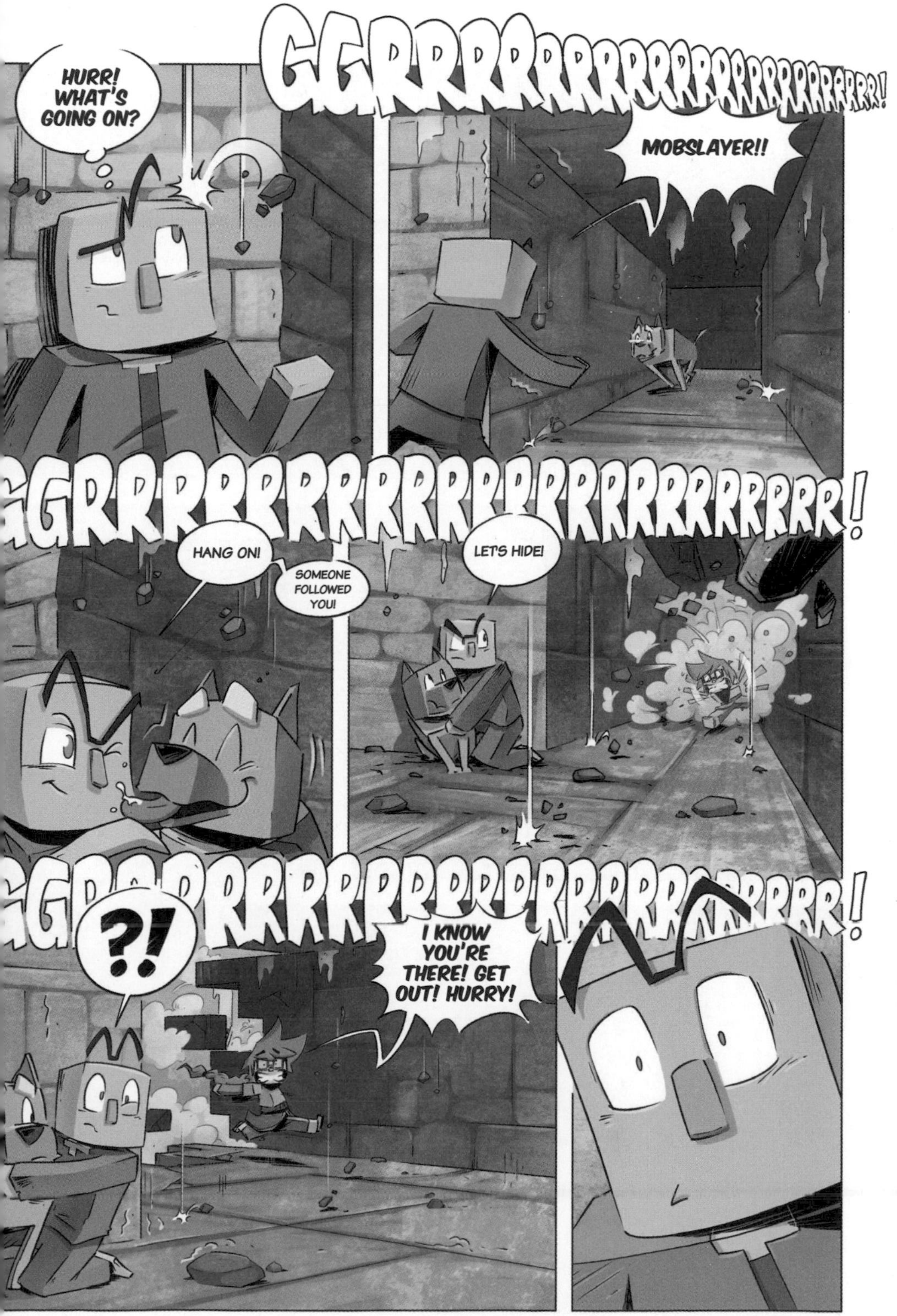
GGRRRRRRRRRRRRRRRRRRRRRRRRR!
HURR! WHAT'S GOING ON?
MOBSLAYER!!
GGRRRRRRRRRRRRRRRRRRRRRRRRR!
HANG ON!
SOMEONE FOLLOWED YOU!
LET'S HIDE!
GGRRRRRRRRRRRRRRRRRRRRRRRRR!
?!
I KNOW YOU'RE THERE! GET OUT! HURRY!

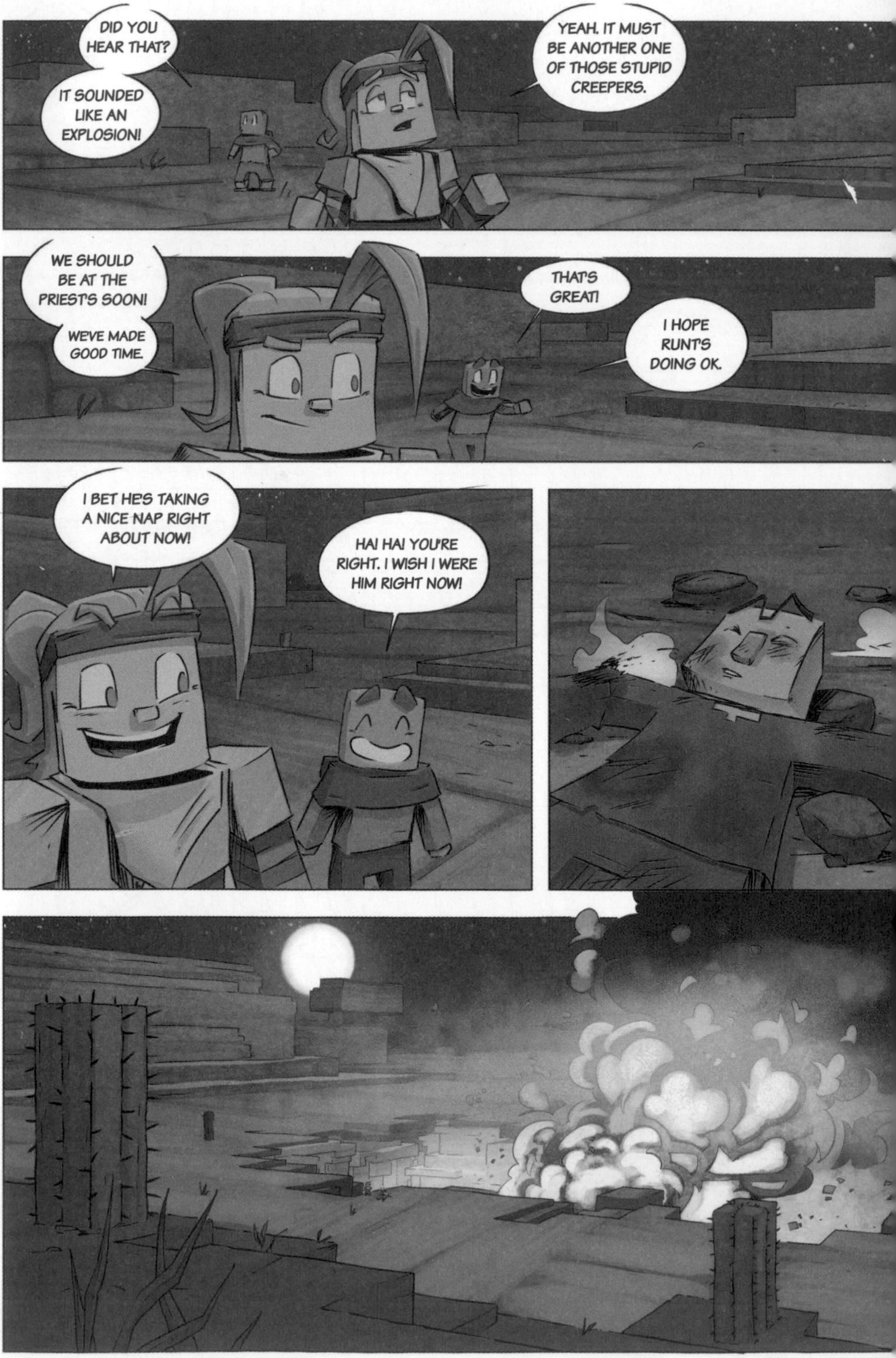
DID YOU HEAR THAT?
IT SOUNDED LIKE AN EXPLOSION!
YEAH. IT MUST BE ANOTHER ONE OF THOSE STUPID CREEPERS.
WE SHOULD BE AT THE PRIEST'S SOON!
WE'VE MADE GOOD TIME.
THAT'S GREAT!
I HOPE RUNT'S DOING OK.
I BET HE'S TAKING A NICE NAP RIGHT ABOUT NOW!
HA! HA! YOU'RE RIGHT. I WISH I WERE HIM RIGHT NOW!

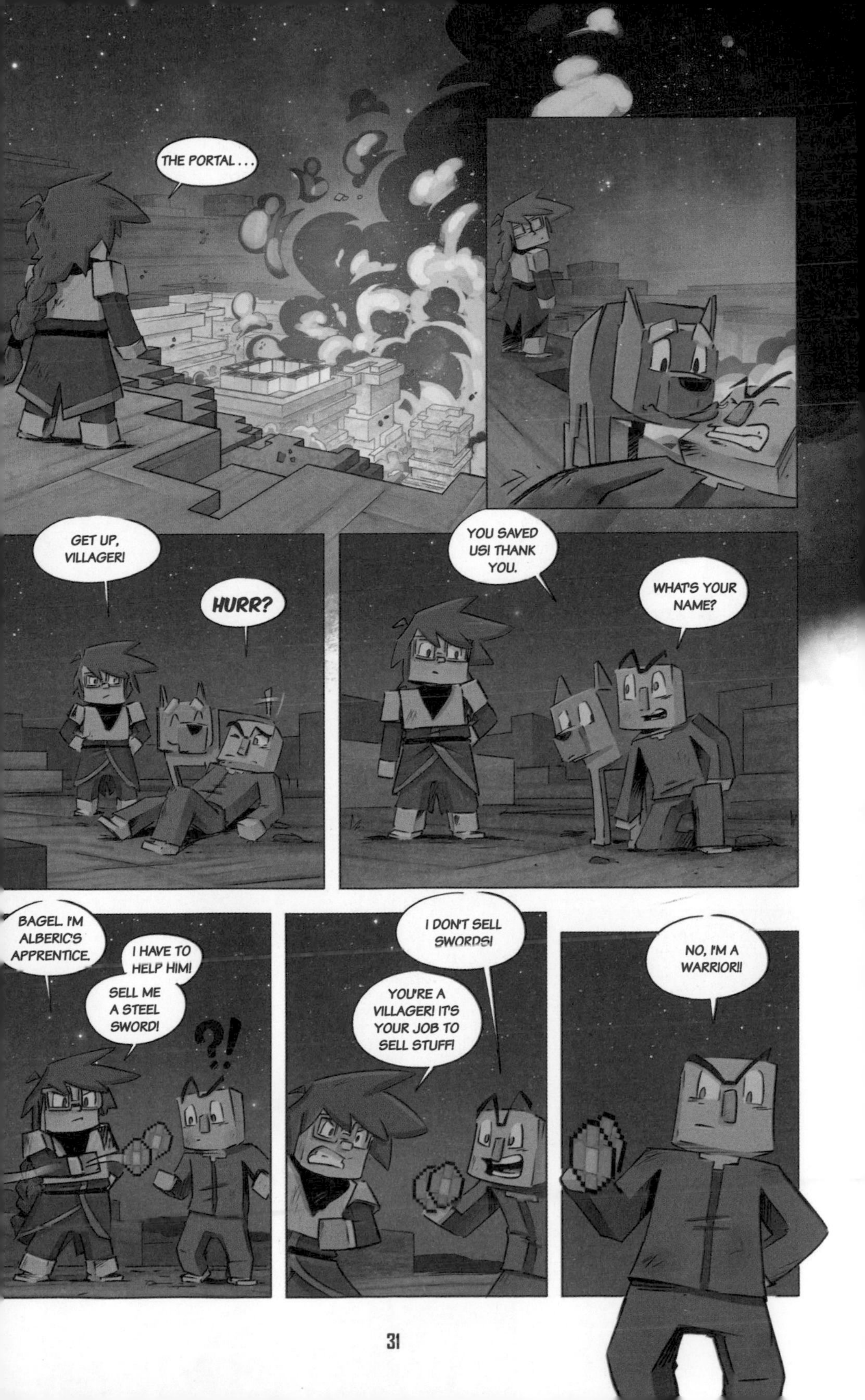
THE PORTAL . . .
GET UP, VILLAGER!
HURR?
YOU SAVED US! THANK YOU.
WHAT'S YOUR NAME?
BAGEL. I'M ALBERIC'S APPRENTICE.
I HAVE TO HELP HIM!
SELL ME A STEEL SWORD!
?!
I DON'T SELL SWORDS!
YOU'RE A VILLAGER! IT'S YOUR JOB TO SELL STUFF!
NO, I'M A WARRIOR!!

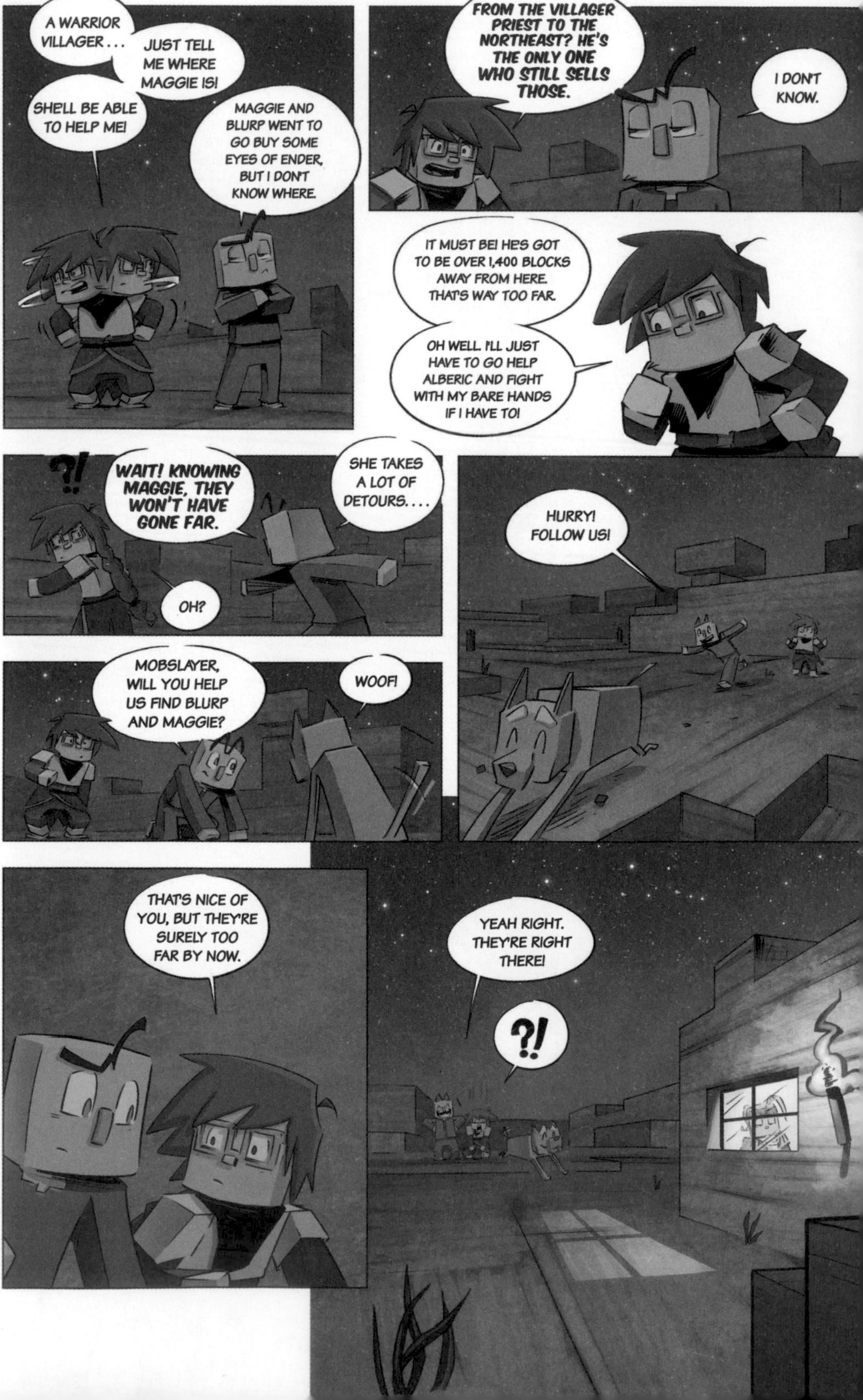
A WARRIOR VILLAGER . . .
JUST TELL ME WHERE MAGGIE IS!
SHE'LL BE ABLE TO HELP ME!
MAGGIE AND BLURP WENT TO GO BUY SOME EYES OF ENDER, BUT I DON'T KNOW WHERE.
FROM THE VILLAGER PRIEST TO THE NORTHEAST? HE'S THE ONLY ONE WHO STILL SELLS THOSE.
I DON'T KNOW.
IT MUST BE! HE'S GOT TO BE OVER 1,400 BLOCKS AWAY FROM HERE. THAT'S WAY TOO FAR.
OH WELL. I'LL JUST HAVE TO GO HELP ALBERIC AND FIGHT WITH MY BARE HANDS IF I HAVE TO!
?!
WAIT! KNOWING MAGGIE, THEY WON'T HAVE GONE FAR.
SHE TAKES A LOT OF DETOURS. . . .
OH?
MOBSLAYER, WILL YOU HELP US FIND BLURP AND MAGGIE?
WOOF!
HURRY! FOLLOW US!
THAT'S NICE OF YOU, BUT THEY'RE SURELY TOO FAR BY NOW.
YEAH RIGHT. THEY'RE RIGHT THERE!
?!

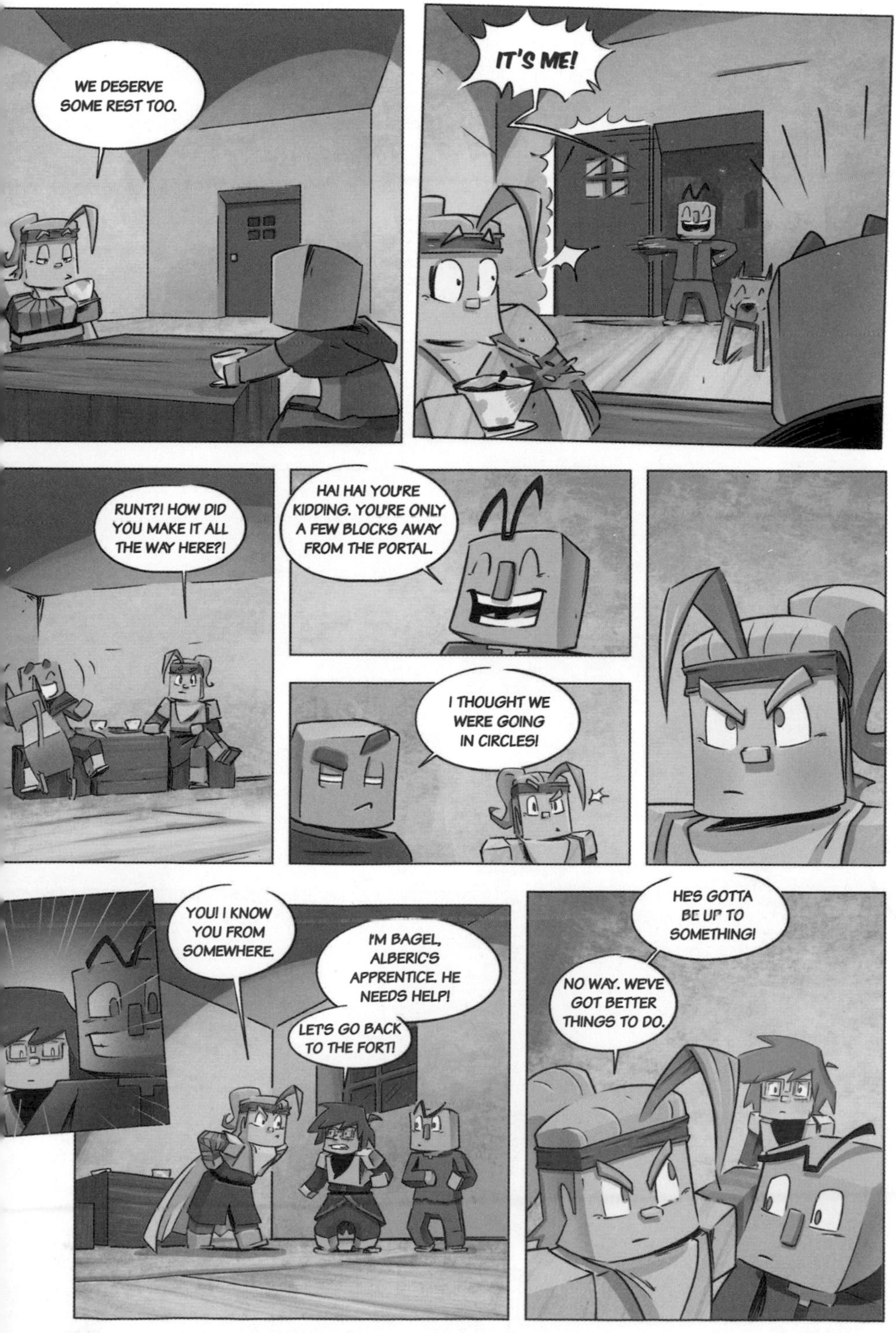
WE DESERVE SOME REST TOO.
IT'S ME!
RUNT?! HOW DID YOU MAKE IT ALL THE WAY HERE?!
HA! HA! YOU'RE KIDDING. YOU'RE ONLY A FEW BLOCKS AWAY FROM THE PORTAL.
I THOUGHT WE WERE GOING IN CIRCLES!
YOU! I KNOW YOU FROM SOMEWHERE.
I'M BAGEL, ALBERIC'S APPRENTICE. HE NEEDS HELP!
LET'S GO BACK TO THE FORT!
HE'S GOTTA BE UP TO SOMETHING!
NO WAY. WE'VE GOT BETTER THINGS TO DO.

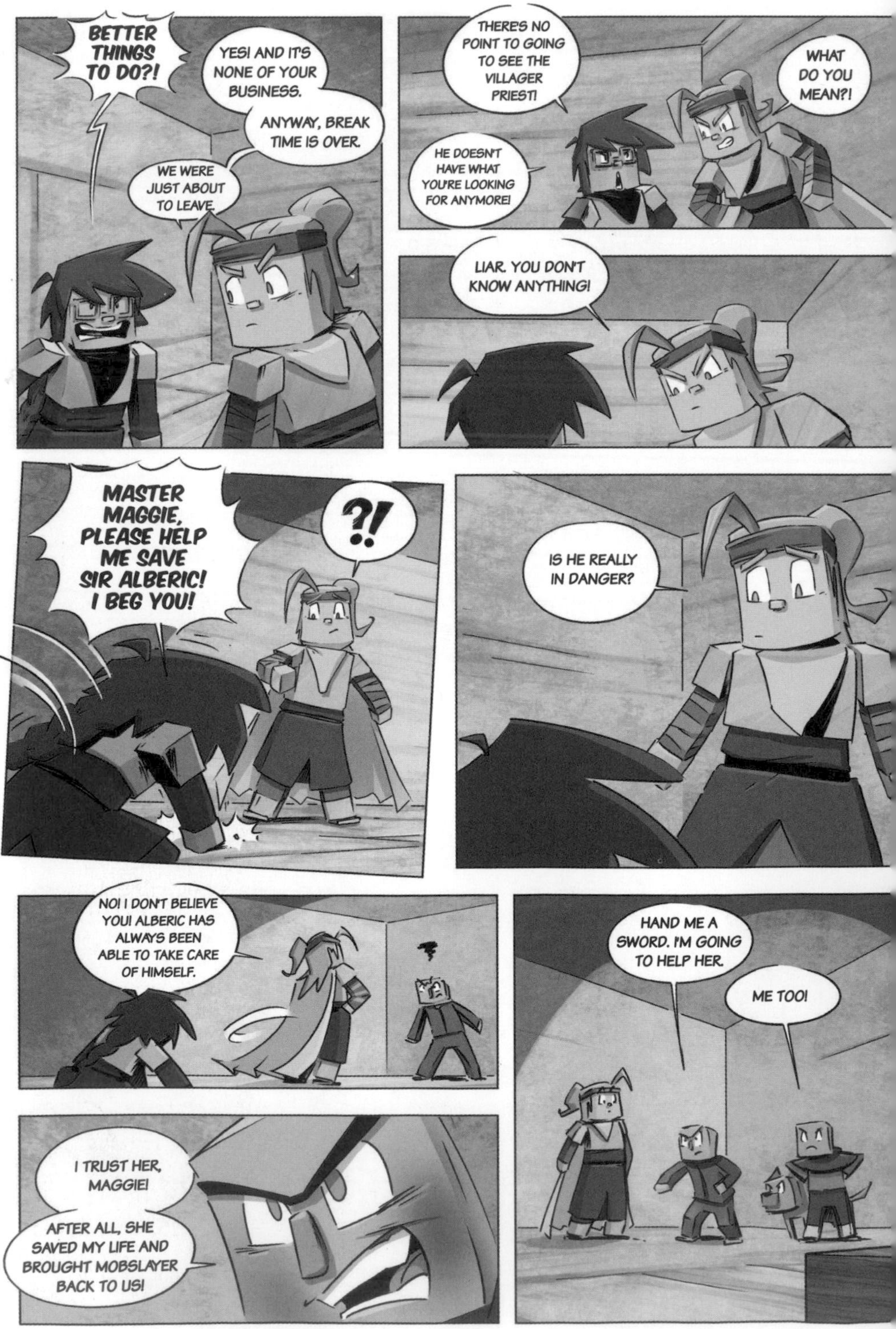
BETTER THINGS TO DO?!
YES! AND IT'S NONE OF YOUR BUSINESS.
ANYWAY, BREAK TIME IS OVER.
WE WERE JUST ABOUT TO LEAVE.
THERE'S NO POINT TO GOING TO SEE THE VILLAGER PRIEST!
WHAT DO YOU MEAN?!
HE DOESN'T HAVE WHAT YOU'RE LOOKING FOR ANYMORE!
LIAR. YOU DON'T KNOW ANYTHING!
MASTER MAGGIE, PLEASE HELP ME SAVE SIR ALBERIC! I BEG YOU!
?!
IS HE REALLY IN DANGER?
NO! I DON'T BELIEVE YOU! ALBERIC HAS ALWAYS BEEN ABLE TO TAKE CARE OF HIMSELF.
I TRUST HER, MAGGIE!
AFTER ALL, SHE SAVED MY LIFE AND BROUGHT MOBSLAYER BACK TO US!
HAND ME A SWORD. I'M GOING TO HELP HER.
ME TOO!

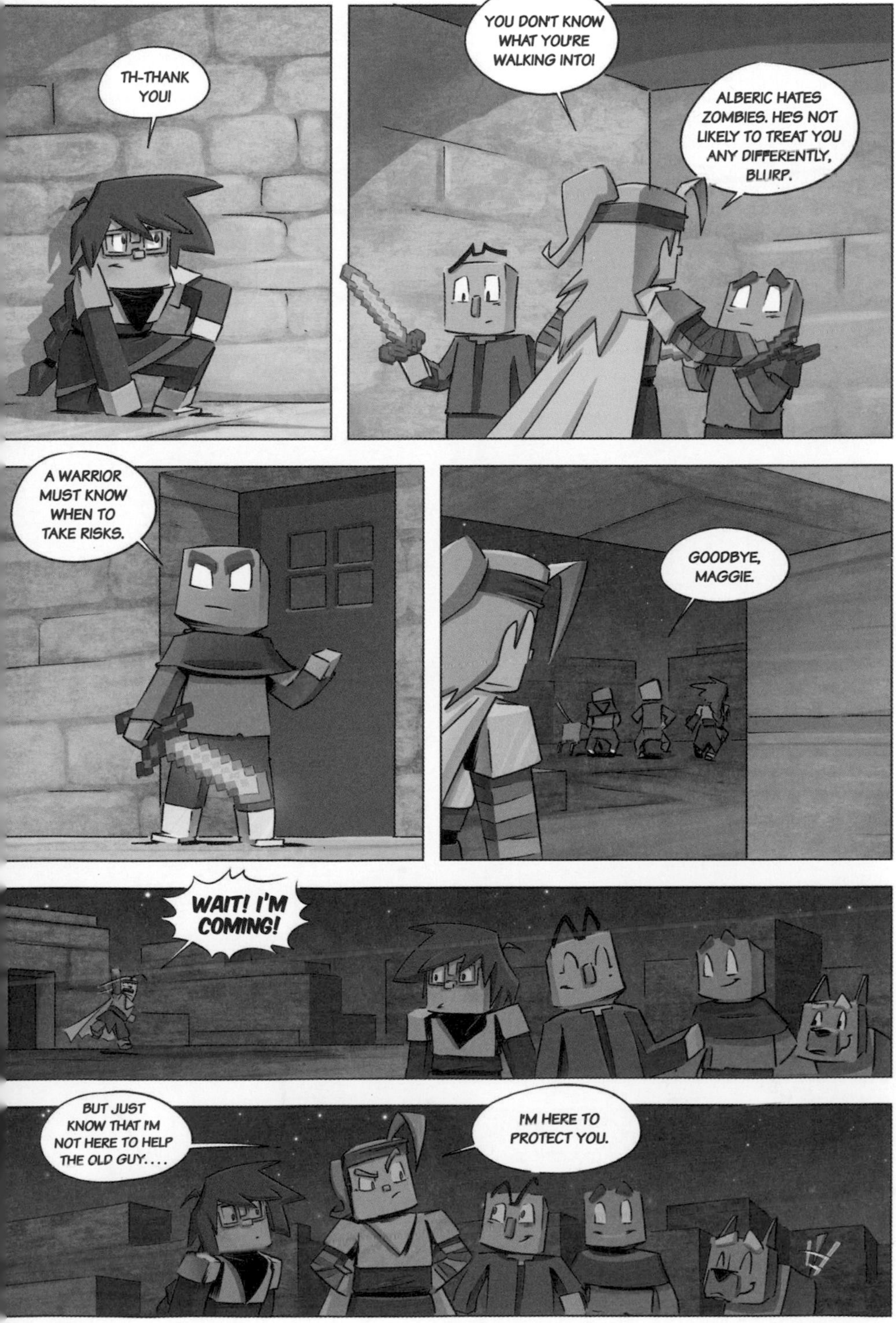
TH-THANK YOU!
YOU DON'T KNOW WHAT YOU'RE WALKING INTO!
ALBERIC HATES ZOMBIES. HE'S NOT LIKELY TO TREAT YOU ANY DIFFERENTLY, BLURP.
A WARRIOR MUST KNOW WHEN TO TAKE RISKS.
GOODBYE, MAGGIE.
WAIT! I'M COMING!
BUT JUST KNOW THAT I'M NOT HERE TO HELP THE OLD GUY. . . .
I'M HERE TO PROTECT YOU.

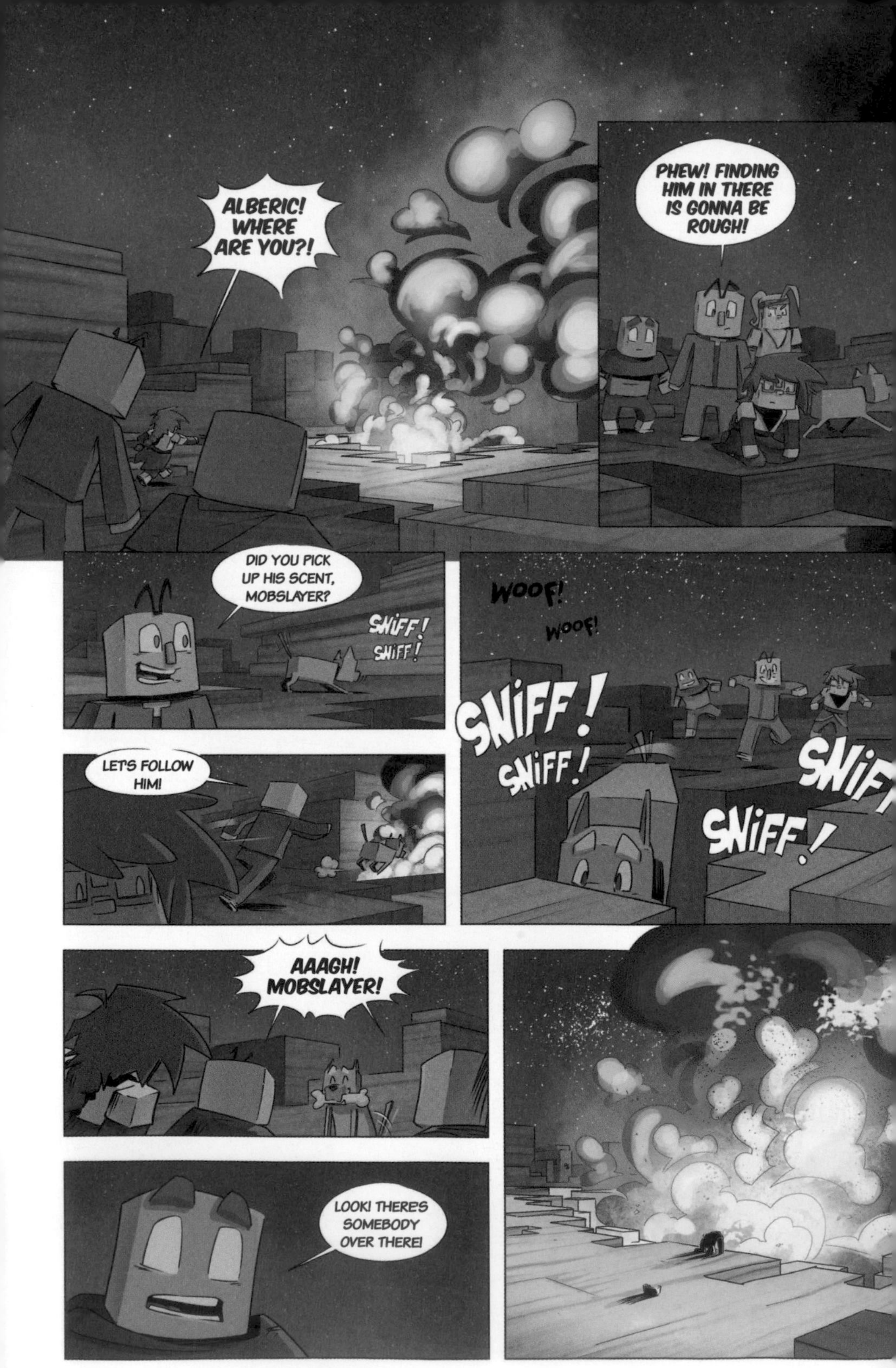
ALBERIC! WHERE ARE YOU?!
PHEW! FINDING HIM IN THERE IS GONNA BE ROUGH!
DID YOU PICK UP HIS SCENT, MOBSLAYER?
SNIFF! SNIFF!
LET'S FOLLOW HIM!
WOOF! WOOF!
SNIFF! SNIFF!
SNIFF! SNIFF!
AAAGH! MOBSLAYER!
LOOK! THERE'S SOMEBODY OVER THERE!

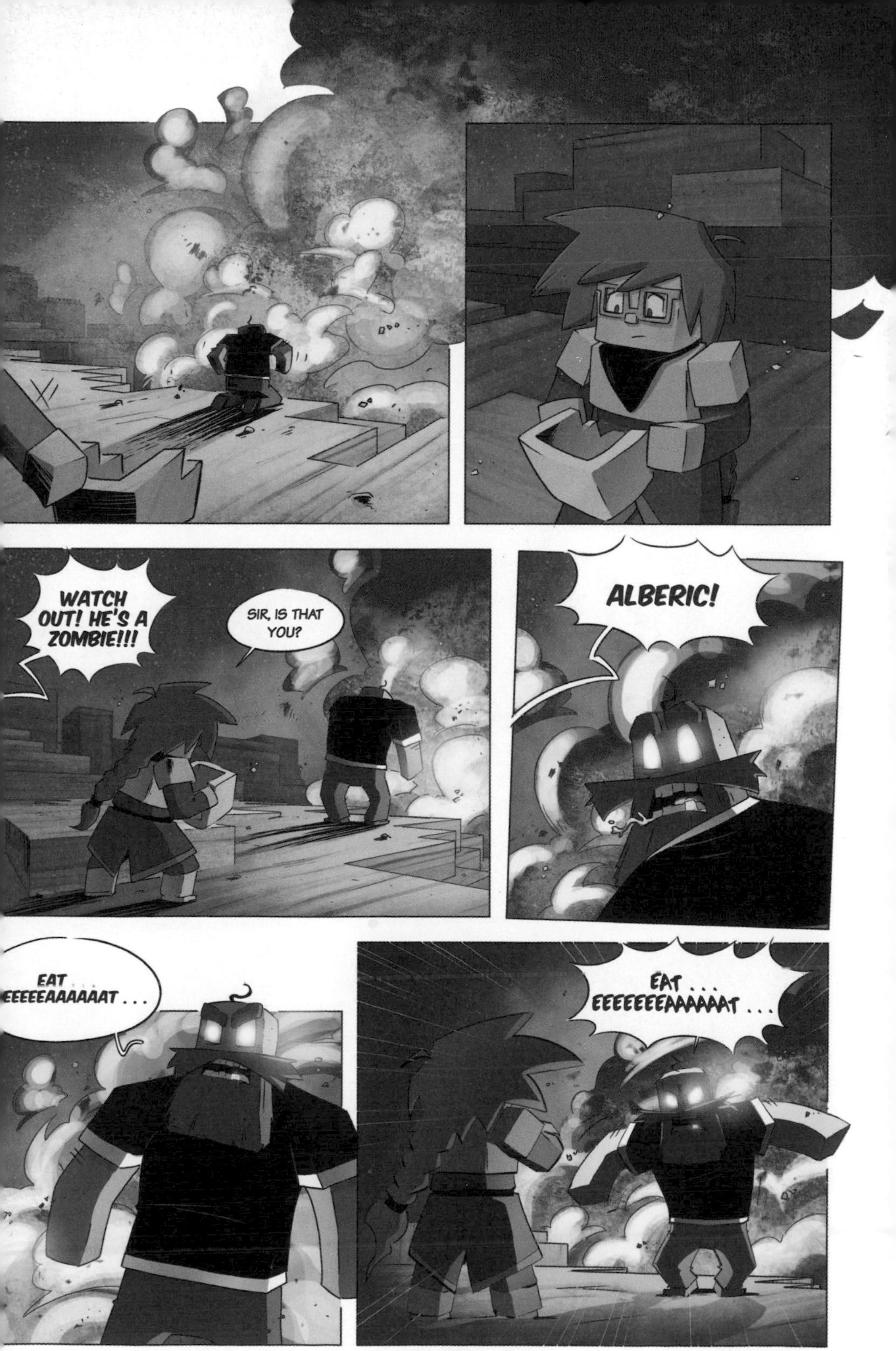
WATCH OUT! HE'S A ZOMBIE!!!
SIR, IS THAT YOU?
ALBERIC!
EAT . . . EEEEEAAAAAAT . . .
EAT . . . EEEEEEEAAAAAAT . . .

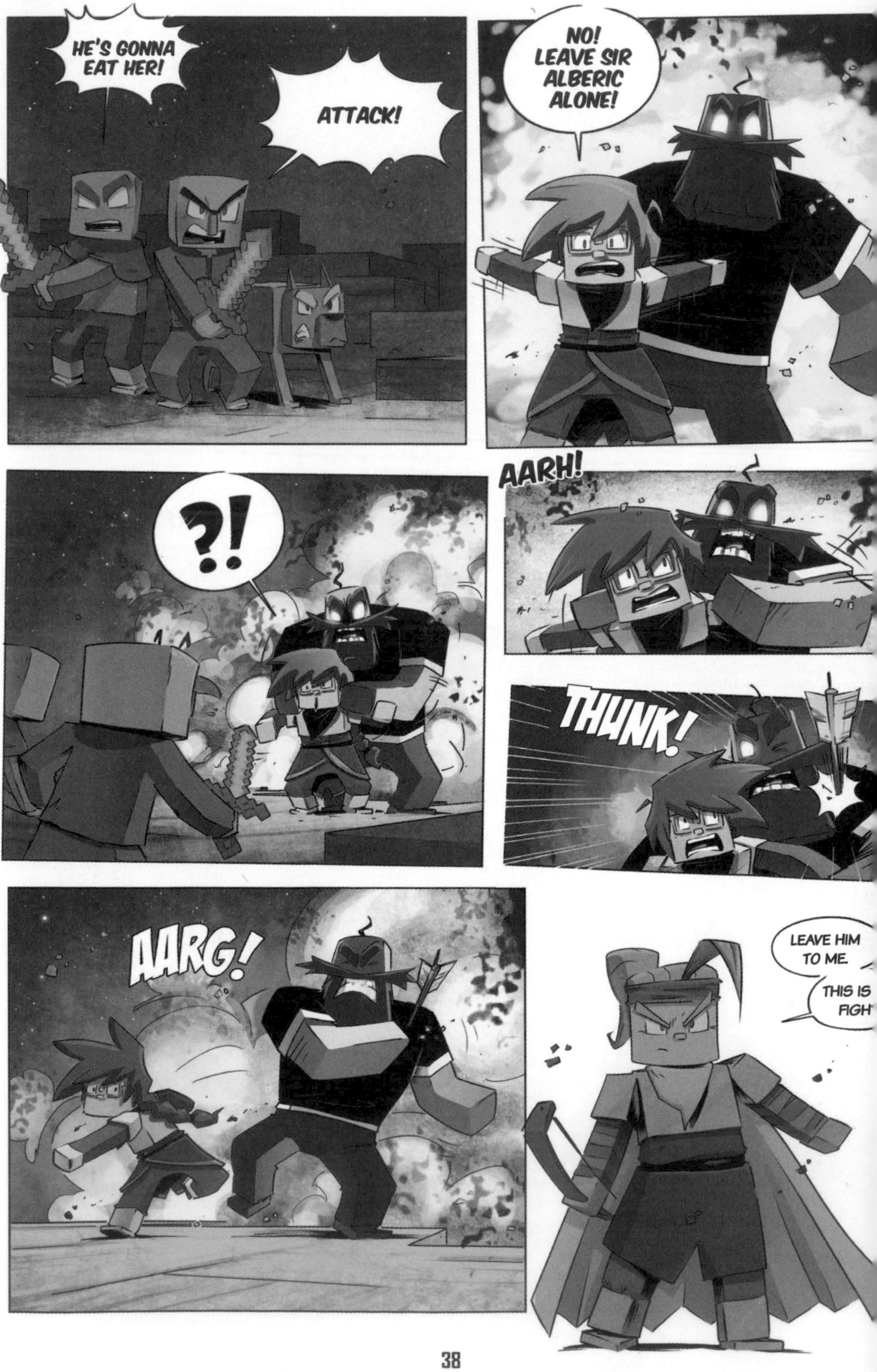
HE'S GONNA EAT HER!
ATTACK!
NO! LEAVE SIR ALBERIC ALONE!
?!
AARH!
THUNK!
AARG!
LEAVE HIM TO ME.
THIS IS
FIGH

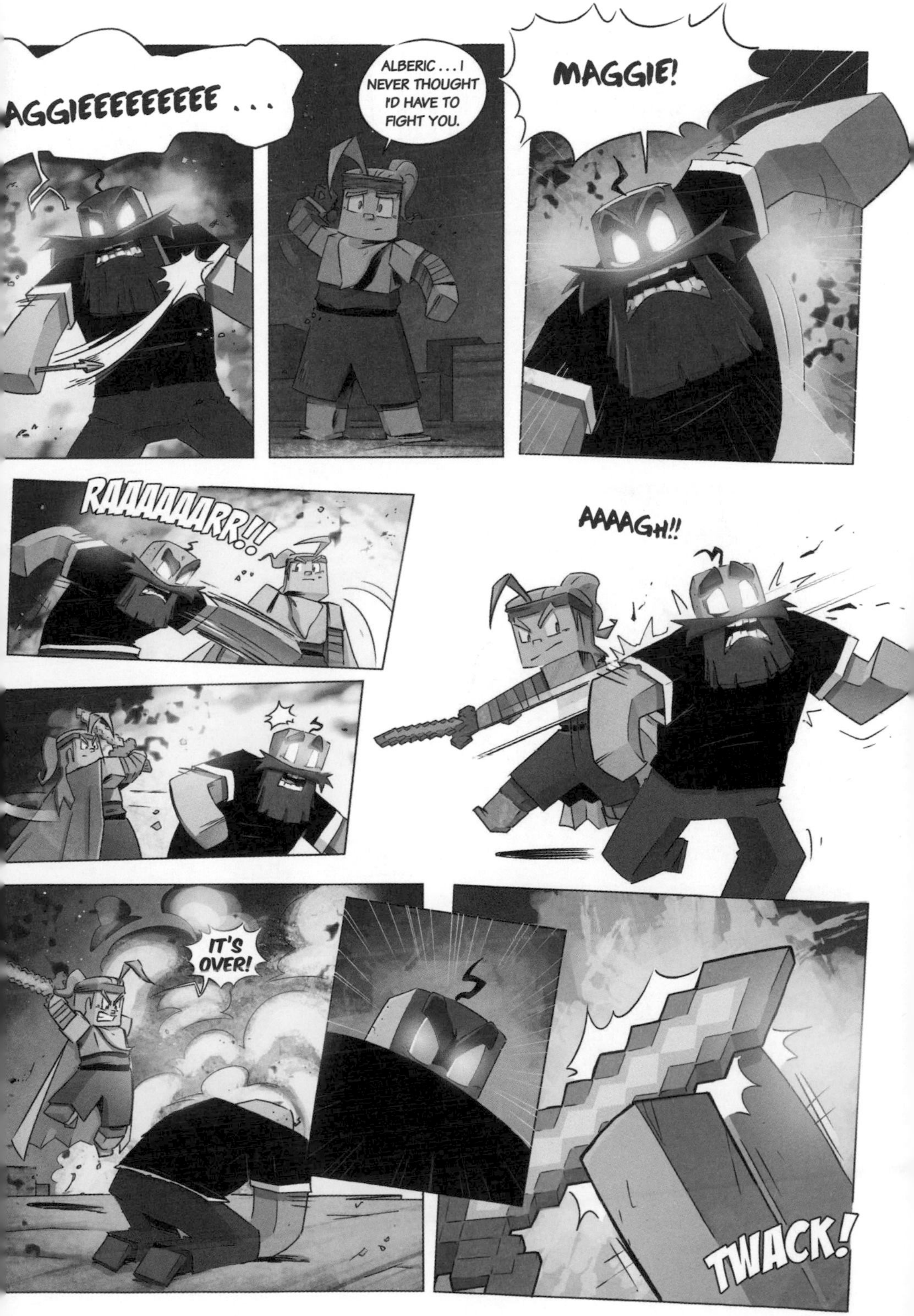
AGGIEEEEEEEEE . . .
ALBERIC . . . I NEVER THOUGHT I'D HAVE TO FIGHT YOU.
MAGGIE!
RAAAAAAARR!!
AAAAGH!!
IT'S OVER!
TWACK!

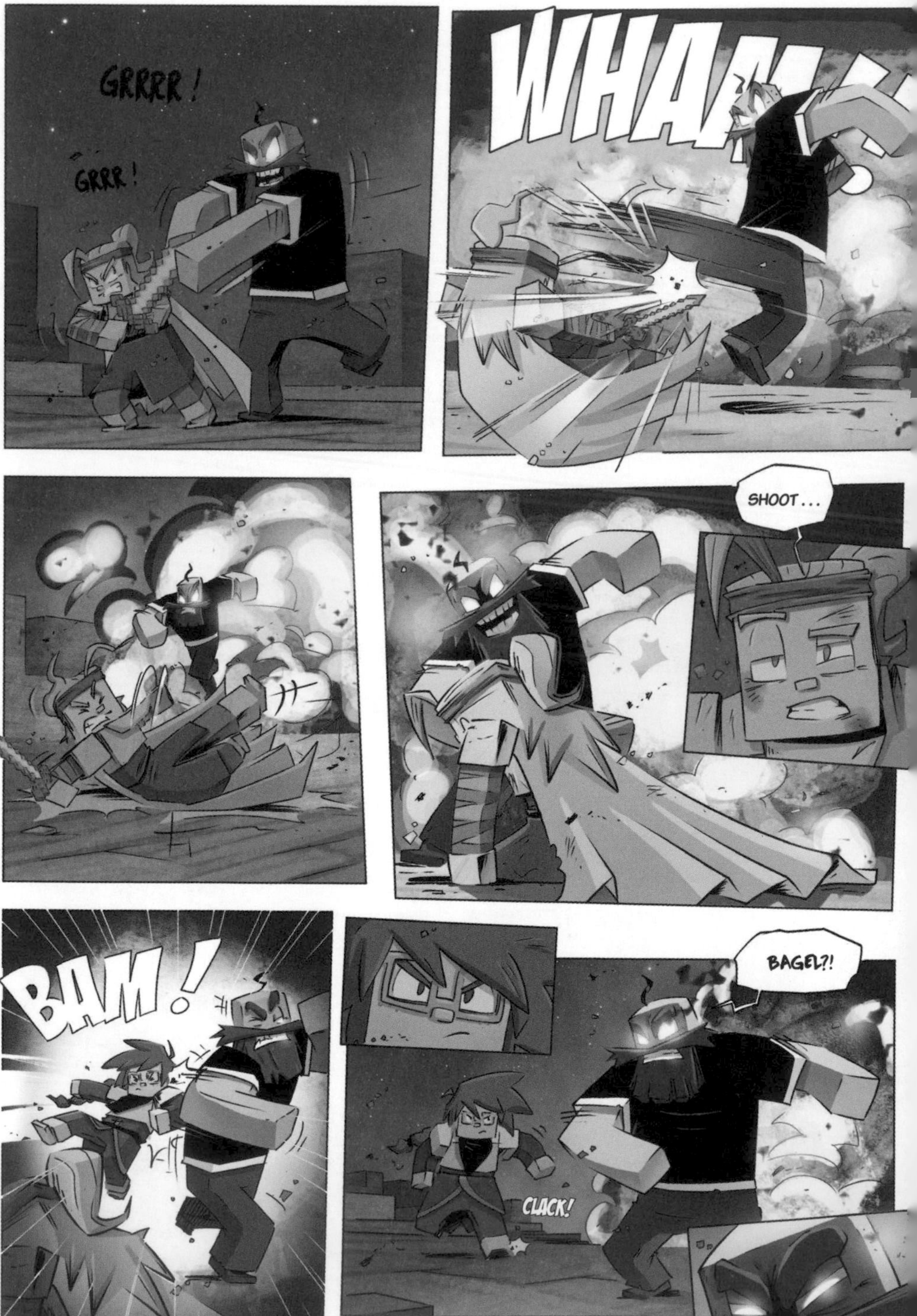
GRRRR!
GRRR!
WHAM
SHOOT...
BAM!
BAGEL?!
CLACK!

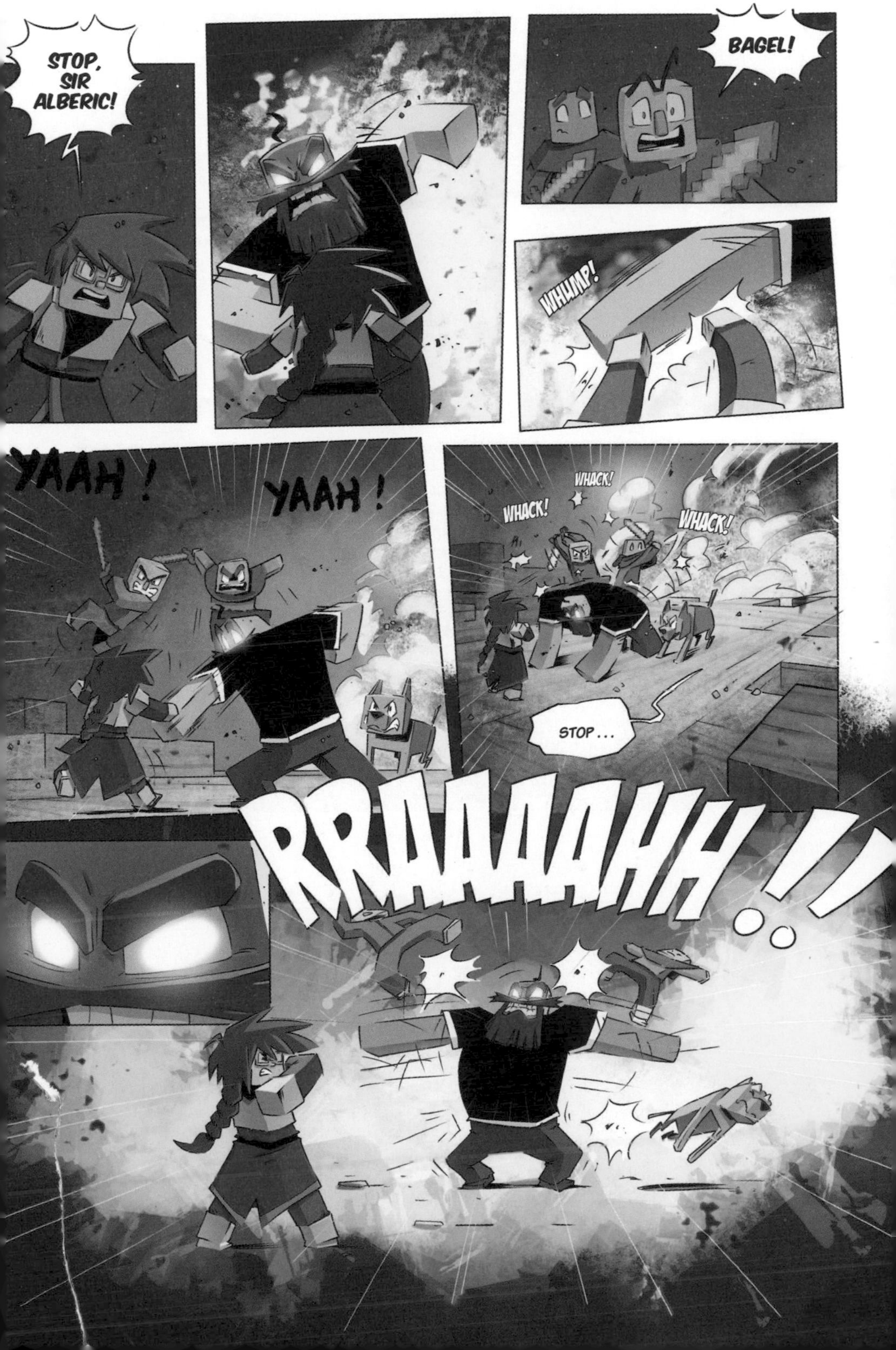
STOP, SIR ALBERIC!
BAGEL!
WHUMP!
YAAH!
YAAH!
WHACK!
WHACK!
WHACK!
STOP...
RRAAAAHH!!

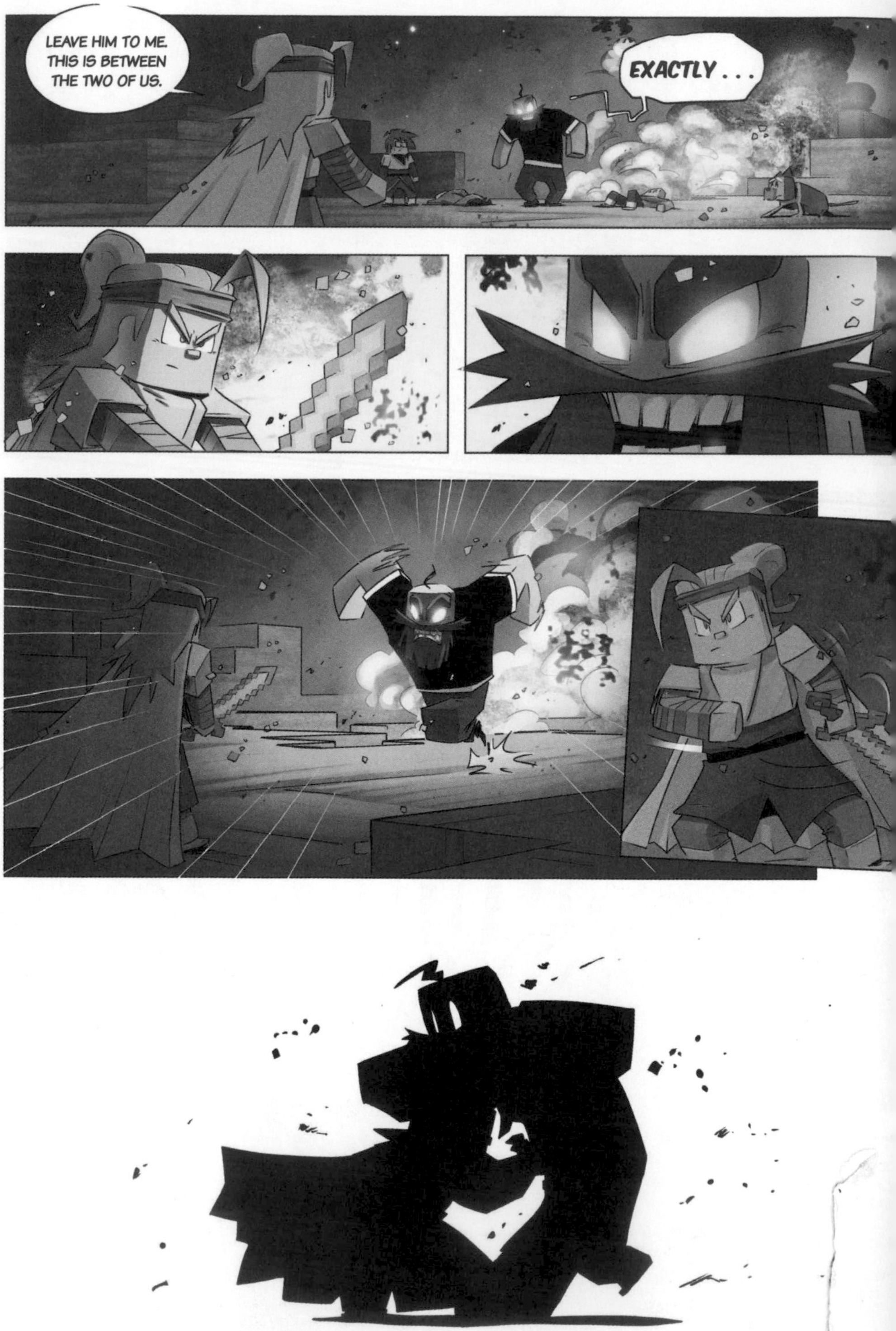
LEAVE HIM TO ME. THIS IS BETWEEN THE TWO OF US.
EXACTLY . . .

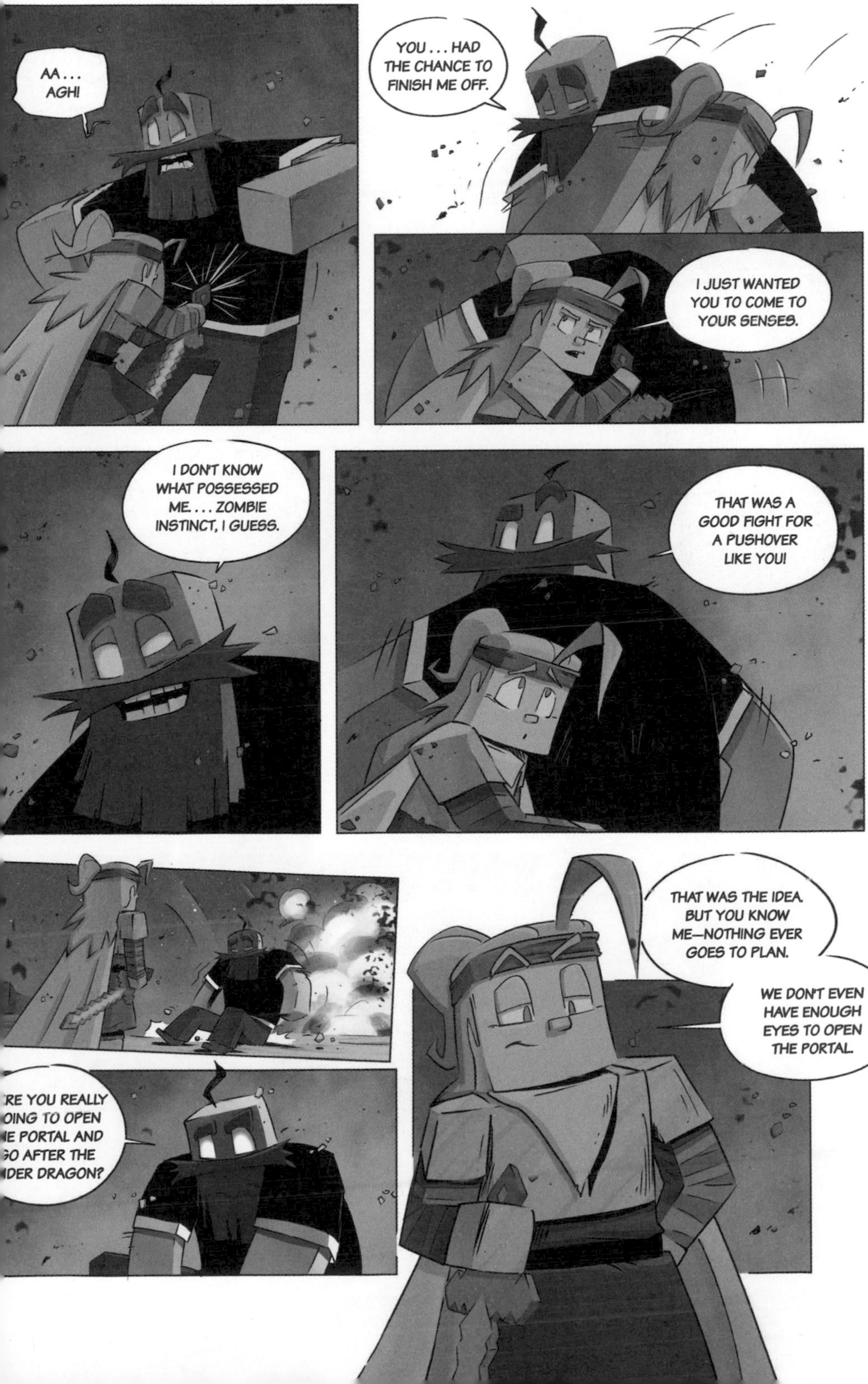
AA . . . AGH!
YOU . . . HAD THE CHANCE TO FINISH ME OFF.
I JUST WANTED YOU TO COME TO YOUR SENSES.
I DON'T KNOW WHAT POSSESSED ME. . . . ZOMBIE INSTINCT, I GUESS.
THAT WAS A GOOD FIGHT FOR A PUSHOVER LIKE YOU!
RE YOU REALLY OING TO OPEN E PORTAL AND O AFTER THE DER DRAGON?
THAT WAS THE IDEA. BUT YOU KNOW ME—NOTHING EVER GOES TO PLAN.
WE DON'T EVEN HAVE ENOUGH EYES TO OPEN THE PORTAL.

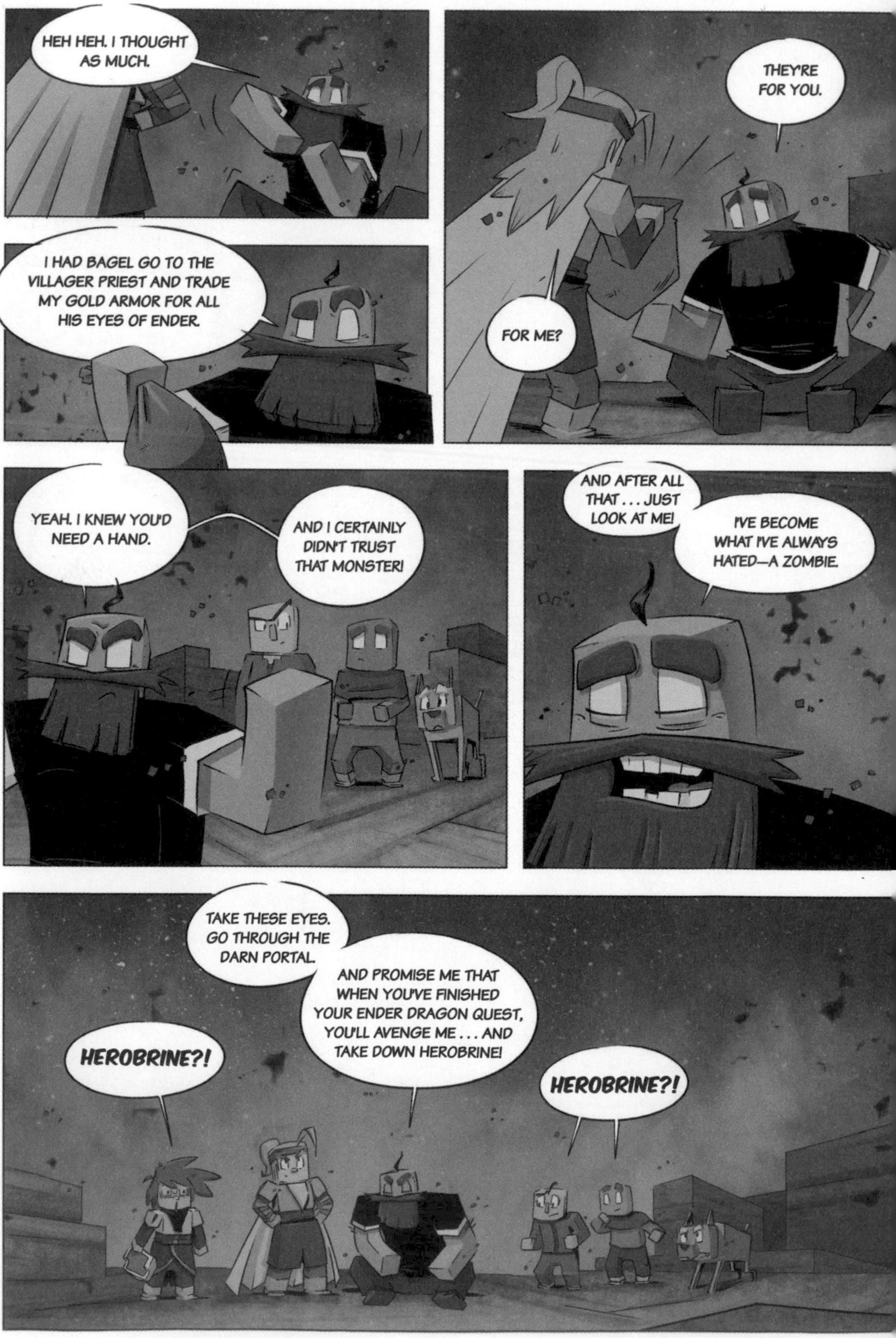
HEH HEH. I THOUGHT AS MUCH.
THEY'RE FOR YOU.
I HAD BAGEL GO TO THE VILLAGER PRIEST AND TRADE MY GOLD ARMOR FOR ALL HIS EYES OF ENDER.
FOR ME?
YEAH. I KNEW YOU'D NEED A HAND.
AND I CERTAINLY DIDN'T TRUST THAT MONSTER!
AND AFTER ALL THAT . . . JUST LOOK AT ME!
I'VE BECOME WHAT I'VE ALWAYS HATED—A ZOMBIE.
TAKE THESE EYES. GO THROUGH THE DARN PORTAL.
AND PROMISE ME THAT WHEN YOU'VE FINISHED YOUR ENDER DRAGON QUEST, YOU'LL AVENGE ME . . . AND TAKE DOWN HEROBRINE!
HEROBRINE?!
HEROBRINE?!

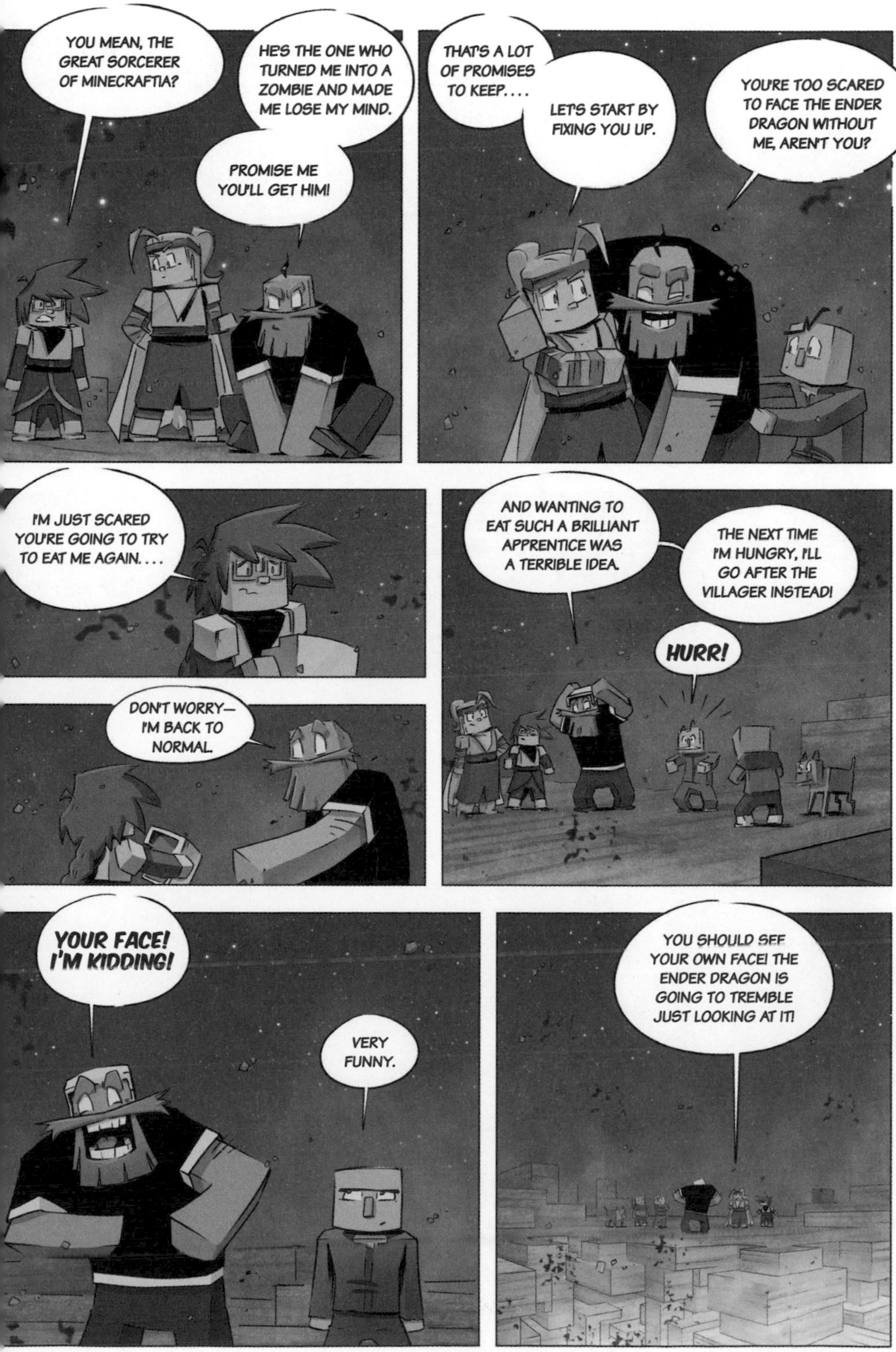
YOU MEAN, THE GREAT SORCERER OF MINECRAFTIA?
HE'S THE ONE WHO TURNED ME INTO A ZOMBIE AND MADE ME LOSE MY MIND.
PROMISE ME YOU'LL GET HIM!
THAT'S A LOT OF PROMISES TO KEEP. . . .
LET'S START BY FIXING YOU UP.
YOU'RE TOO SCARED TO FACE THE ENDER DRAGON WITHOUT ME, AREN'T YOU?
I'M JUST SCARED YOU'RE GOING TO TRY TO EAT ME AGAIN. . . .
DON'T WORRY— I'M BACK TO NORMAL.
AND WANTING TO EAT SUCH A BRILLIANT APPRENTICE WAS A TERRIBLE IDEA.
THE NEXT TIME I'M HUNGRY, I'LL GO AFTER THE VILLAGER INSTEAD!
HURR!
YOUR FACE! I'M KIDDING!
VERY FUNNY.
YOU SHOULD SEE YOUR OWN FACE! THE ENDER DRAGON IS GOING TO TREMBLE JUST LOOKING AT IT!

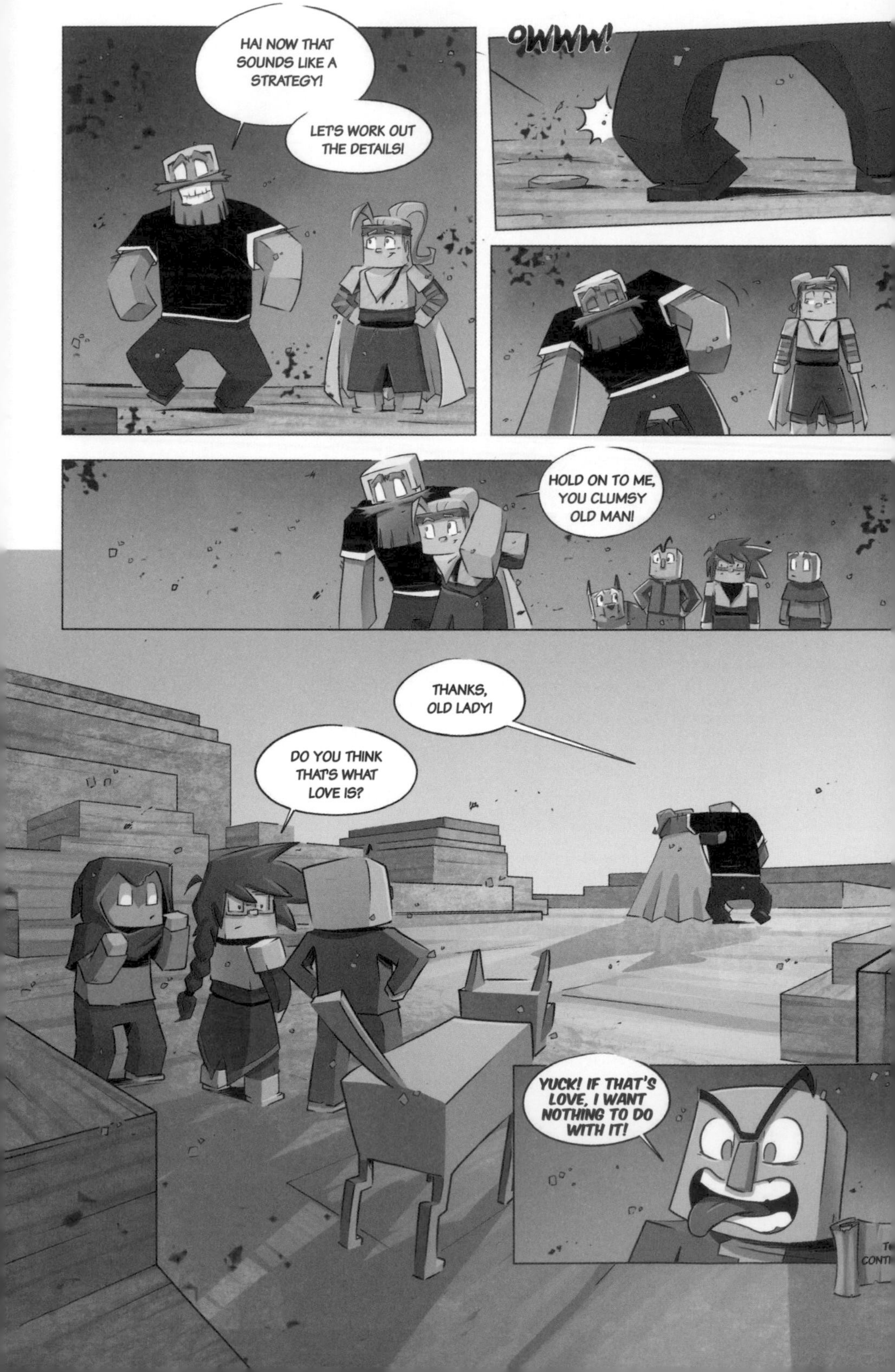
HA! NOW THAT SOUNDS LIKE A STRATEGY!
LET'S WORK OUT THE DETAILS!
OWWW!
HOLD ON TO ME, YOU CLUMSY OLD MAN!
THANKS, OLD LADY!
DO YOU THINK THAT'S WHAT LOVE IS?
YUCK! IF THAT'S LOVE, I WANT NOTHING TO DO WITH IT!

PART TWO

WELCOME TO THE END

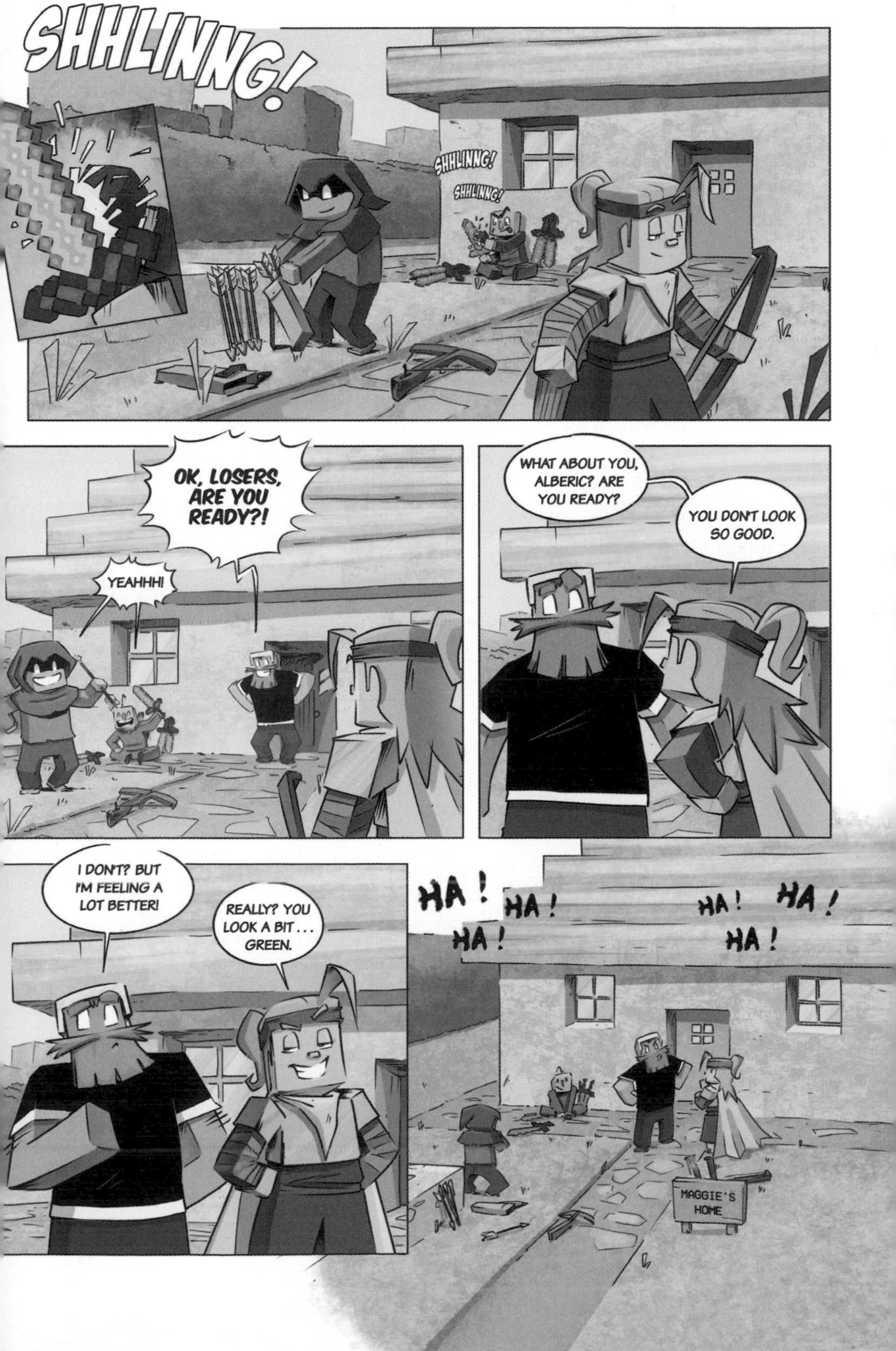
SHHLINNG!
SHHLINNG!
SHHLINNG!
OK, LOSERS, ARE YOU READY?!
YEAHHH!
WHAT ABOUT YOU, ALBERIC? ARE YOU READY?
YOU DON'T LOOK SO GOOD.
I DON'T? BUT I'M FEELING A LOT BETTER!
REALLY? YOU LOOK A BIT . . . GREEN.
HA! HA! HA! HA! HA! HA!
MAGGIE'S HOME

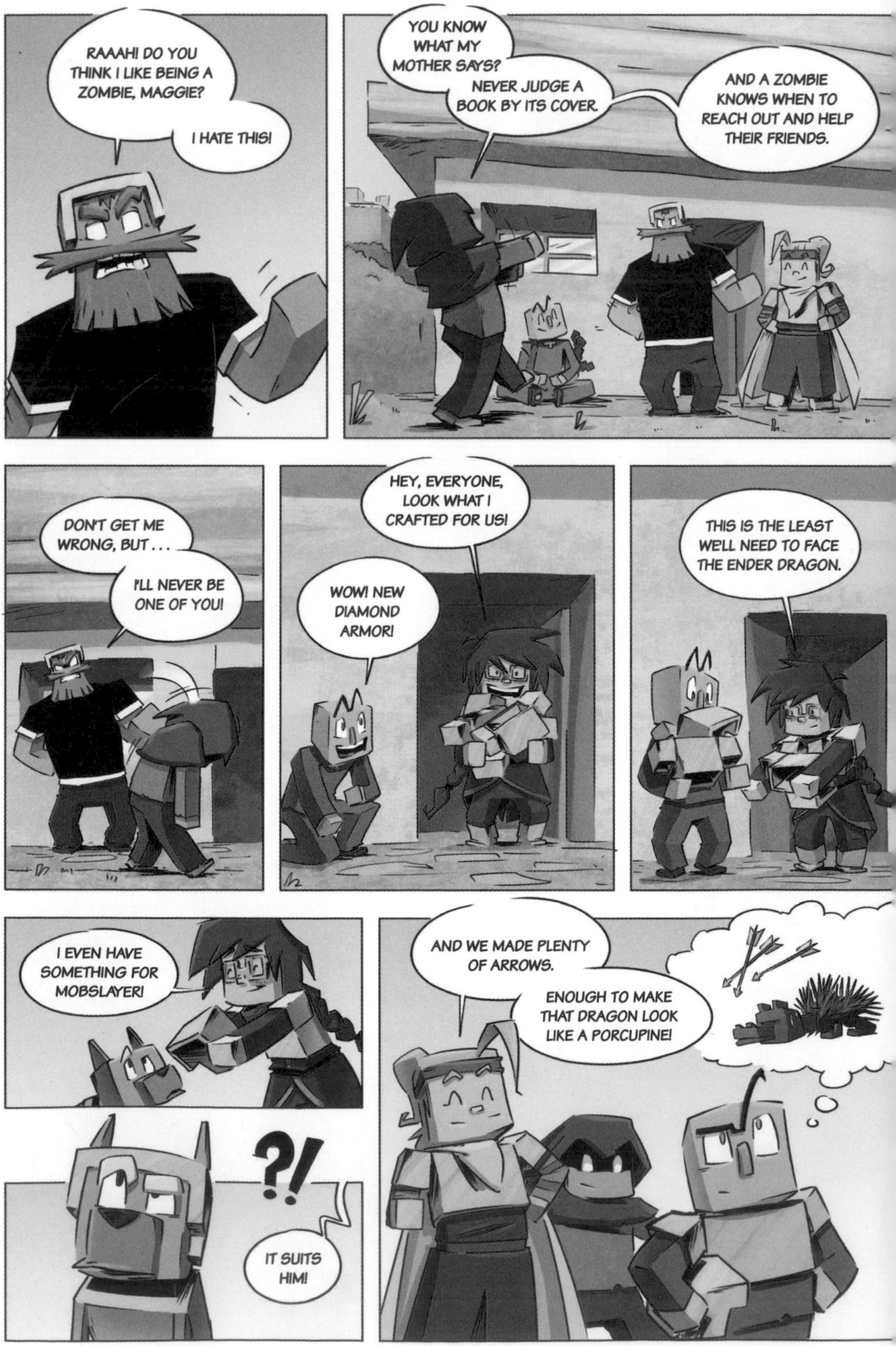
RAAAH! DO YOU THINK I LIKE BEING A ZOMBIE, MAGGIE?
I HATE THIS!
YOU KNOW WHAT MY MOTHER SAYS?
NEVER JUDGE A BOOK BY ITS COVER.
AND A ZOMBIE KNOWS WHEN TO REACH OUT AND HELP THEIR FRIENDS.
DON'T GET ME WRONG, BUT . . .
I'LL NEVER BE ONE OF YOU!
HEY, EVERYONE, LOOK WHAT I CRAFTED FOR US!
WOW! NEW DIAMOND ARMOR!
THIS IS THE LEAST WE'LL NEED TO FACE THE ENDER DRAGON.
I EVEN HAVE SOMETHING FOR MOBSLAYER!
?!
IT SUITS HIM!
AND WE MADE PLENTY OF ARROWS.
ENOUGH TO MAKE THAT DRAGON LOOK LIKE A PORCUPINE!

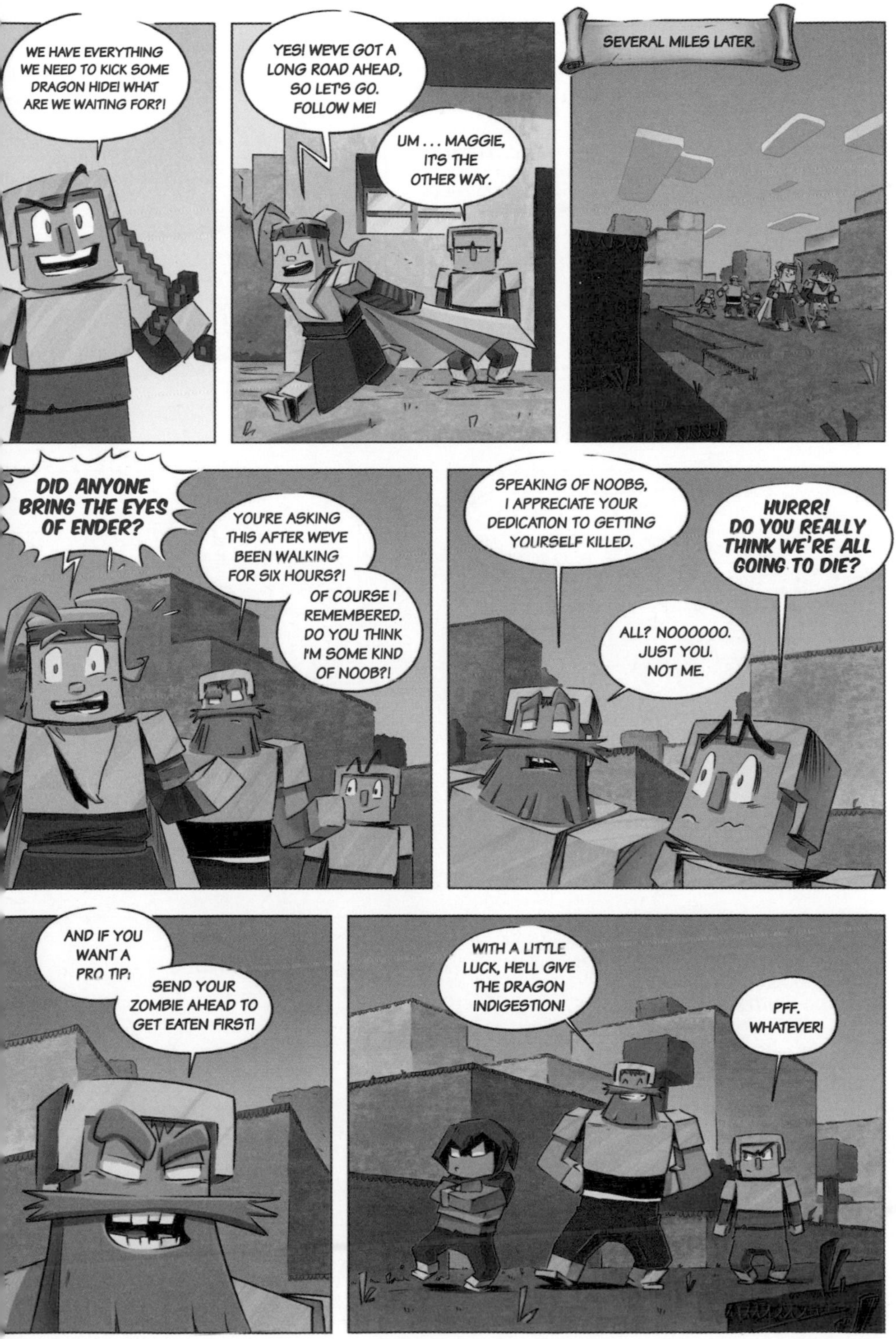
WE HAVE EVERYTHING WE NEED TO KICK SOME DRAGON HIDE! WHAT ARE WE WAITING FOR?!
YES! WE'VE GOT A LONG ROAD AHEAD, SO LET'S GO. FOLLOW ME!
UM . . . MAGGIE, IT'S THE OTHER WAY.
SEVERAL MILES LATER
DID ANYONE BRING THE EYES OF ENDER?
YOU'RE ASKING THIS AFTER WE'VE BEEN WALKING FOR SIX HOURS?!
OF COURSE I REMEMBERED. DO YOU THINK I'M SOME KIND OF NOOB?!
SPEAKING OF NOOBS, I APPRECIATE YOUR DEDICATION TO GETTING YOURSELF KILLED.
HURRR! DO YOU REALLY THINK WE'RE ALL GOING TO DIE?
ALL? NOOOOOO. JUST YOU. NOT ME.
AND IF YOU WANT A PRO TIP:
SEND YOUR ZOMBIE AHEAD TO GET EATEN FIRST!
WITH A LITTLE LUCK, HE'LL GIVE THE DRAGON INDIGESTION!
PFF. WHATEVER!

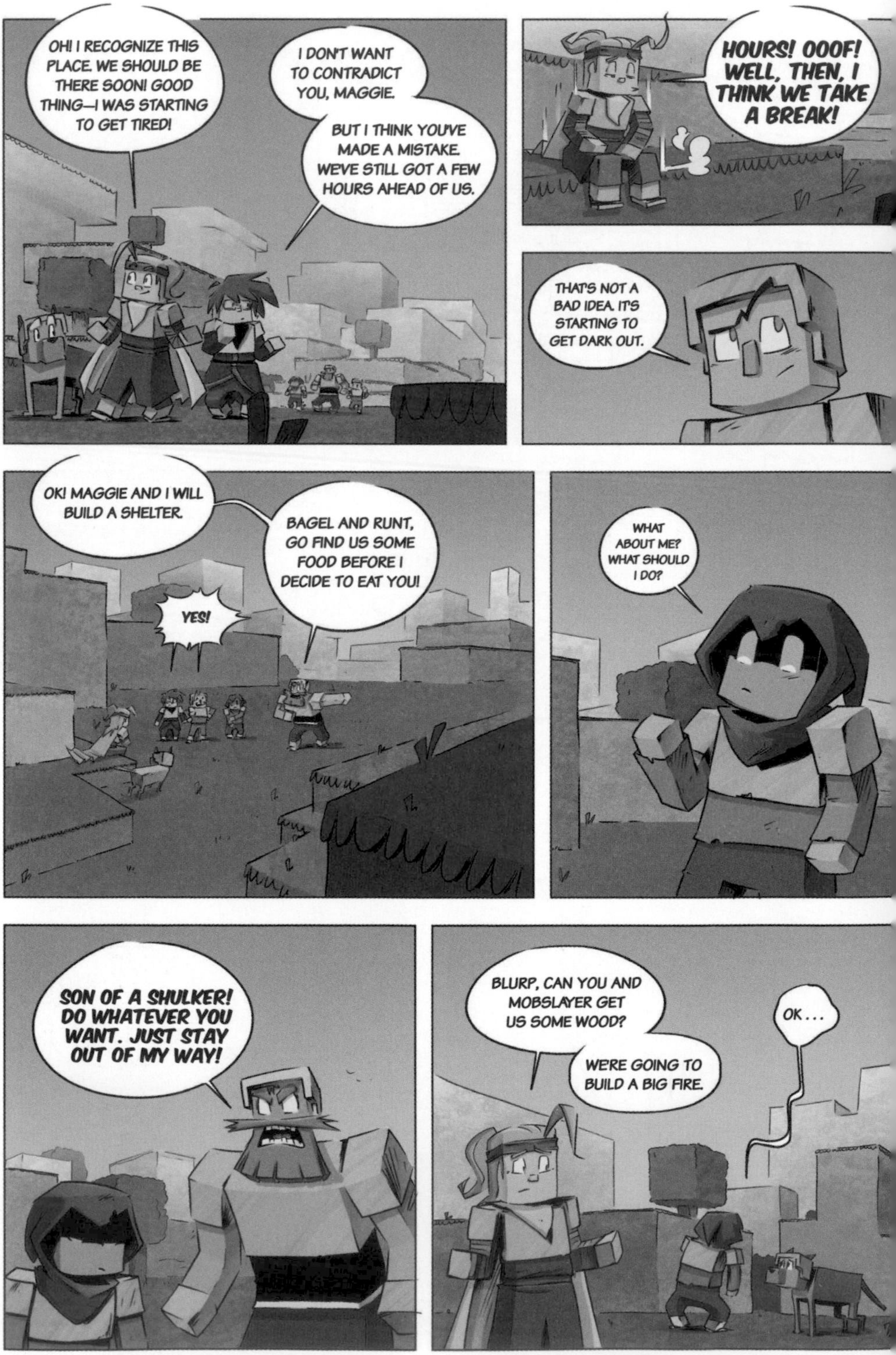

OH! I RECOGNIZE THIS PLACE. WE SHOULD BE THERE SOON! GOOD THING—I WAS STARTING TO GET TIRED!
I DON'T WANT TO CONTRADICT YOU, MAGGIE.
BUT I THINK YOU'VE MADE A MISTAKE. WE'VE STILL GOT A FEW HOURS AHEAD OF US.
HOURS! OOOF! WELL, THEN, I THINK WE TAKE A BREAK!
THAT'S NOT A BAD IDEA. IT'S STARTING TO GET DARK OUT.
OK! MAGGIE AND I WILL BUILD A SHELTER.
BAGEL AND RUNT, GO FIND US SOME FOOD BEFORE I DECIDE TO EAT YOU!
YES!
WHAT ABOUT ME? WHAT SHOULD I DO?
SON OF A SHULKER! DO WHATEVER YOU WANT. JUST STAY OUT OF MY WAY!
BLURP, CAN YOU AND MOBSLAYER GET US SOME WOOD?
WE'RE GOING TO BUILD A BIG FIRE.
OK . . .

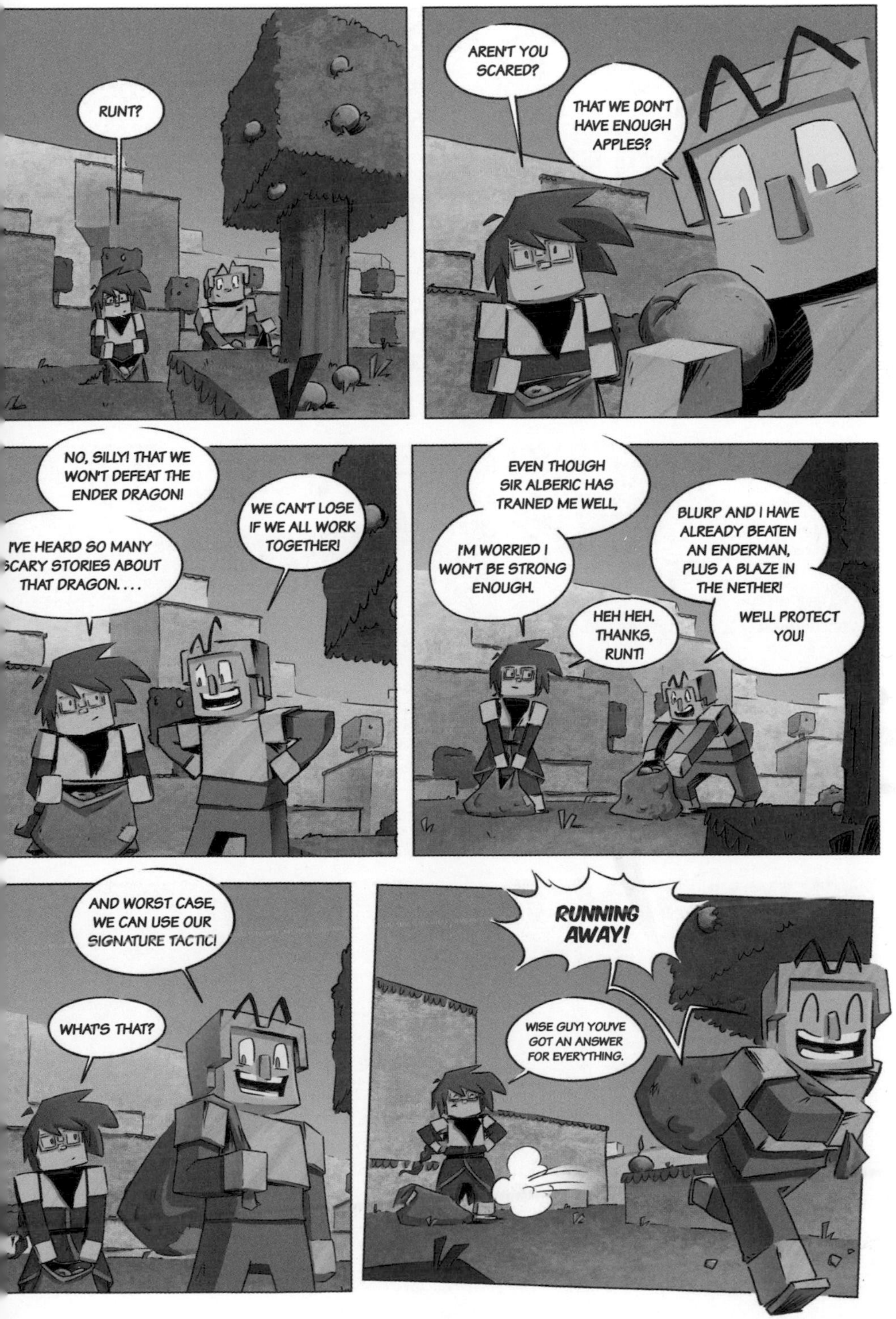
RUNT?
AREN'T YOU SCARED?
THAT WE DON'T HAVE ENOUGH APPLES?
NO, SILLY! THAT WE WON'T DEFEAT THE ENDER DRAGON!
I'VE HEARD SO MANY SCARY STORIES ABOUT THAT DRAGON. . . .
WE CAN'T LOSE IF WE ALL WORK TOGETHER!
EVEN THOUGH SIR ALBERIC HAS TRAINED ME WELL,
I'M WORRIED I WON'T BE STRONG ENOUGH.
BLURP AND I HAVE ALREADY BEATEN AN ENDERMAN, PLUS A BLAZE IN THE NETHER!
WE'LL PROTECT YOU!
HEH HEH. THANKS, RUNT!
AND WORST CASE, WE CAN USE OUR SIGNATURE TACTIC!
WHAT'S THAT?
RUNNING AWAY!
WISE GUY! YOU'VE GOT AN ANSWER FOR EVERYTHING.

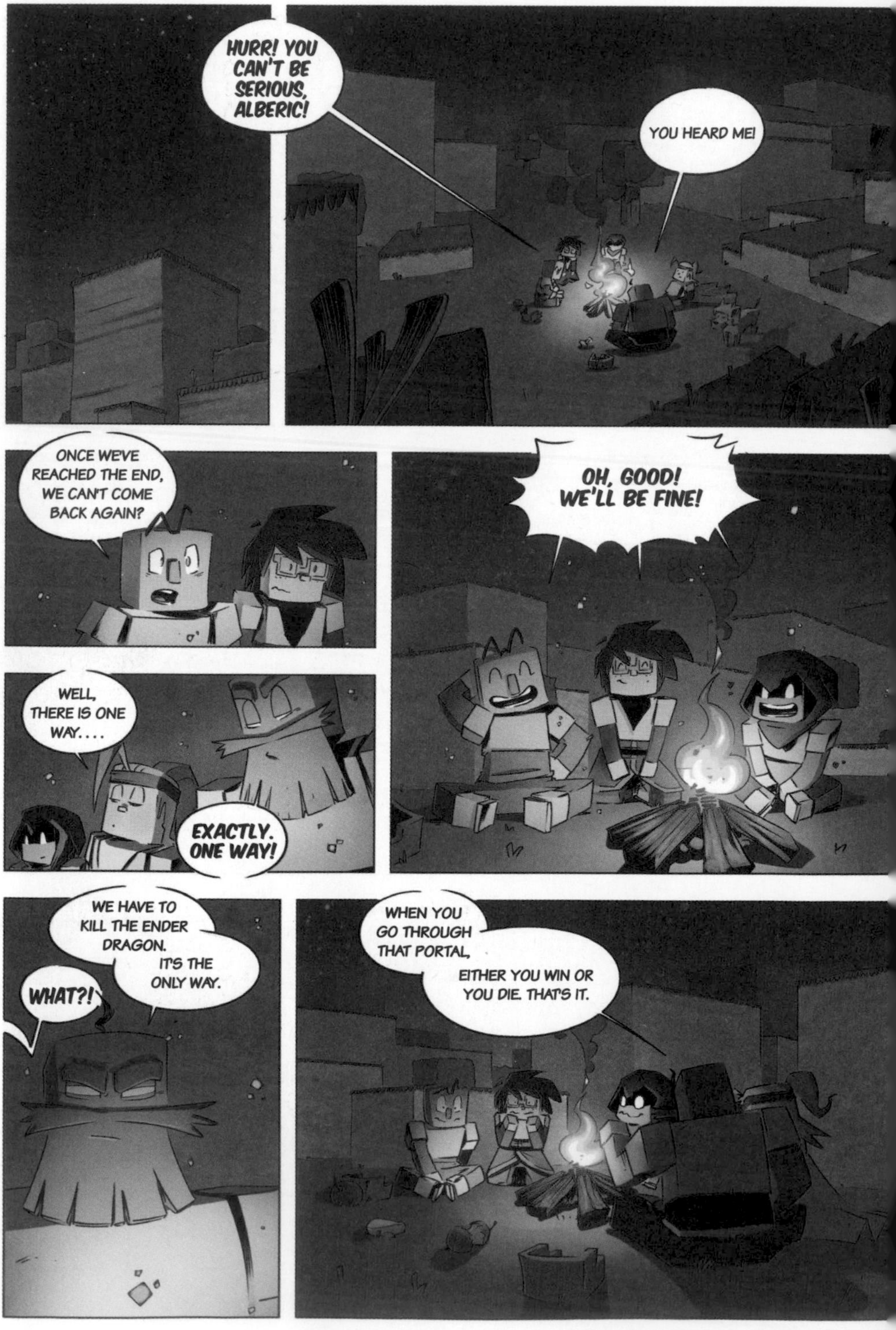
HURR! YOU CAN'T BE SERIOUS, ALBERIC!
YOU HEARD ME!
ONCE WE'VE REACHED THE END, WE CAN'T COME BACK AGAIN?
WELL, THERE IS ONE WAY....
EXACTLY. ONE WAY!
OH, GOOD! WE'LL BE FINE!
WE HAVE TO KILL THE ENDER DRAGON.
IT'S THE ONLY WAY.
WHAT?!
WHEN YOU GO THROUGH THAT PORTAL,
EITHER YOU WIN OR YOU DIE. THAT'S IT.

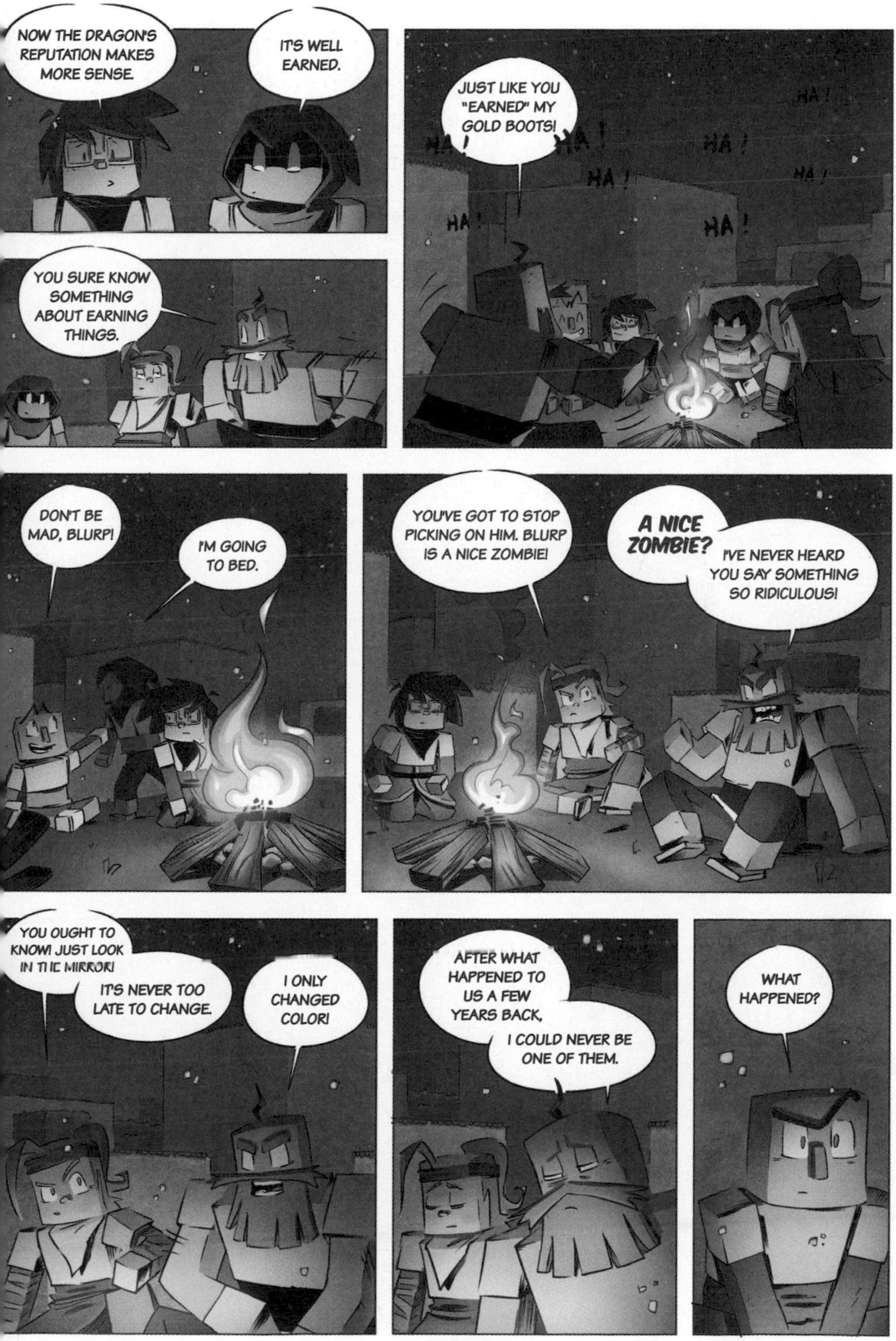
NOW THE DRAGON'S REPUTATION MAKES MORE SENSE.
IT'S WELL EARNED.
YOU SURE KNOW SOMETHING ABOUT EARNING THINGS.
JUST LIKE YOU "EARNED" MY GOLD BOOTS!
HA! HA! HA! HA! HA! HA! HA! HA!
DON'T BE MAD, BLURP!
I'M GOING TO BED.
YOU'VE GOT TO STOP PICKING ON HIM. BLURP IS A NICE ZOMBIE!
A NICE ZOMBIE?
I'VE NEVER HEARD YOU SAY SOMETHING SO RIDICULOUS!
YOU OUGHT TO KNOW! JUST LOOK IN THE MIRROR!
IT'S NEVER TOO LATE TO CHANGE.
I ONLY CHANGED COLOR!
AFTER WHAT HAPPENED TO US A FEW YEARS BACK,
I COULD NEVER BE ONE OF THEM.
WHAT HAPPENED?

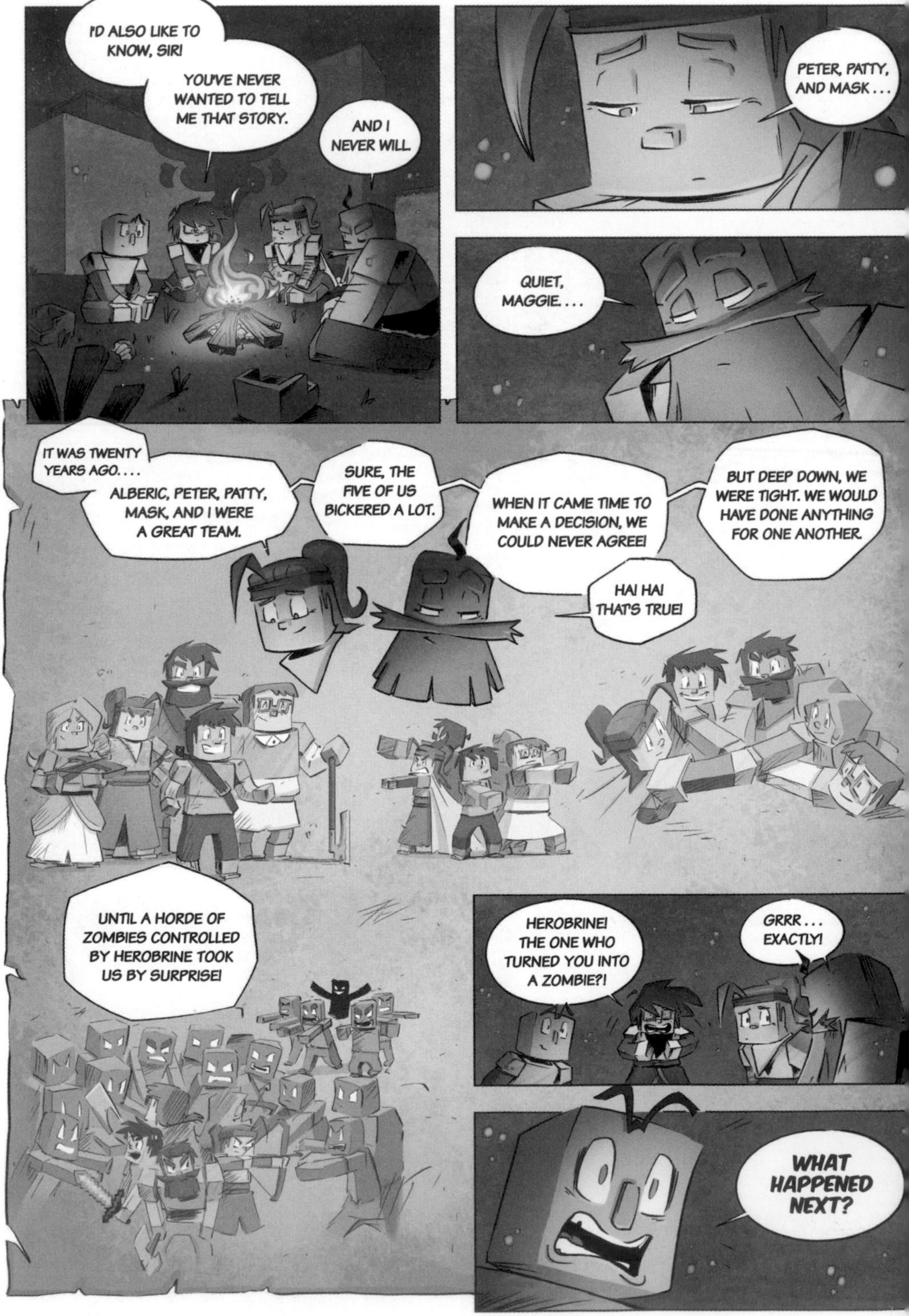
I'D ALSO LIKE TO KNOW, SIR!
YOU'VE NEVER WANTED TO TELL ME THAT STORY.
AND I NEVER WILL.
PETER, PATTY, AND MASK . . .
QUIET, MAGGIE. . . .
IT WAS TWENTY YEARS AGO. . . .
ALBERIC, PETER, PATTY, MASK, AND I WERE A GREAT TEAM.
SURE, THE FIVE OF US BICKERED A LOT.
WHEN IT CAME TIME TO MAKE A DECISION, WE COULD NEVER AGREE!
BUT DEEP DOWN, WE WERE TIGHT. WE WOULD HAVE DONE ANYTHING FOR ONE ANOTHER.
HA! HA! THAT'S TRUE!
UNTIL A HORDE OF ZOMBIES CONTROLLED BY HEROBRINE TOOK US BY SURPRISE!
HEROBRINE! THE ONE WHO TURNED YOU INTO A ZOMBIE?!
GRRR . . . EXACTLY!
WHAT HAPPENED NEXT?

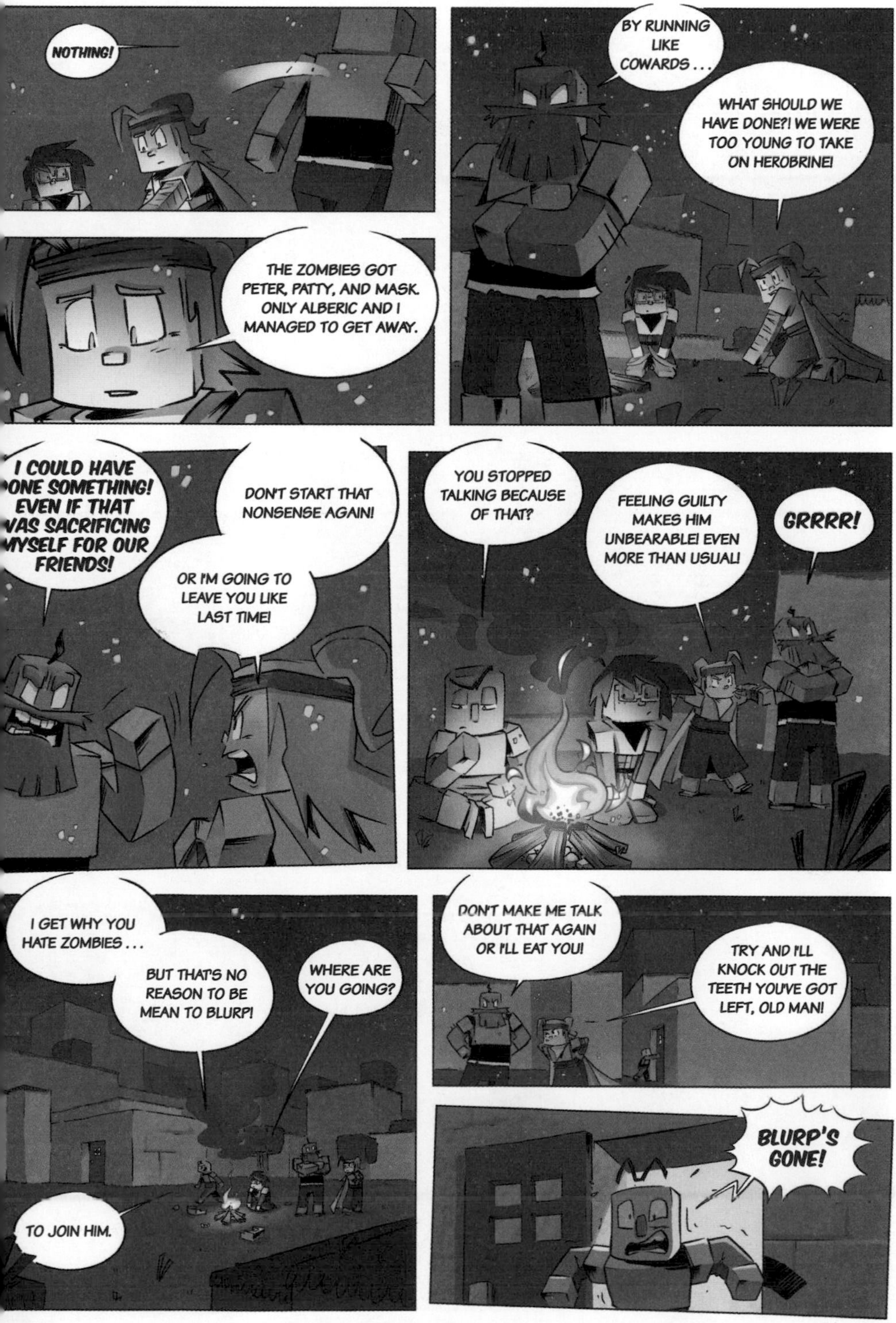
NOTHING!
BY RUNNING LIKE COWARDS . . .
WHAT SHOULD WE HAVE DONE?! WE WERE TOO YOUNG TO TAKE ON HEROBRINE!
THE ZOMBIES GOT PETER, PATTY, AND MASK. ONLY ALBERIC AND I MANAGED TO GET AWAY.
I COULD HAVE ONE SOMETHING! EVEN IF THAT VAS SACRIFICING MYSELF FOR OUR FRIENDS!
DON'T START THAT NONSENSE AGAIN!
OR I'M GOING TO LEAVE YOU LIKE LAST TIME!
YOU STOPPED TALKING BECAUSE OF THAT?
FEELING GUILTY MAKES HIM UNBEARABLE! EVEN MORE THAN USUAL!
GRRRR!
I GET WHY YOU HATE ZOMBIES . . .
BUT THAT'S NO REASON TO BE MEAN TO BLURP!
WHERE ARE YOU GOING?
TO JOIN HIM.
DON'T MAKE ME TALK ABOUT THAT AGAIN OR I'LL EAT YOU!
TRY AND I'LL KNOCK OUT THE TEETH YOU'VE GOT LEFT, OLD MAN!
BLURP'S GONE!

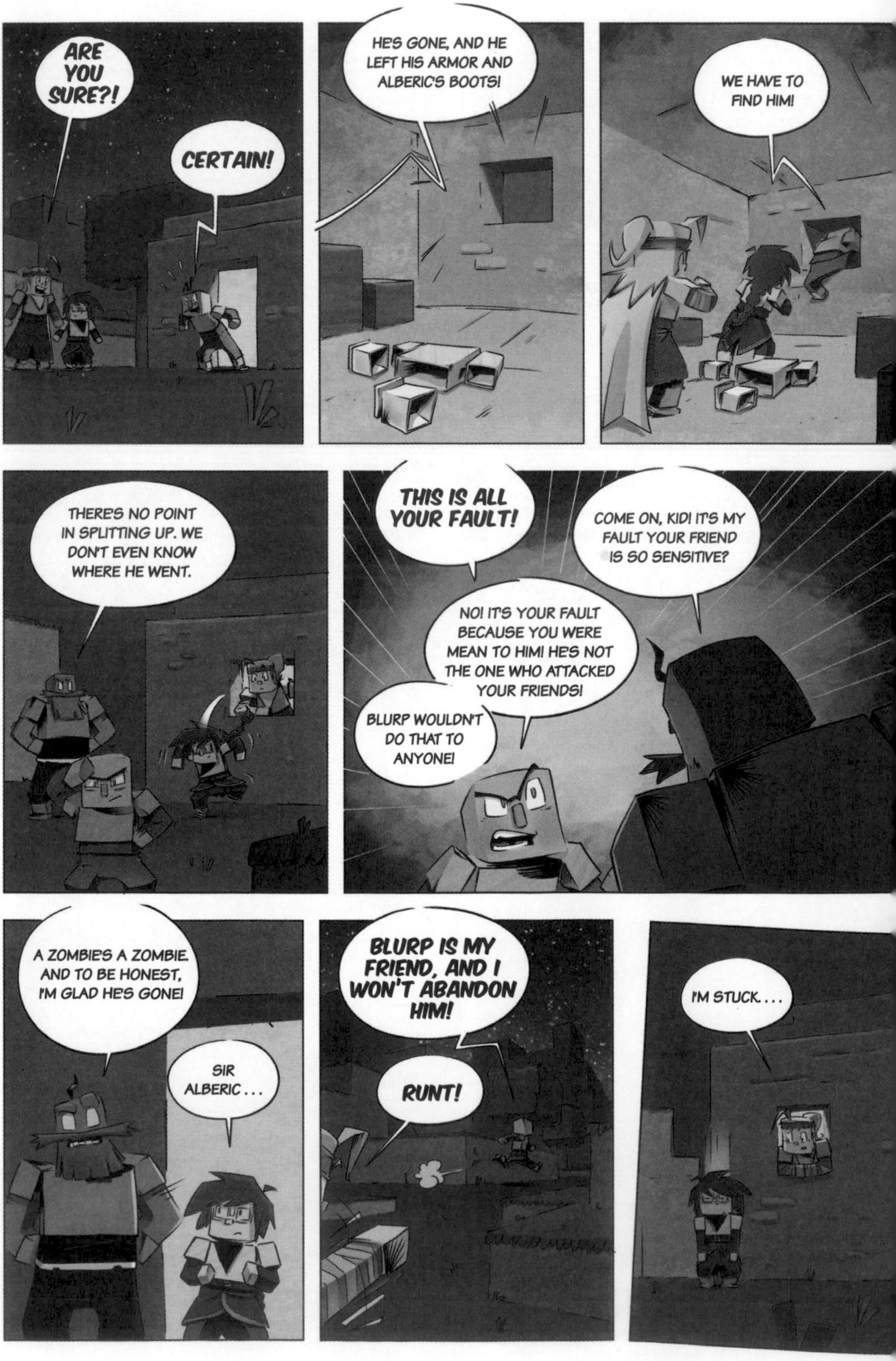
ARE YOU SURE?!
CERTAIN!
HE'S GONE, AND HE LEFT HIS ARMOR AND ALBERIC'S BOOTS!
WE HAVE TO FIND HIM!
THERE'S NO POINT IN SPLITTING UP. WE DON'T EVEN KNOW WHERE HE WENT.
THIS IS ALL YOUR FAULT!
COME ON, KID! IT'S MY FAULT YOUR FRIEND IS SO SENSITIVE?
NO! IT'S YOUR FAULT BECAUSE YOU WERE MEAN TO HIM! HE'S NOT THE ONE WHO ATTACKED YOUR FRIENDS!
BLURP WOULDN'T DO THAT TO ANYONE!
A ZOMBIE'S A ZOMBIE. AND TO BE HONEST, I'M GLAD HE'S GONE!
SIR ALBERIC . . .
BLURP IS MY FRIEND, AND I WON'T ABANDON HIM!
RUNT!
I'M STUCK. . . .

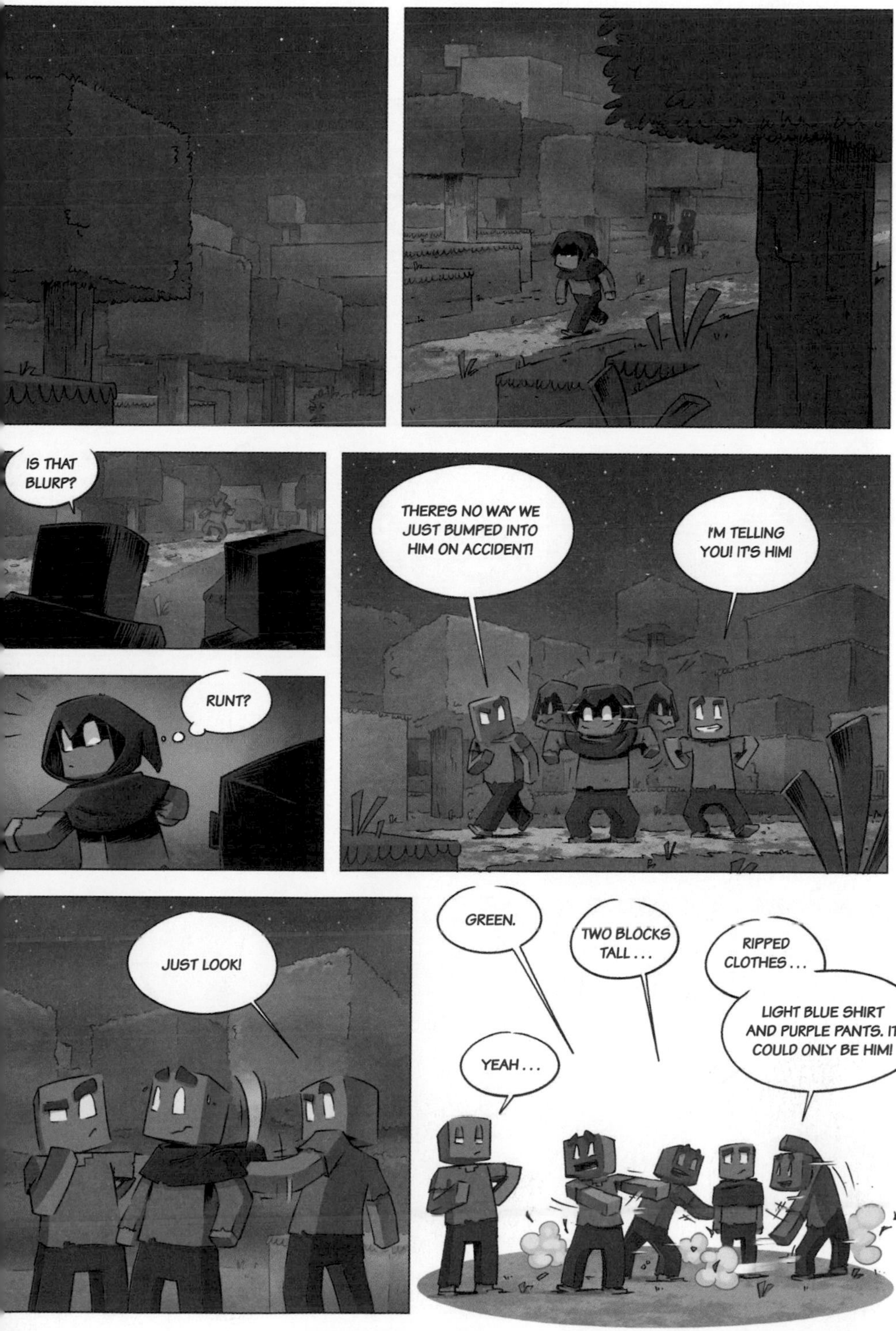
IS THAT BLURP?
RUNT?
THERE'S NO WAY WE JUST BUMPED INTO HIM ON ACCIDENT!
I'M TELLING YOU! IT'S HIM!
JUST LOOK!
GREEN.
TWO BLOCKS TALL . . .
RIPPED CLOTHES . . .
LIGHT BLUE SHIRT AND PURPLE PANTS. IT COULD ONLY BE HIM!
YEAH . . .

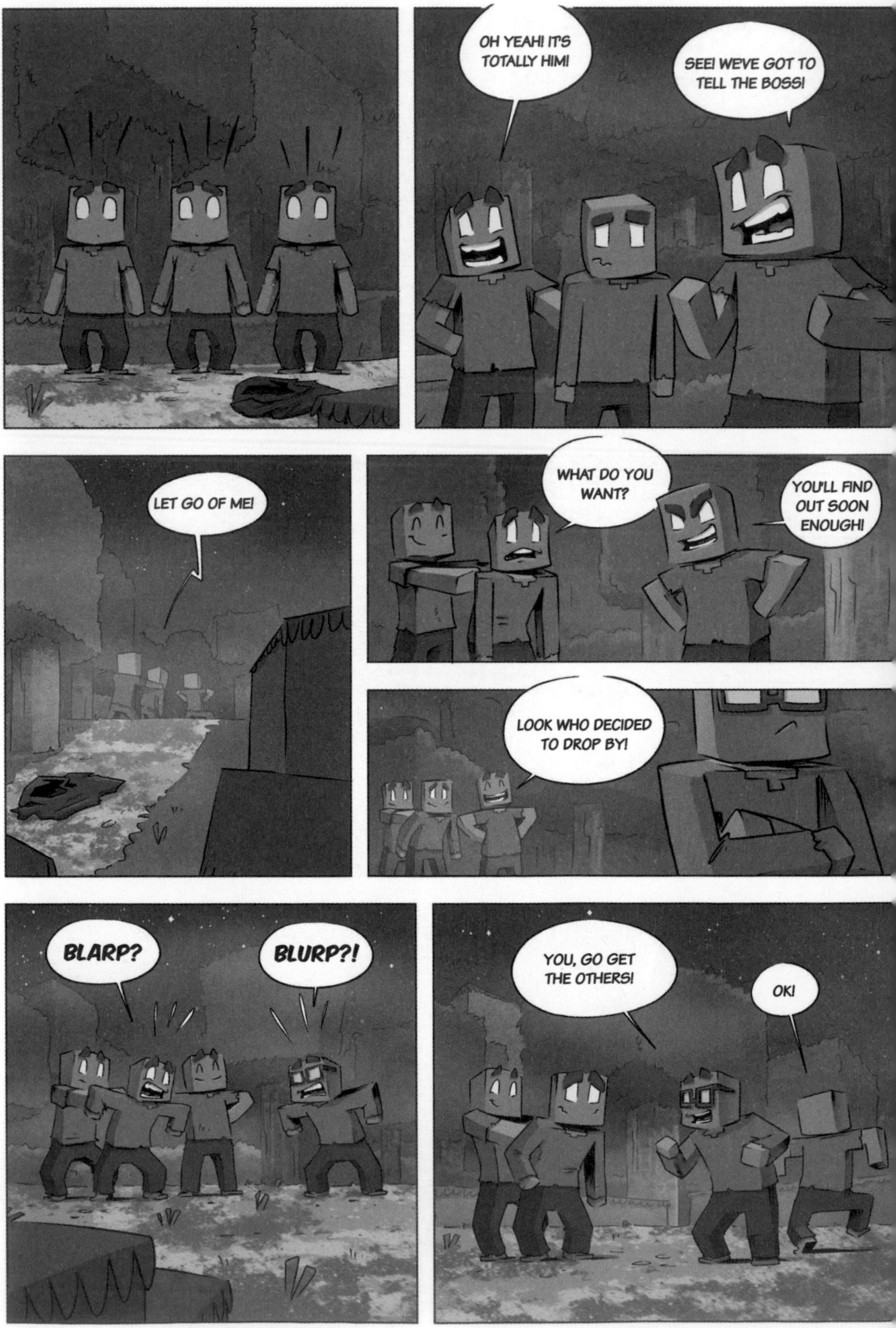
OH YEAH! IT'S TOTALLY HIM!
SEE! WE'VE GOT TO TELL THE BOSS!
LET GO OF ME!
WHAT DO YOU WANT?
YOU'LL FIND OUT SOON ENOUGH!
LOOK WHO DECIDED TO DROP BY!
BLARP?
BLURP?!
YOU, GO GET THE OTHERS!
OK!

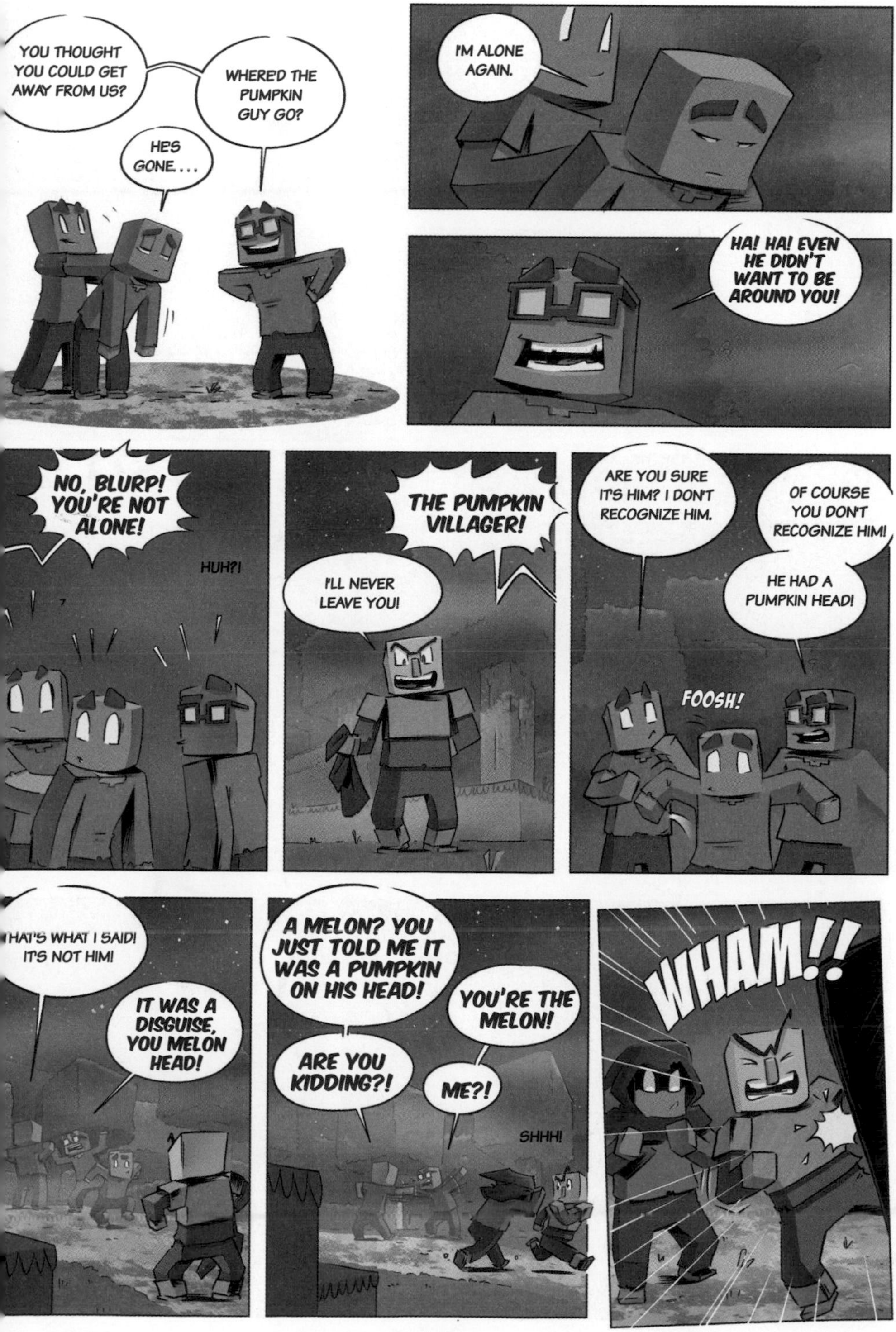
YOU THOUGHT YOU COULD GET AWAY FROM US?
WHERE'D THE PUMPKIN GUY GO?
HE'S GONE. . . .
I'M ALONE AGAIN.
HA! HA! EVEN HE DIDN'T WANT TO BE AROUND YOU!
NO, BLURP! YOU'RE NOT ALONE!
HUH?!
THE PUMPKIN VILLAGER!
I'LL NEVER LEAVE YOU!
ARE YOU SURE IT'S HIM? I DON'T RECOGNIZE HIM.
OF COURSE YOU DON'T RECOGNIZE HIM!
HE HAD A PUMPKIN HEAD!
FOOSH!
THAT'S WHAT I SAID! IT'S NOT HIM!
IT WAS A DISGUISE, YOU MELON HEAD!
A MELON? YOU JUST TOLD ME IT WAS A PUMPKIN ON HIS HEAD!
ARE YOU KIDDING?!
YOU'RE THE MELON!
ME?!
SHHH!
WHAM!!

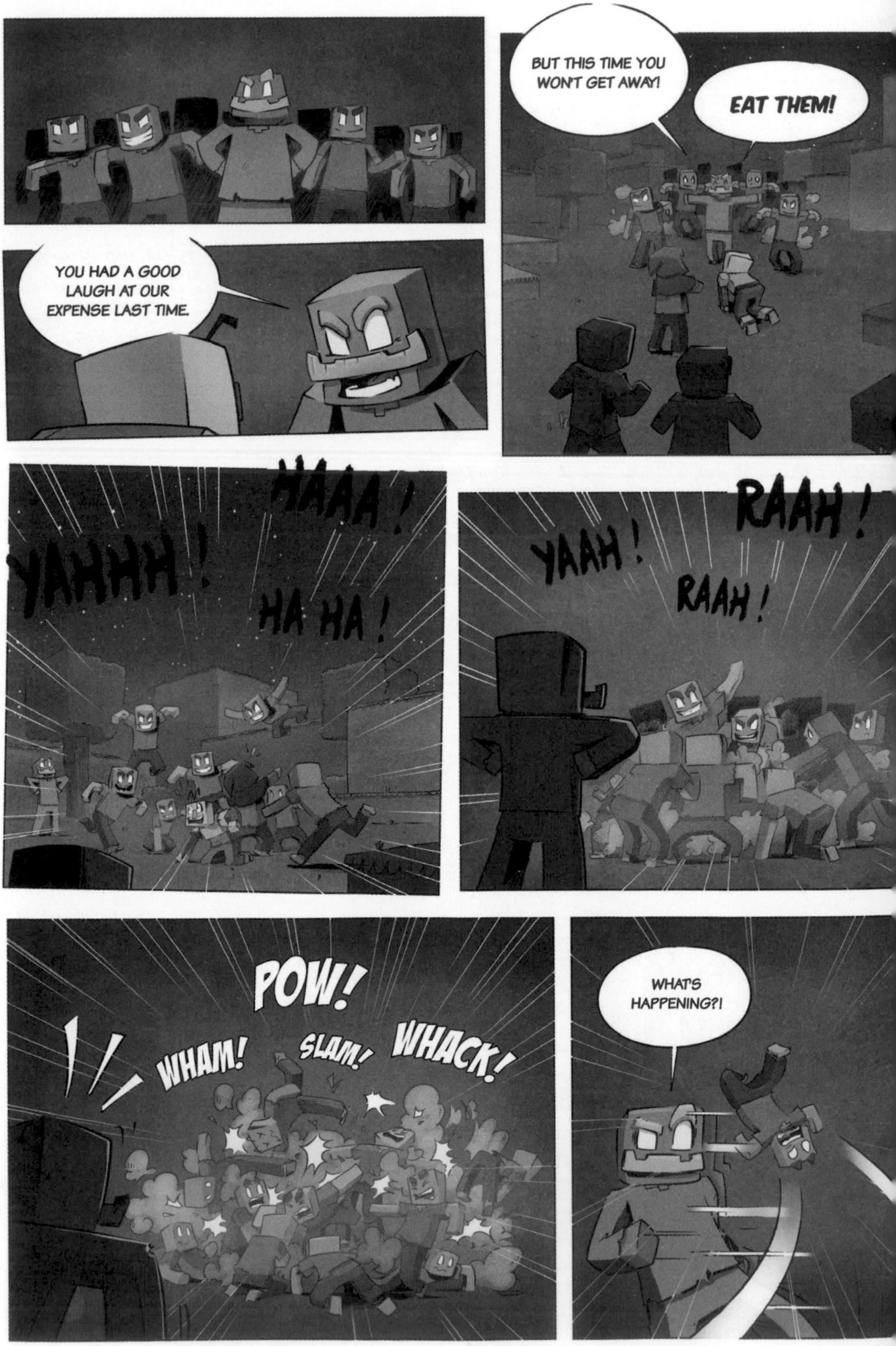
YOU HAD A GOOD LAUGH AT OUR EXPENSE LAST TIME.
BUT THIS TIME YOU WON'T GET AWAY!
EAT THEM!
HAAA!
YAHHH!
HA HA!
RAAH!
YAAH!
RAAH!
POW!
WHAM!
SLAM!
WHACK!
WHAT'S HAPPENING?!

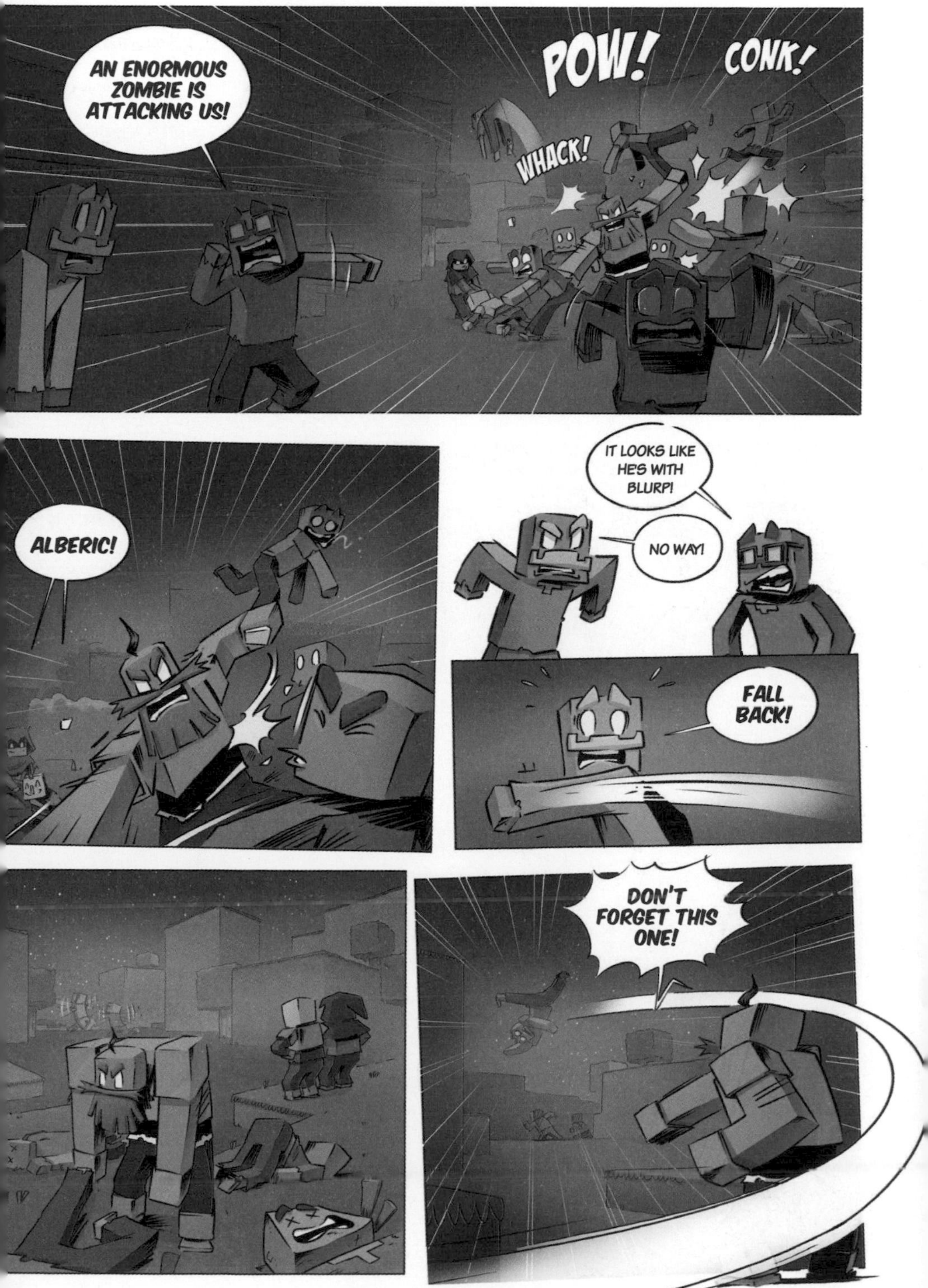
AN ENORMOUS ZOMBIE IS ATTACKING US!
POW!
CONK!
WHACK!
ALBERIC!
IT LOOKS LIKE HE'S WITH BLURP!
NO WAY!
FALL BACK!
DON'T FORGET THIS ONE!

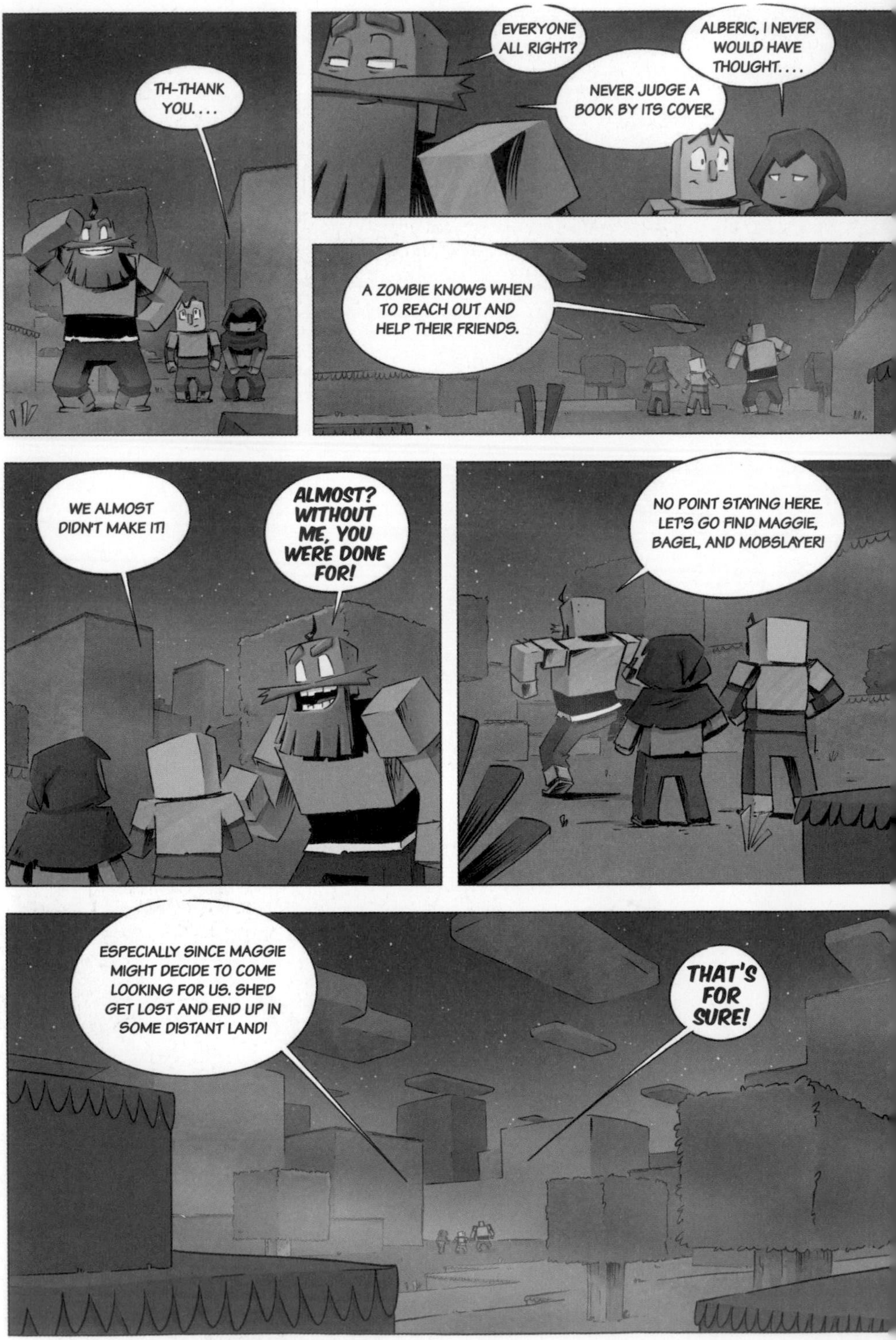
TH-THANK YOU. . . .
EVERYONE ALL RIGHT?
ALBERIC, I NEVER WOULD HAVE THOUGHT. . . .
NEVER JUDGE A BOOK BY ITS COVER.
A ZOMBIE KNOWS WHEN TO REACH OUT AND HELP THEIR FRIENDS.
WE ALMOST DIDN'T MAKE IT!
ALMOST? WITHOUT ME, YOU WERE DONE FOR!
NO POINT STAYING HERE. LET'S GO FIND MAGGIE, BAGEL, AND MOBSLAYER!
ESPECIALLY SINCE MAGGIE MIGHT DECIDE TO COME LOOKING FOR US. SHE'D GET LOST AND END UP IN SOME DISTANT LAND!
THAT'S FOR SURE!

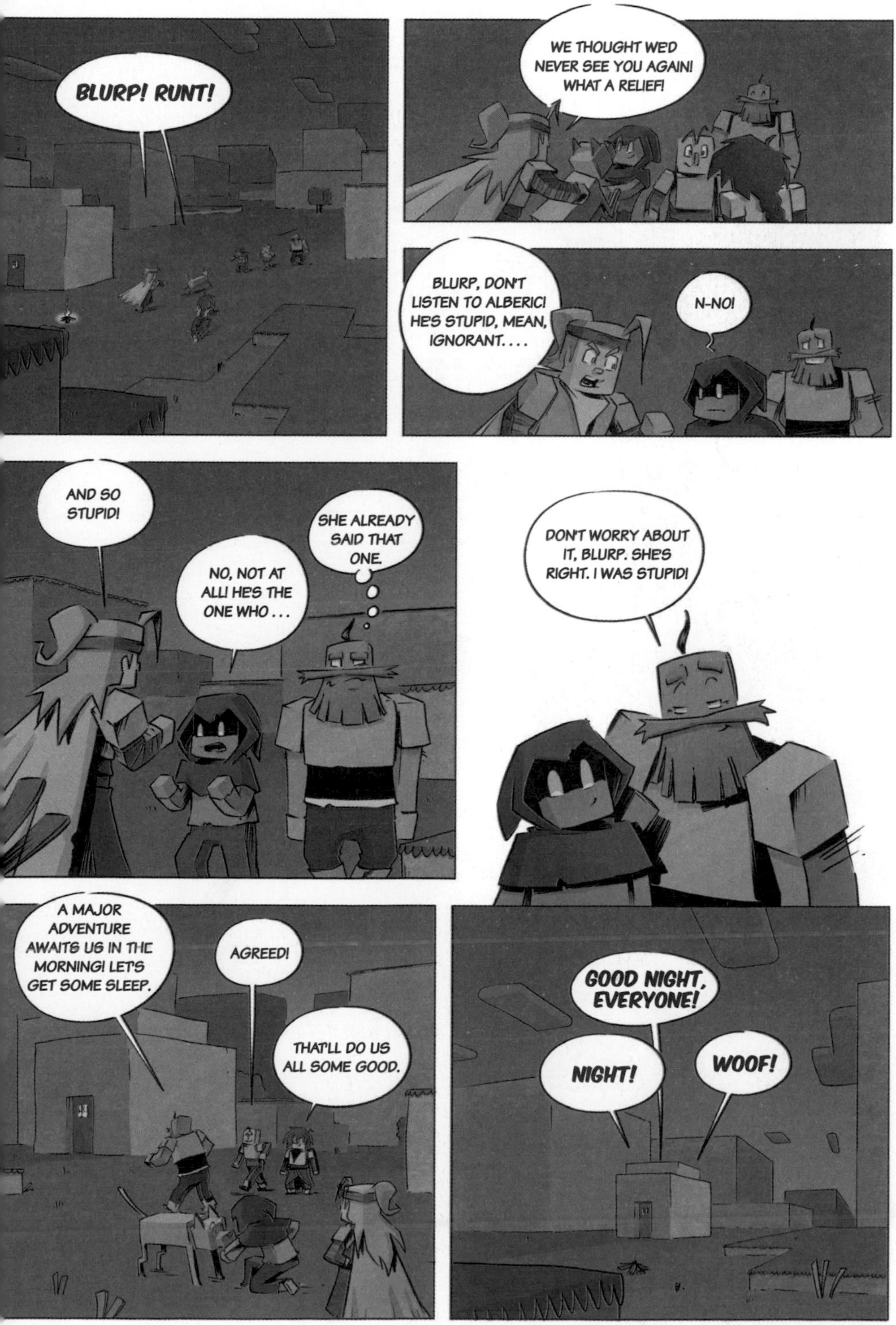
BLURP! RUNT!
WE THOUGHT WE'D NEVER SEE YOU AGAIN! WHAT A RELIEF!
BLURP, DON'T LISTEN TO ALBERIC! HE'S STUPID, MEAN, IGNORANT. . . .
N-NO!
AND SO STUPID!
NO, NOT AT ALL! HE'S THE ONE WHO . . .
SHE ALREADY SAID THAT ONE.
DON'T WORRY ABOUT IT, BLURP. SHE'S RIGHT. I WAS STUPID!
A MAJOR ADVENTURE AWAITS US IN THE MORNING! LET'S GET SOME SLEEP.
AGREED!
THAT'LL DO US ALL SOME GOOD.
GOOD NIGHT, EVERYONE!
NIGHT!
WOOF!

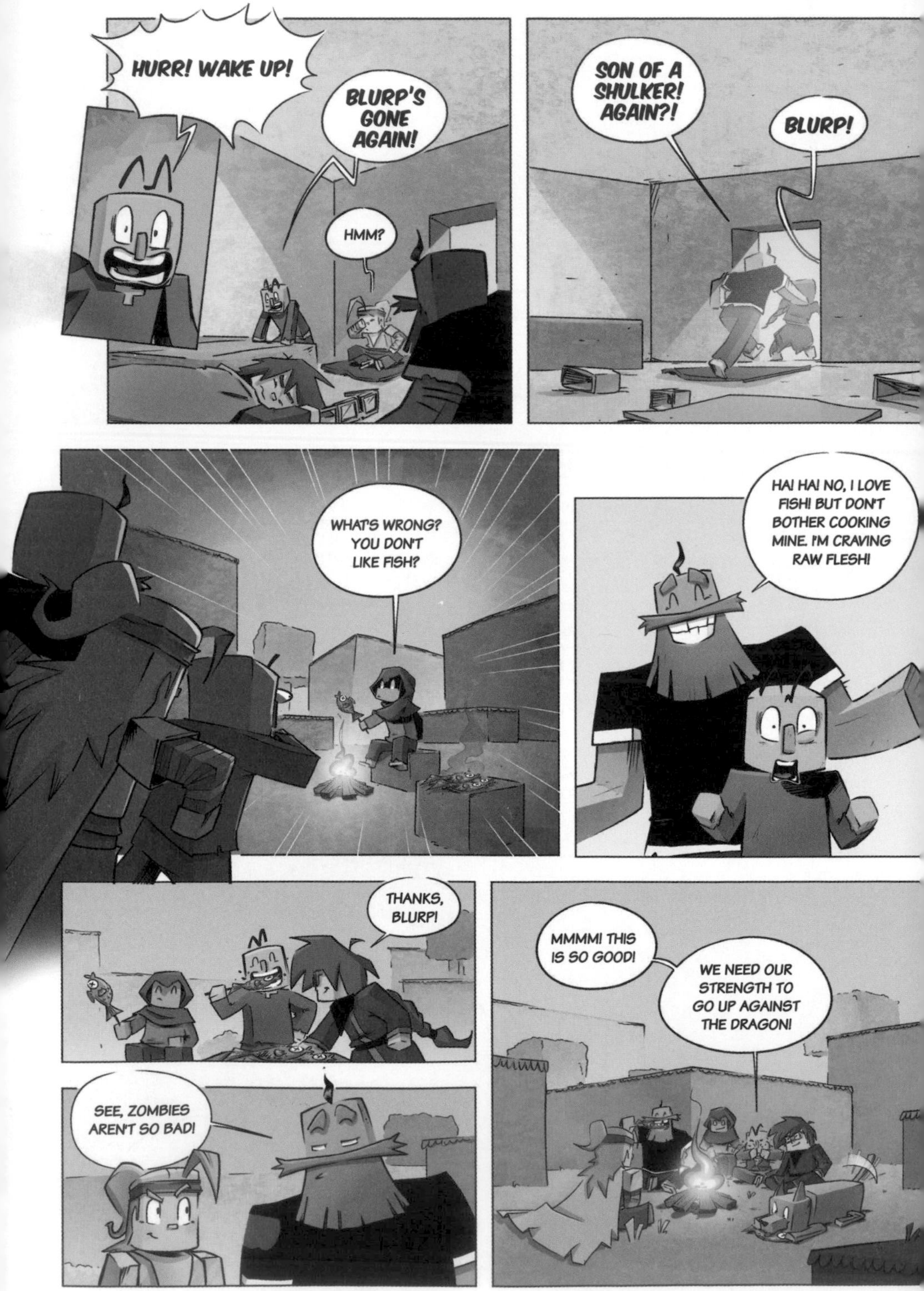
HURR! WAKE UP!
BLURP'S GONE AGAIN!
HMM?
SON OF A SHULKER! AGAIN?!
BLURP!
WHAT'S WRONG? YOU DON'T LIKE FISH?
HA! HA! NO, I LOVE FISH! BUT DON'T BOTHER COOKING MINE. I'M CRAVING RAW FLESH!
THANKS, BLURP!
SEE, ZOMBIES AREN'T SO BAD!
MMMM! THIS IS SO GOOD!
WE NEED OUR STRENGTH TO GO UP AGAINST THE DRAGON!

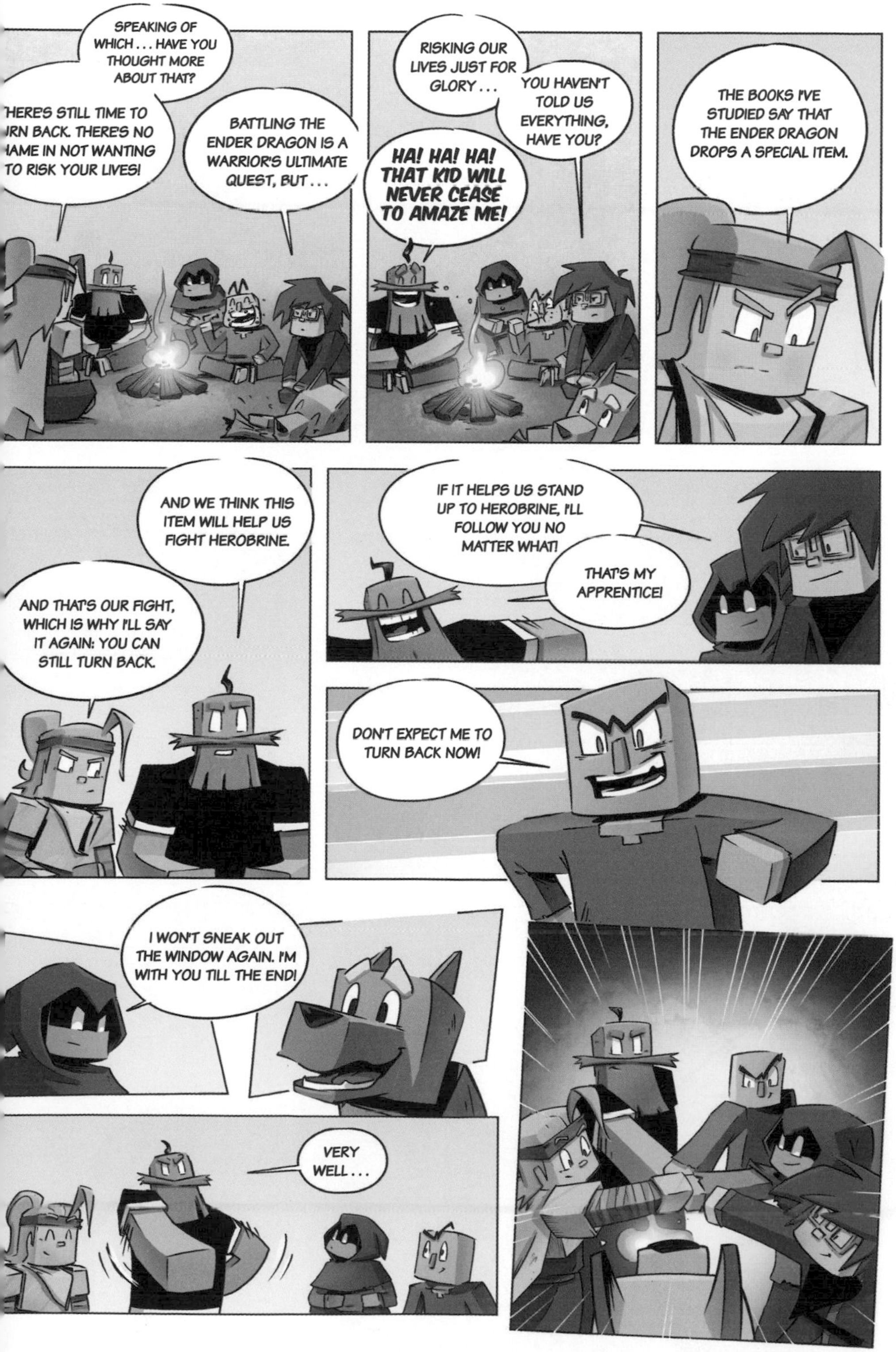
SPEAKING OF WHICH . . . HAVE YOU THOUGHT MORE ABOUT THAT?
THERE'S STILL TIME TO URN BACK. THERE'S NO HAME IN NOT WANTING TO RISK YOUR LIVES!
BATTLING THE ENDER DRAGON IS A WARRIOR'S ULTIMATE QUEST, BUT . . .
RISKING OUR LIVES JUST FOR GLORY . . .
YOU HAVEN'T TOLD US EVERYTHING, HAVE YOU?
HA! HA! HA! THAT KID WILL NEVER CEASE TO AMAZE ME!
THE BOOKS I'VE STUDIED SAY THAT THE ENDER DRAGON DROPS A SPECIAL ITEM.
AND WE THINK THIS ITEM WILL HELP US FIGHT HEROBRINE.
AND THAT'S OUR FIGHT, WHICH IS WHY I'LL SAY IT AGAIN: YOU CAN STILL TURN BACK.
IF IT HELPS US STAND UP TO HEROBRINE, I'LL FOLLOW YOU NO MATTER WHAT!
THAT'S MY APPRENTICE!
DON'T EXPECT ME TO TURN BACK NOW!
I WON'T SNEAK OUT THE WINDOW AGAIN. I'M WITH YOU TILL THE END!
VERY WELL . . .

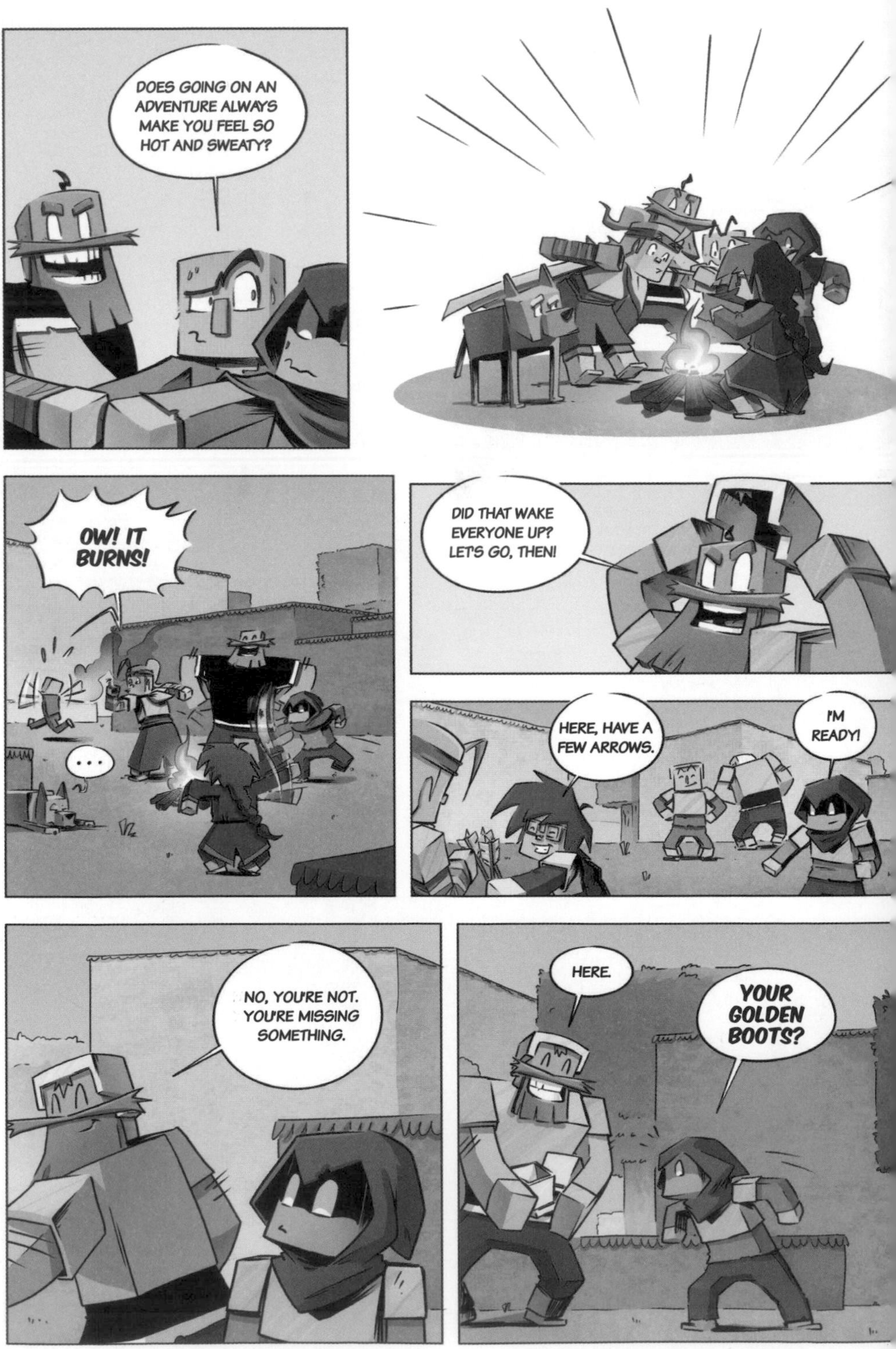
DOES GOING ON AN ADVENTURE ALWAYS MAKE YOU FEEL SO HOT AND SWEATY?
OW! IT BURNS!
...
DID THAT WAKE EVERYONE UP? LET'S GO, THEN!
HERE, HAVE A FEW ARROWS.
I'M READY!
NO, YOU'RE NOT. YOU'RE MISSING SOMETHING.
HERE.
YOUR GOLDEN BOOTS?

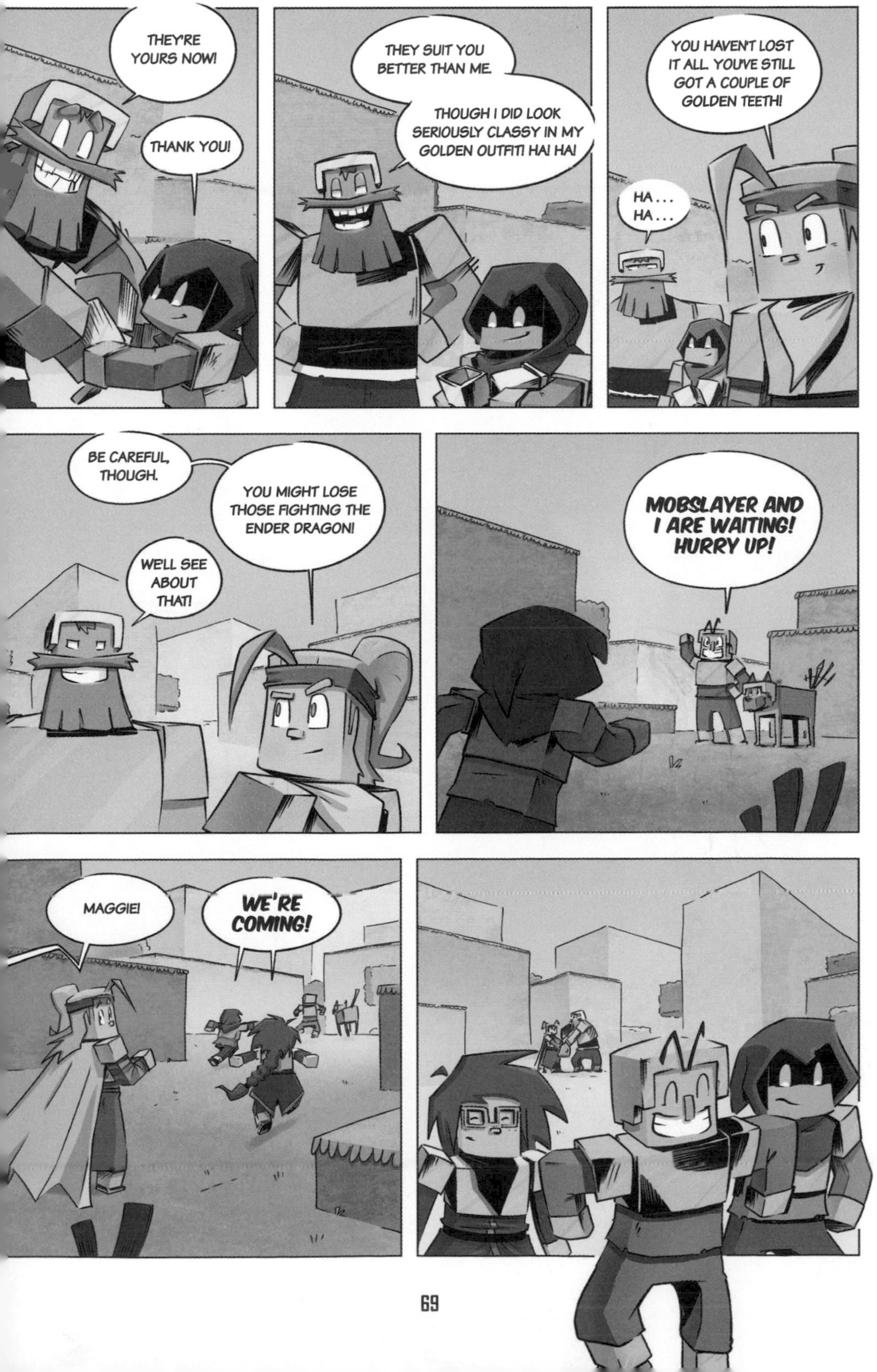
THEY'RE YOURS NOW!
THANK YOU!
THEY SUIT YOU BETTER THAN ME.
THOUGH I DID LOOK SERIOUSLY CLASSY IN MY GOLDEN OUTFIT! HA! HA!
YOU HAVEN'T LOST IT ALL. YOU'VE STILL GOT A COUPLE OF GOLDEN TEETH!
HA . . . HA . . .
BE CAREFUL, THOUGH.
YOU MIGHT LOSE THOSE FIGHTING THE ENDER DRAGON!
WE'LL SEE ABOUT THAT!
MOBSLAYER AND I ARE WAITING! HURRY UP!
MAGGIE!
WE'RE COMING!

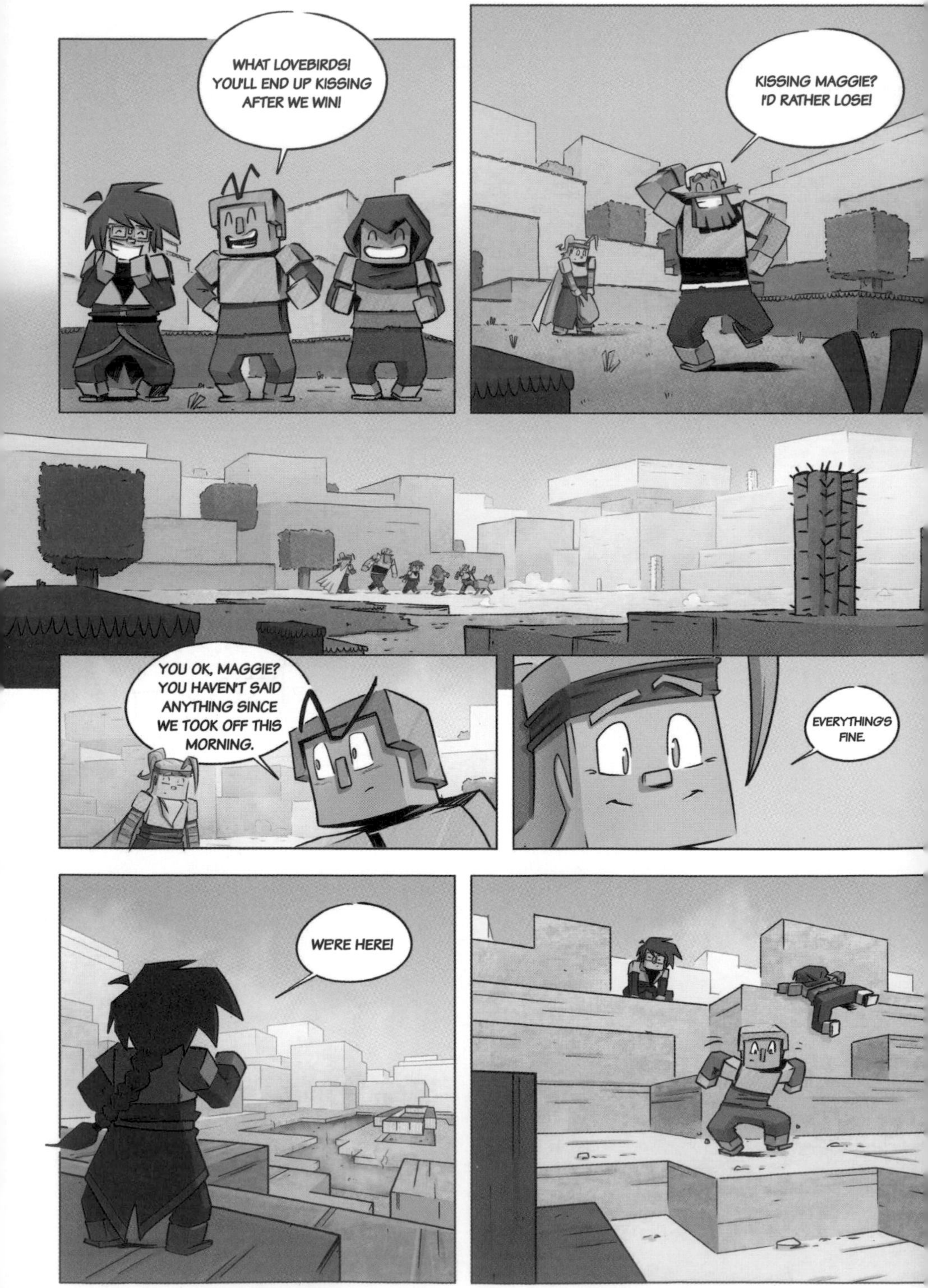
WHAT LOVEBIRDS! YOU'LL END UP KISSING AFTER WE WIN!
KISSING MAGGIE? I'D RATHER LOSE!
YOU OK, MAGGIE? YOU HAVEN'T SAID ANYTHING SINCE WE TOOK OFF THIS MORNING.
EVERYTHING'S FINE.
WE'RE HERE!

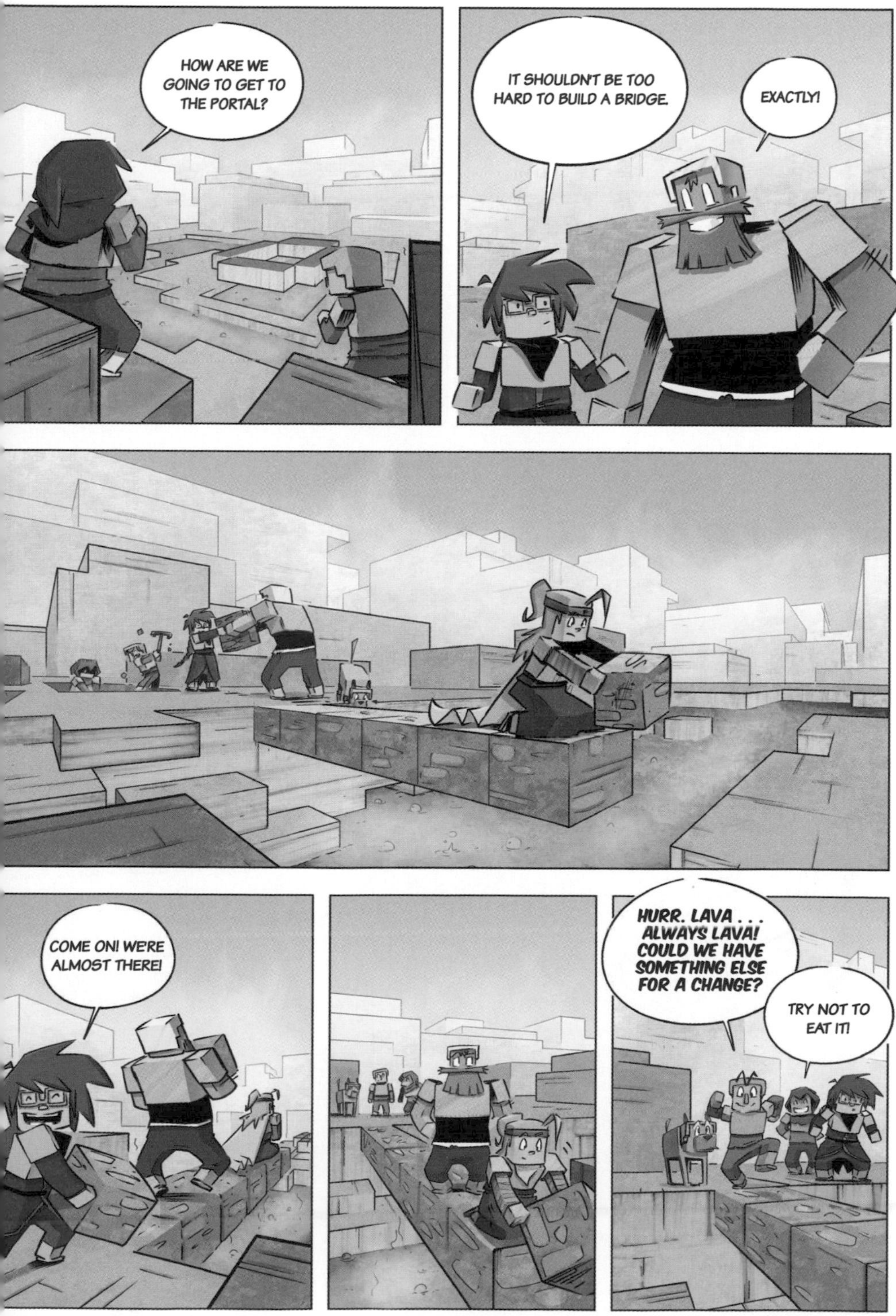
HOW ARE WE GOING TO GET TO THE PORTAL?
IT SHOULDN'T BE TOO HARD TO BUILD A BRIDGE.
EXACTLY!
COME ON! WE'RE ALMOST THERE!
HURR. LAVA . . . ALWAYS LAVA! COULD WE HAVE SOMETHING ELSE FOR A CHANGE?
TRY NOT TO EAT IT!

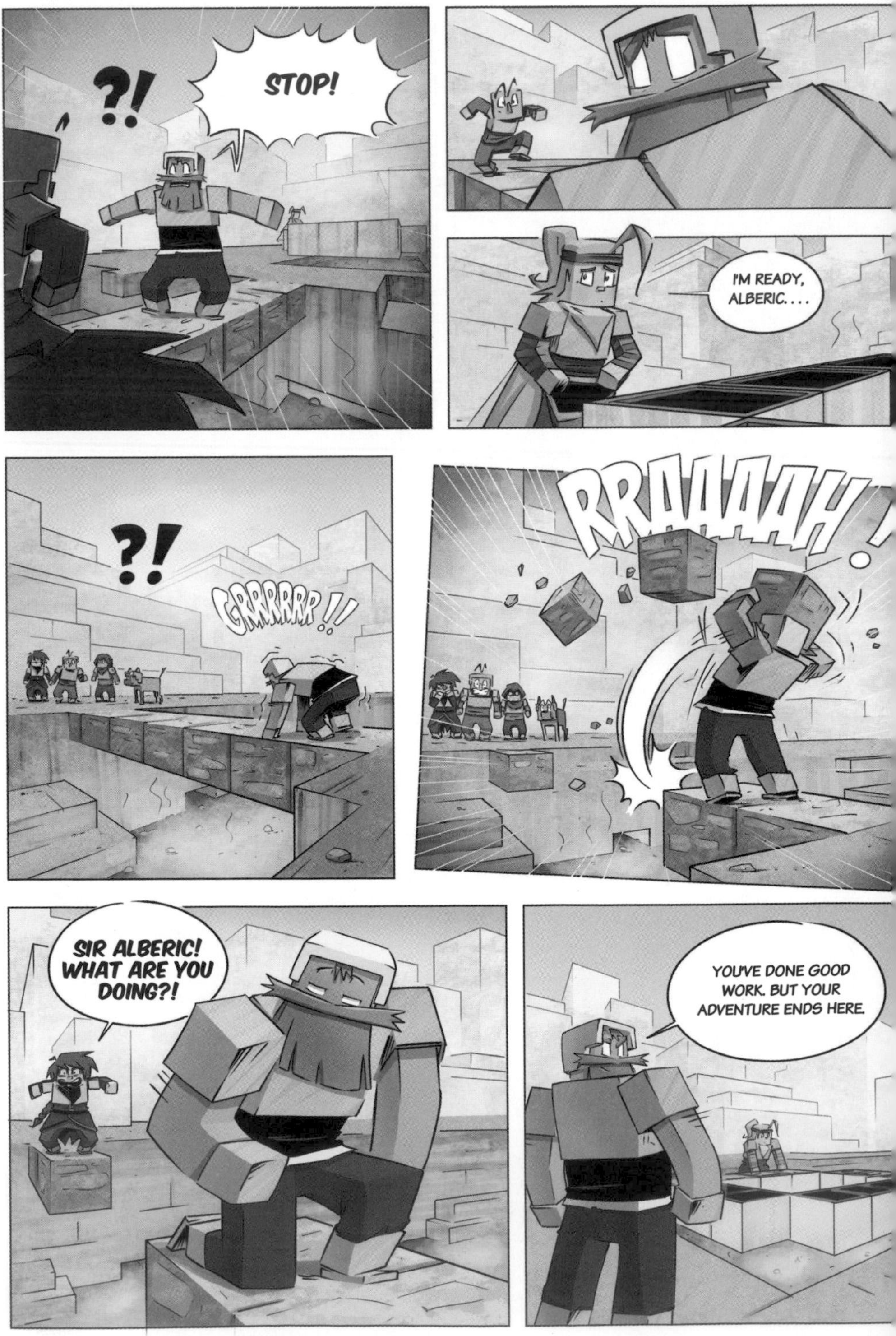
?!
STOP!
I'M READY, ALBERIC. . . .
?!
GRRRRRR!!
RRAAAAAH!
SIR ALBERIC! WHAT ARE YOU DOING?!
YOU'VE DONE GOOD WORK. BUT YOUR ADVENTURE ENDS HERE.

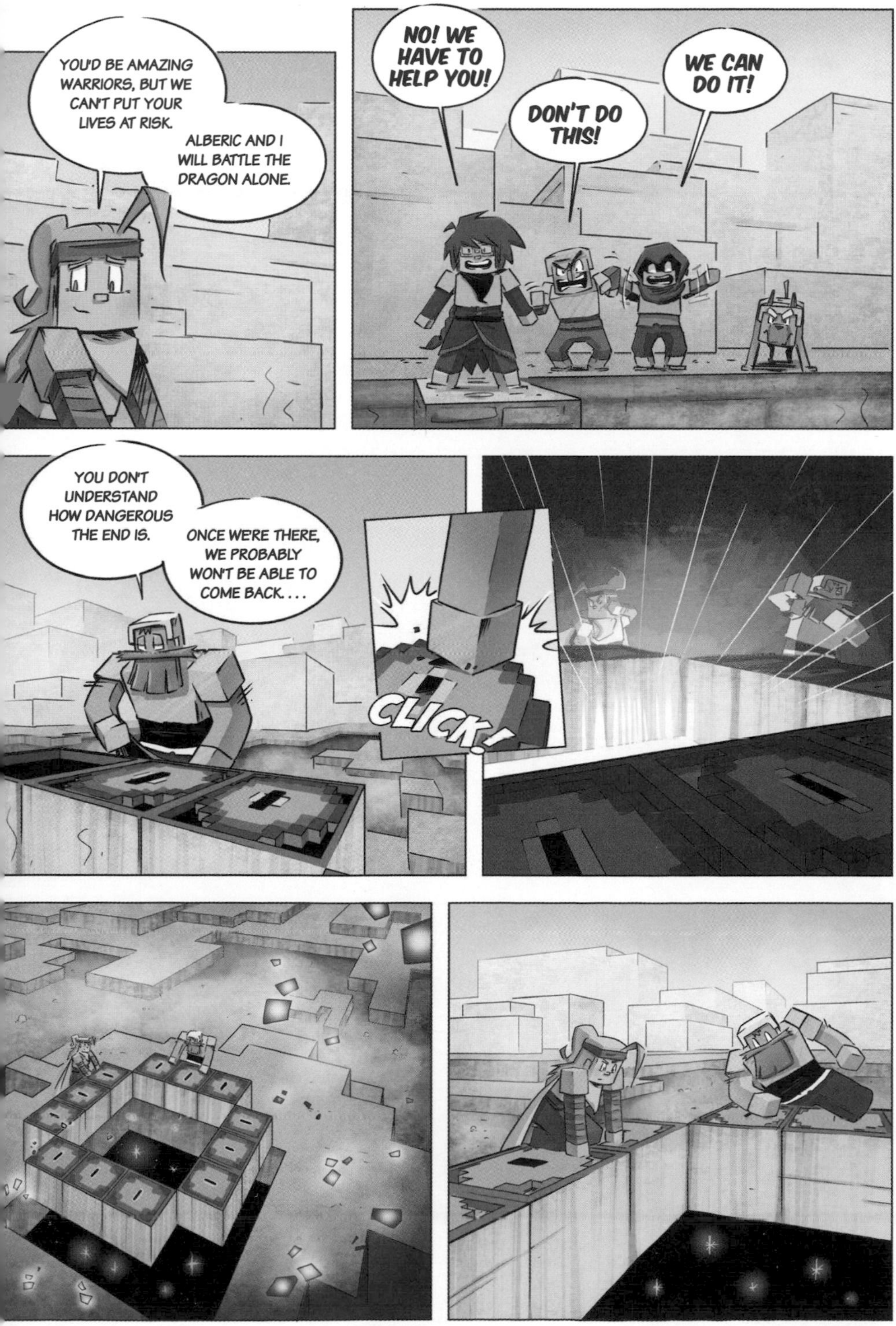
YOU'D BE AMAZING WARRIORS, BUT WE CAN'T PUT YOUR LIVES AT RISK.
ALBERIC AND I WILL BATTLE THE DRAGON ALONE.
NO! WE HAVE TO HELP YOU!
DON'T DO THIS!
WE CAN DO IT!
YOU DON'T UNDERSTAND HOW DANGEROUS THE END IS.
ONCE WE'RE THERE, WE PROBABLY WON'T BE ABLE TO COME BACK. . . .
CLICK!

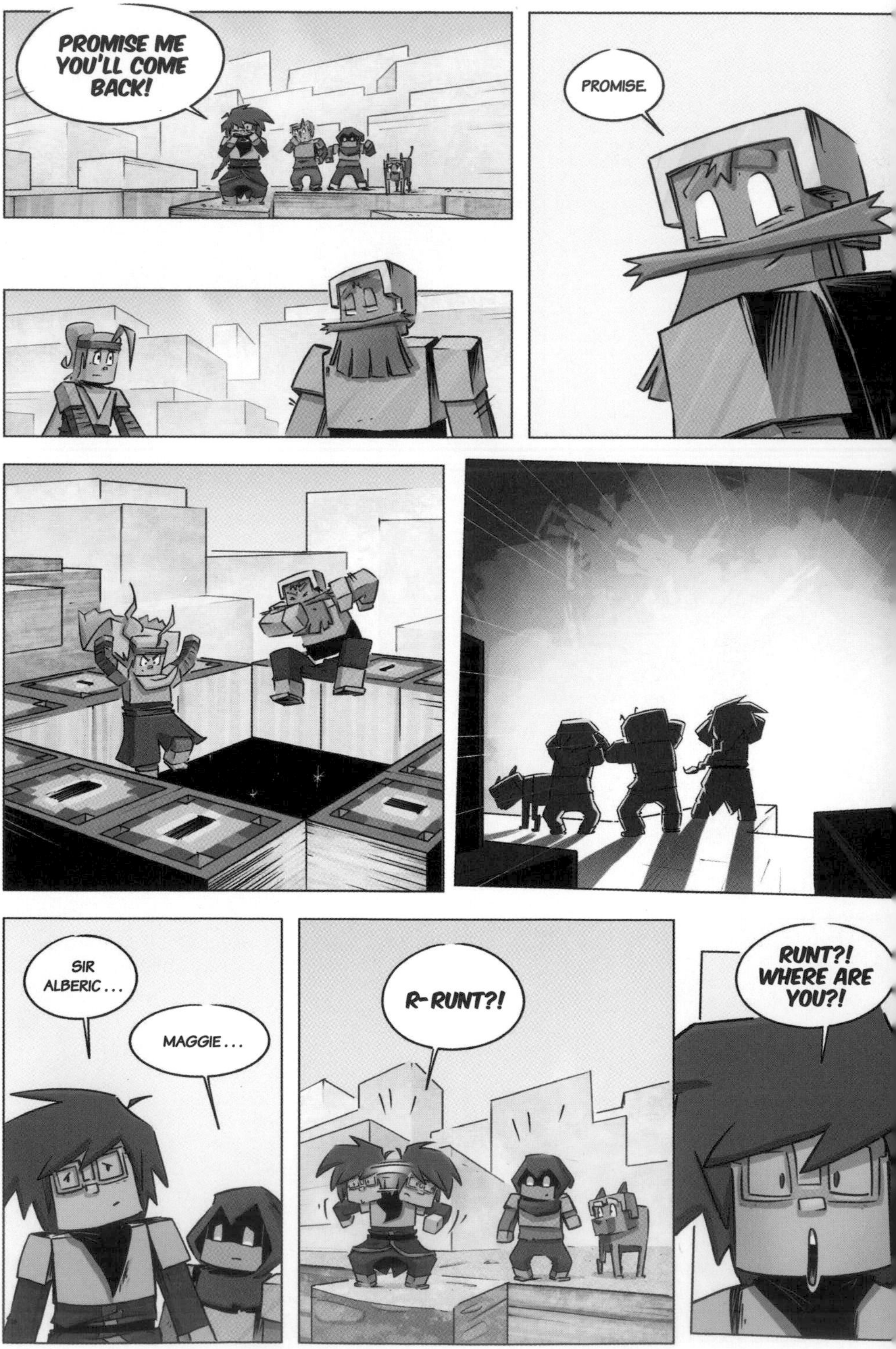
PROMISE ME YOU'LL COME BACK!
PROMISE.
SIR ALBERIC . . .
MAGGIE . . .
R-RUNT?!
RUNT?! WHERE ARE YOU?!

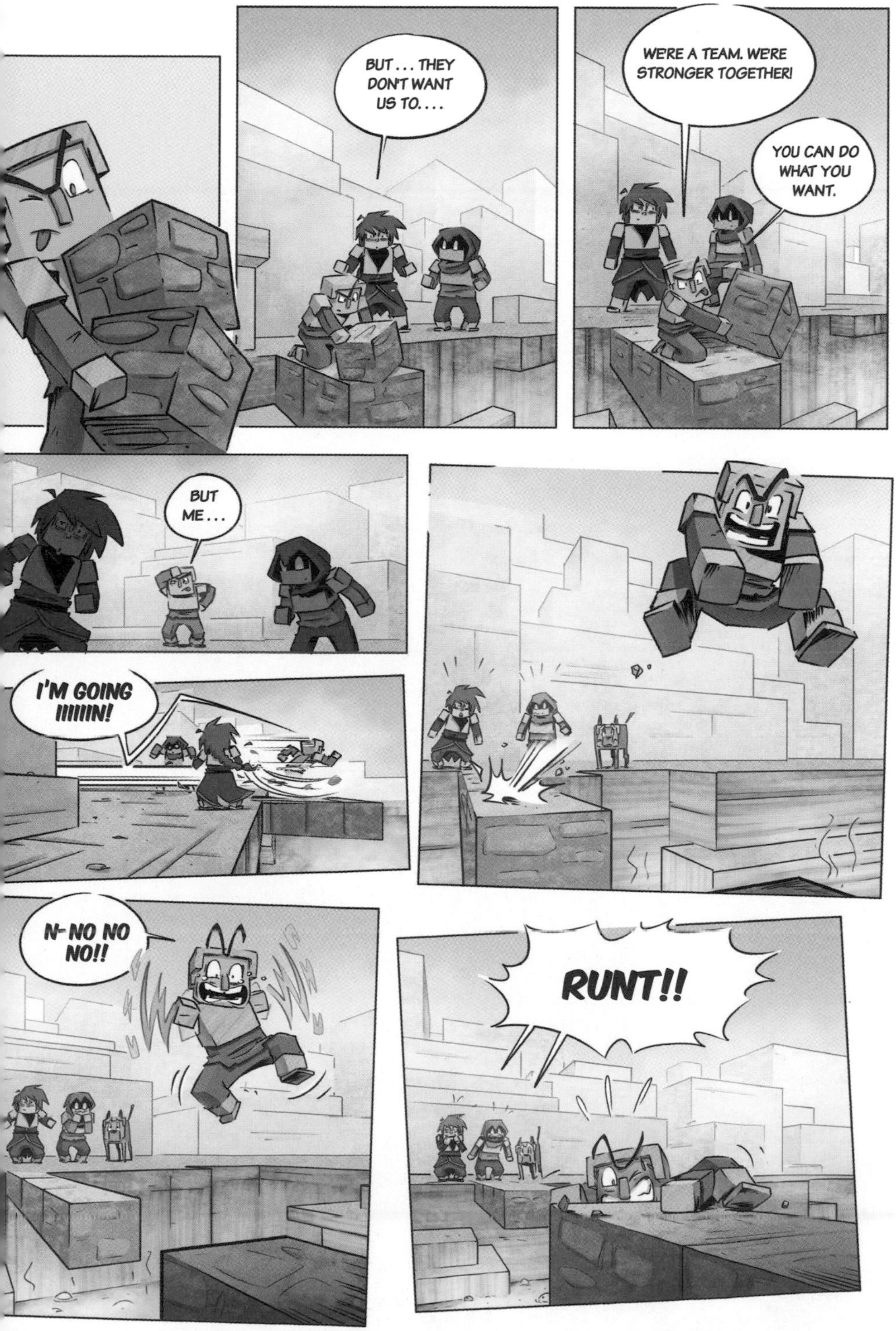
BUT . . . THEY DON'T WANT US TO. . . .
WE'RE A TEAM. WE'RE STRONGER TOGETHER!
YOU CAN DO WHAT YOU WANT.
BUT ME . . .
I'M GOING IIIIIIIN!
N-NO NO NO!!
RUNT!!

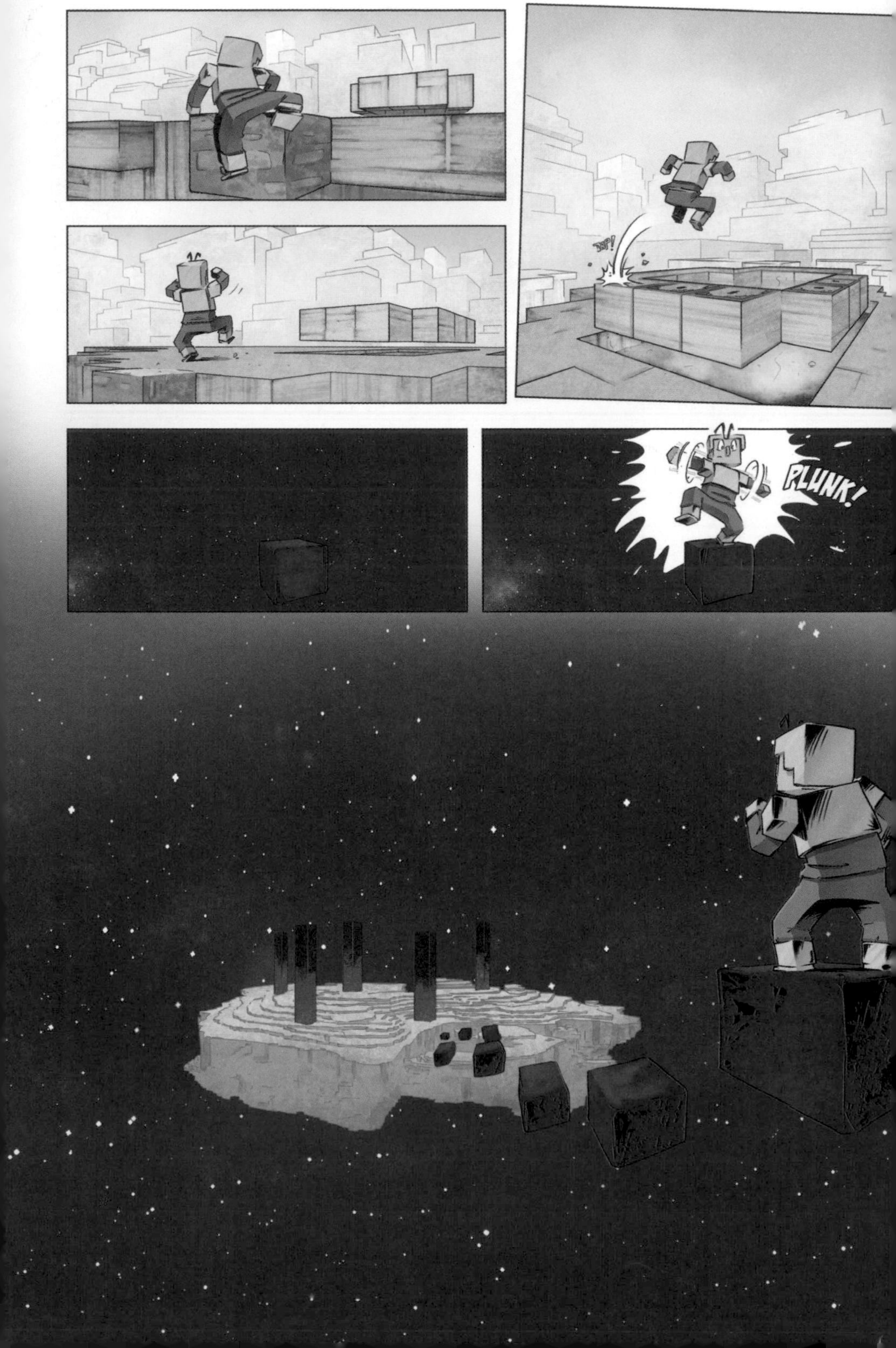
TAP!
PLUNK!

EEEEEEEEERRRRRREEEEEEEEE!!

DON'T LOOK ANY OF THEM IN THE EYE AND WE'LL BE FINE!

I KNOW! DON'T TREAT ME LIKE A NOOB!

OH, WELL DONE! YOU LOOKED AT THAT ONE!

I DID NOT!

?!

WHOOSH!

WHOOSH!

WHOOSH!

WHOOSH!

WHOOSH!

RUNT?!!

OOPS! I THINK I MIGHT HAVE GLANCED AT ONE . . .

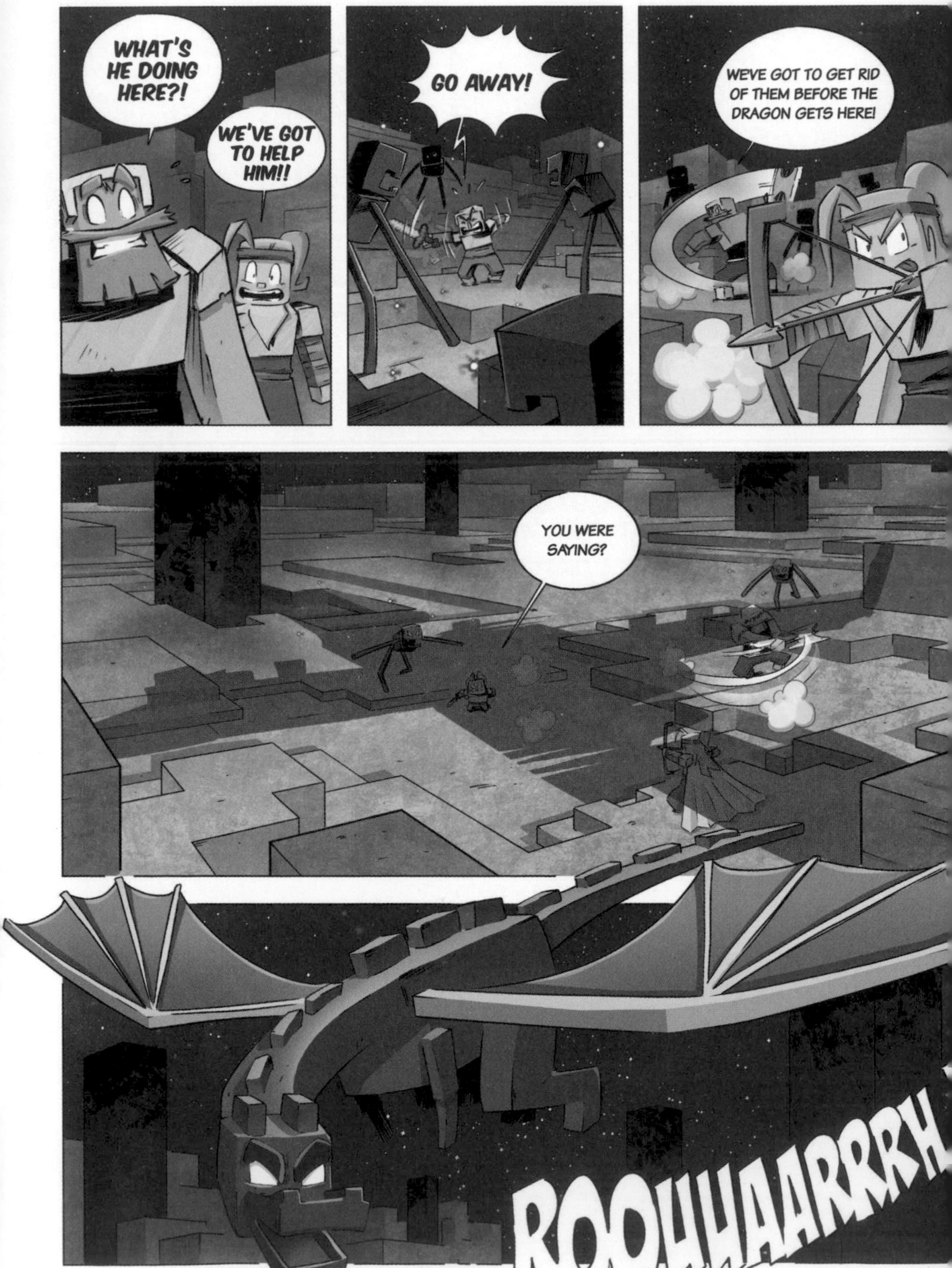
WHAT'S HE DOING HERE?!
WE'VE GOT TO HELP HIM!!
GO AWAY!
WE'VE GOT TO GET RID OF THEM BEFORE THE DRAGON GETS HERE!
YOU WERE SAYING?
ROOUUAARRRH

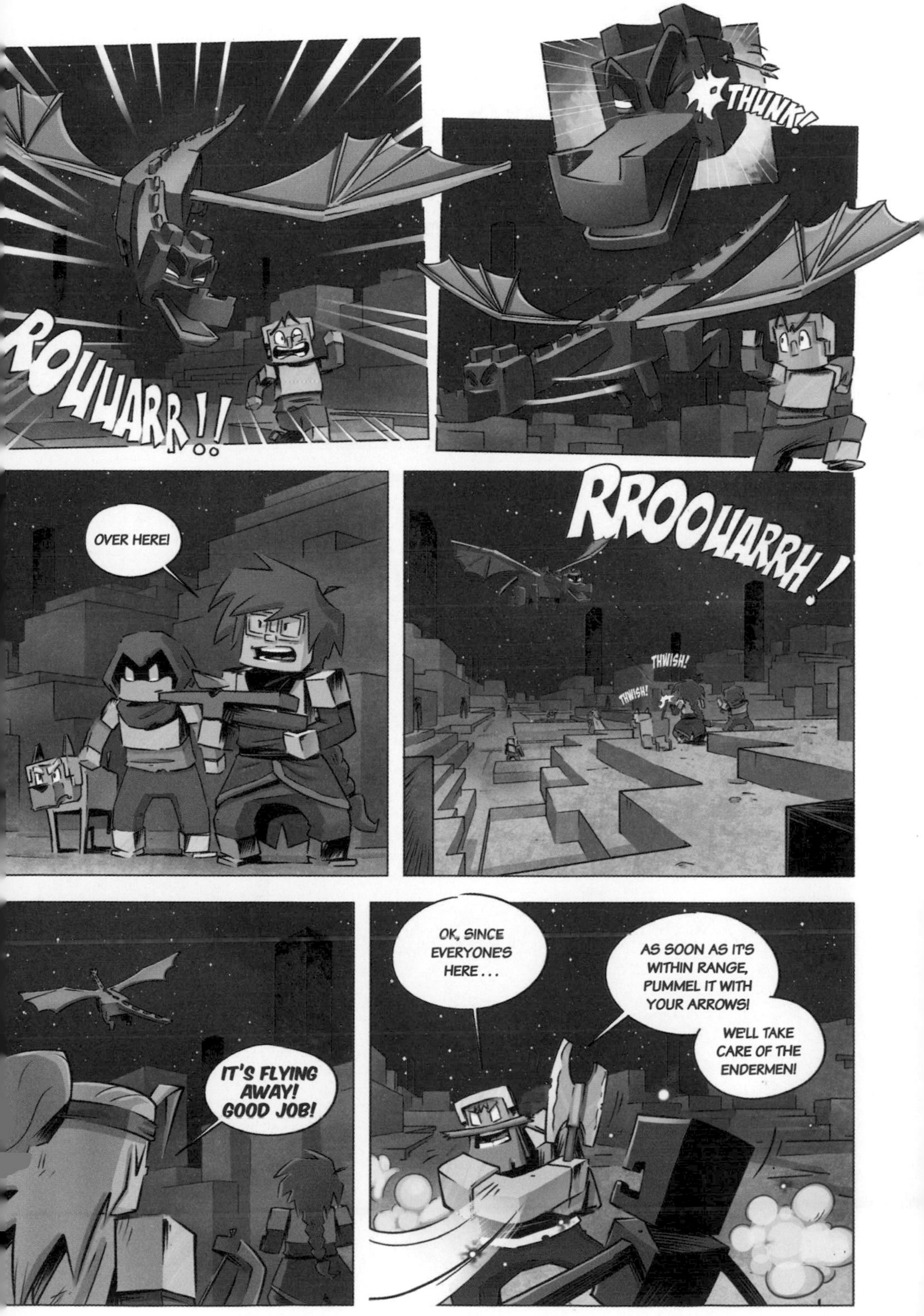
ROUUARR!!
THUNK!
OVER HERE!
RROOUARRH!
THWISH!
THWISH!
IT'S FLYING AWAY! GOOD JOB!
OK, SINCE EVERYONE'S HERE . . .
AS SOON AS IT'S WITHIN RANGE, PUMMEL IT WITH YOUR ARROWS!
WE'LL TAKE CARE OF THE ENDERMEN!

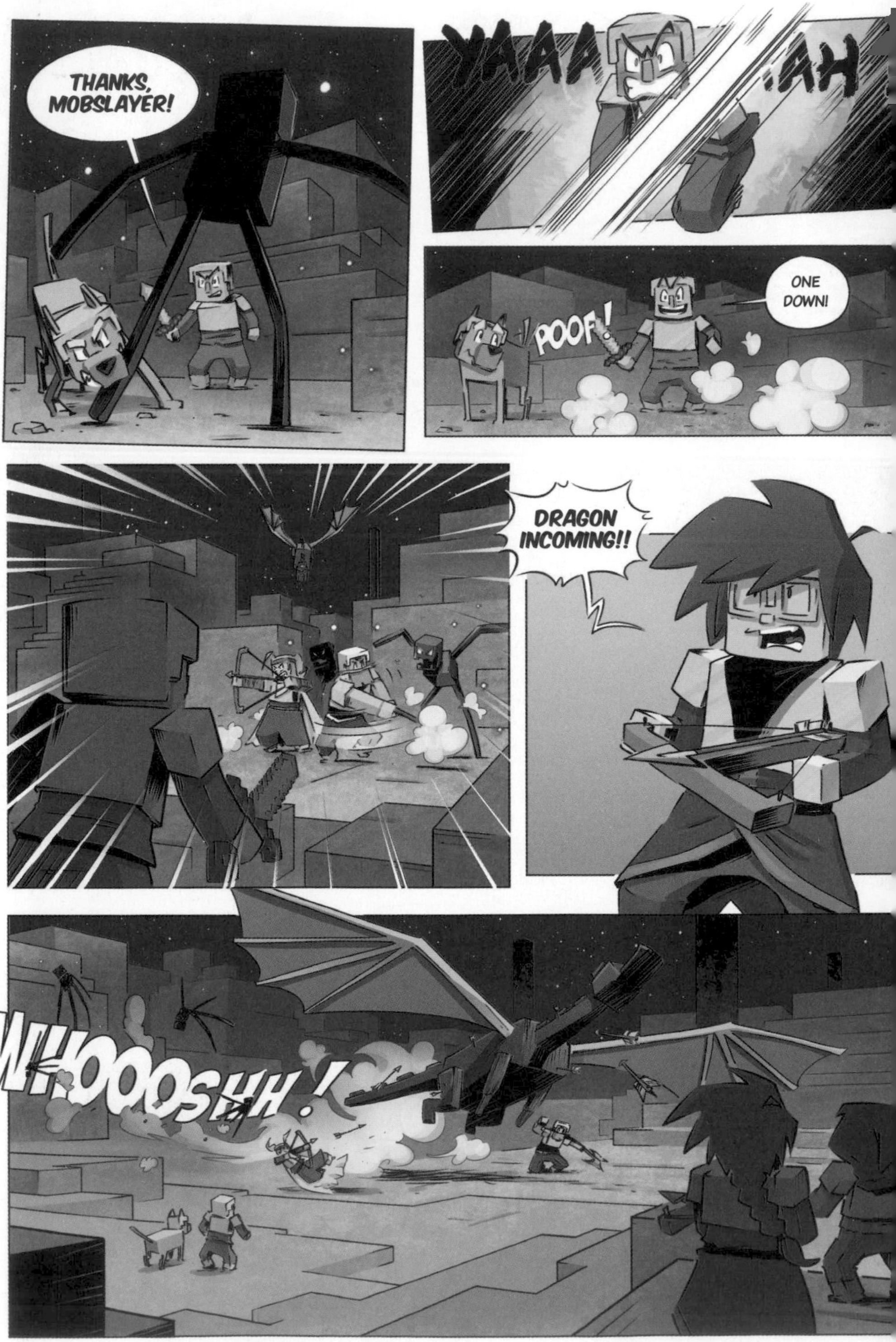
THANKS, MOBSLAYER!
YAAAAH!
ONE DOWN!
POOF!
DRAGON INCOMING!!
WHOOOSHH!

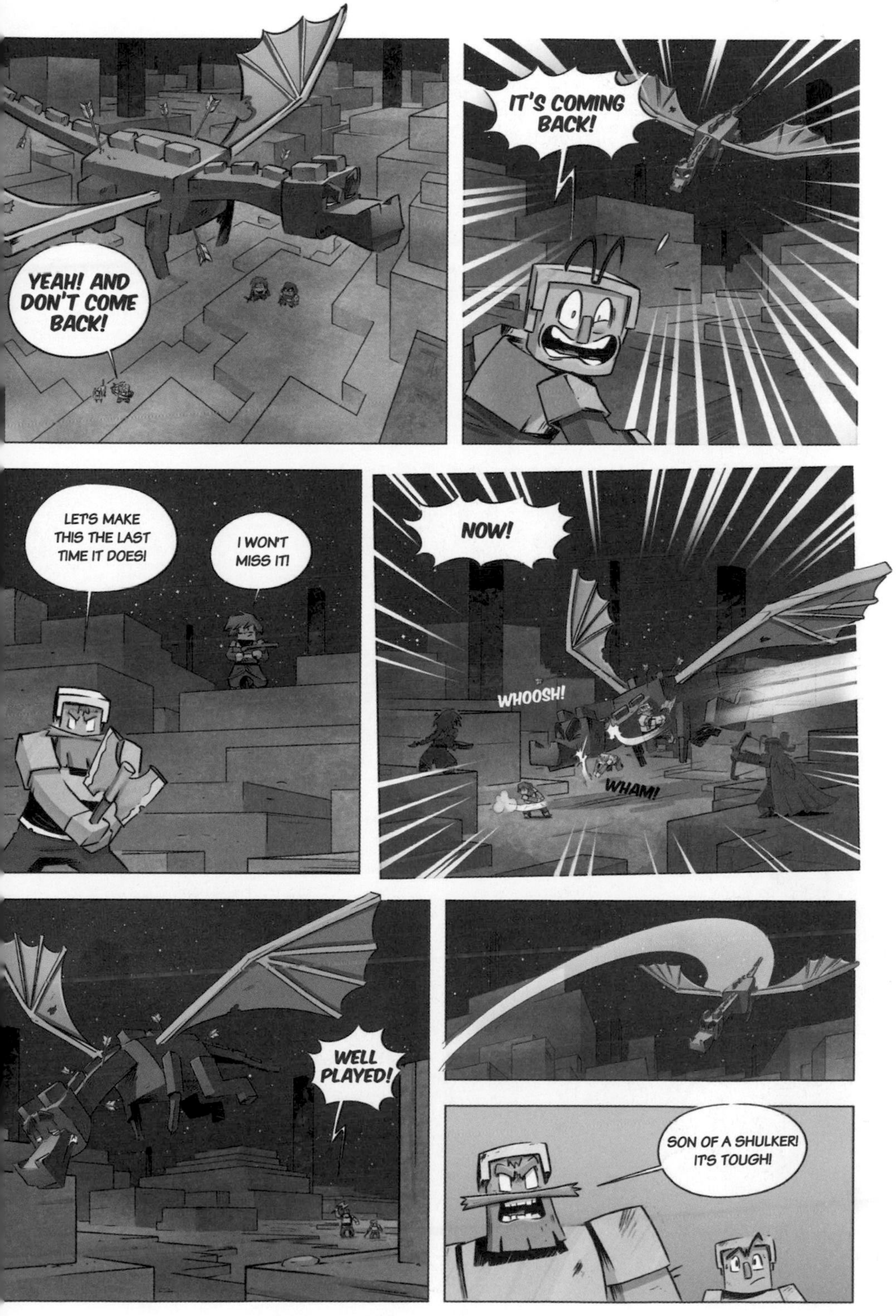
YEAH! AND DON'T COME BACK!
IT'S COMING BACK!
LET'S MAKE THIS THE LAST TIME IT DOES!
I WON'T MISS IT!
NOW!
WHOOSH!
WHAM!
WELL PLAYED!
SON OF A SHULKER! IT'S TOUGH!

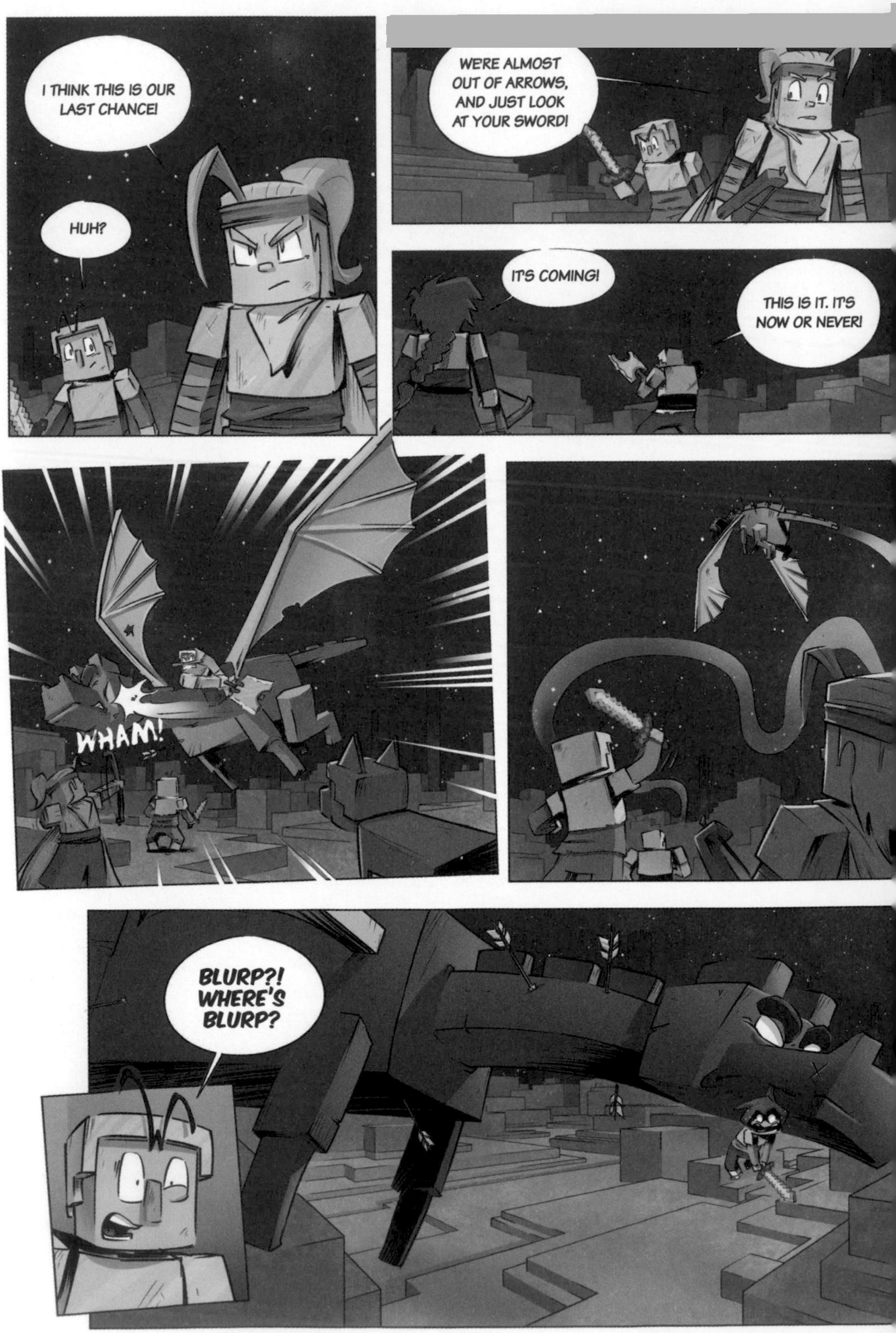
I THINK THIS IS OUR LAST CHANCE!
HUH?
WE'RE ALMOST OUT OF ARROWS, AND JUST LOOK AT YOUR SWORD!
IT'S COMING!
THIS IS IT. IT'S NOW OR NEVER!
WHAM!
BLURP?! WHERE'S BLURP?

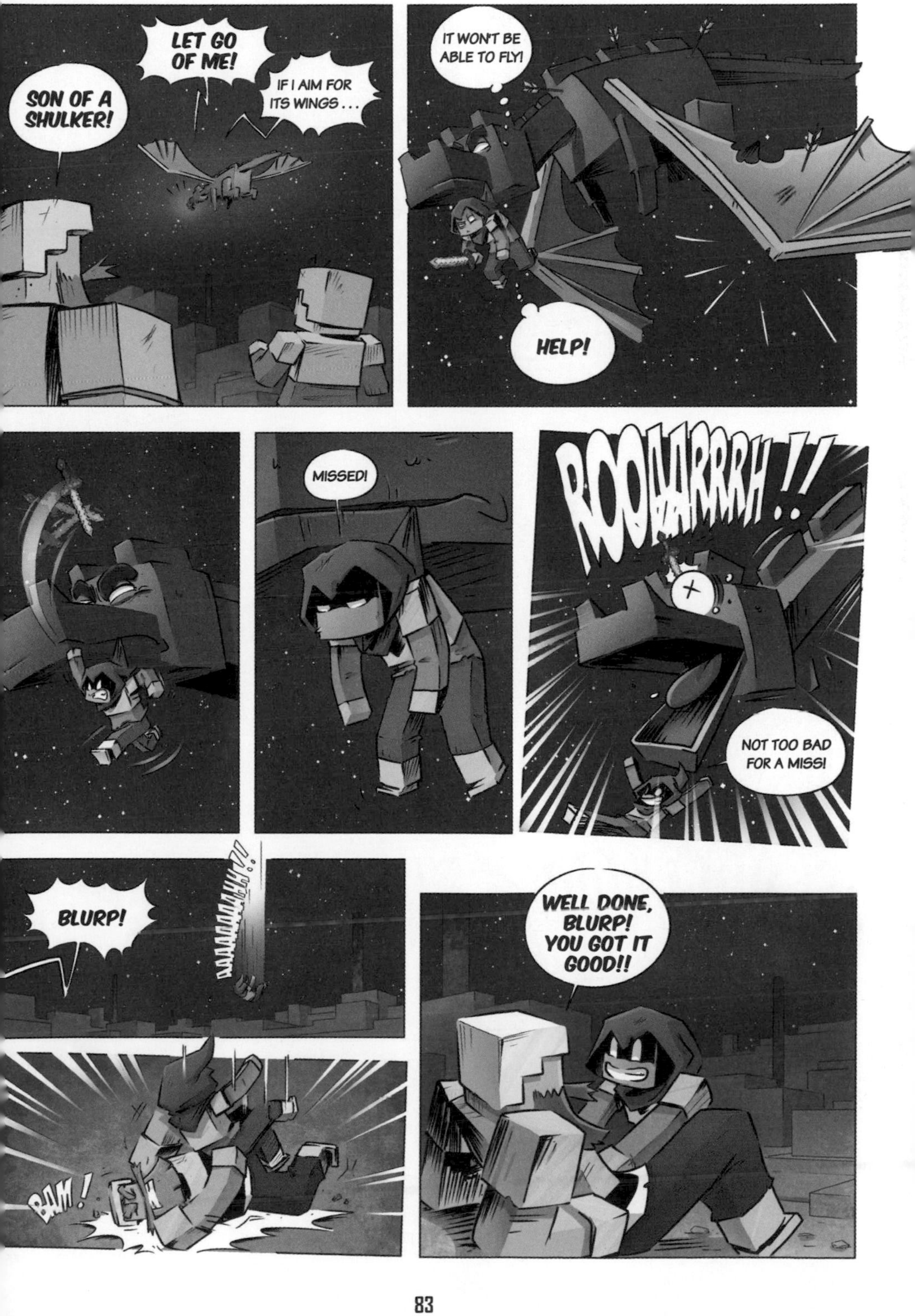
SON OF A SHULKER!
LET GO OF ME!
IF I AIM FOR ITS WINGS . . .
IT WON'T BE ABLE TO FLY!
HELP!
MISSED!
ROOAARRRH !!
NOT TOO BAD FOR A MISS!
BLURP!
AAAAAAAAHH!!
BAM!
WELL DONE, BLURP! YOU GOT IT GOOD!!

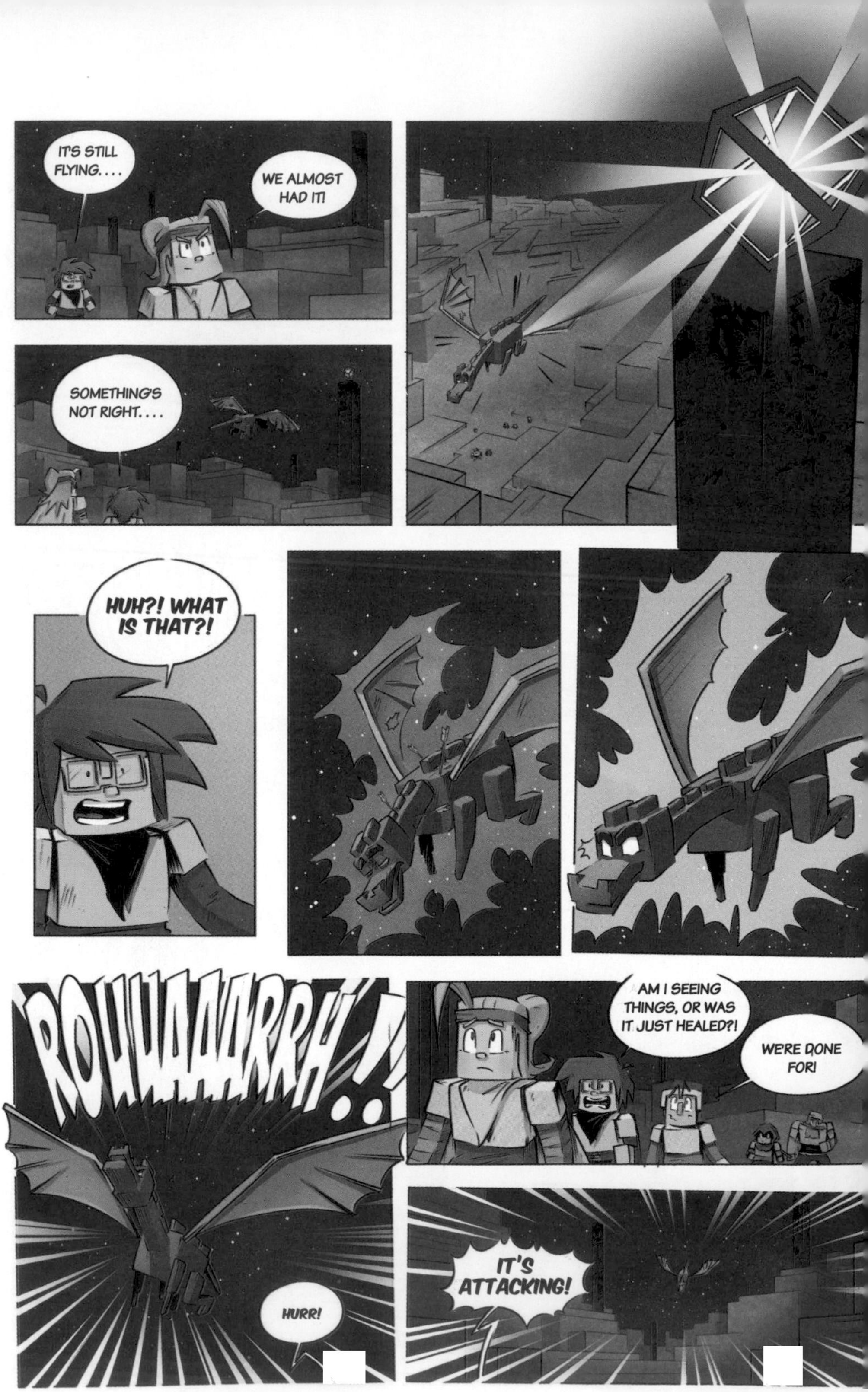
IT'S STILL FLYING....
WE ALMOST HAD IT!
SOMETHING'S NOT RIGHT....
HUH?! WHAT IS THAT?!
ROUUAAARRH..!!
HURR!
AM I SEEING THINGS, OR WAS IT JUST HEALED?!
WE'RE DONE FOR!
IT'S ATTACKING!

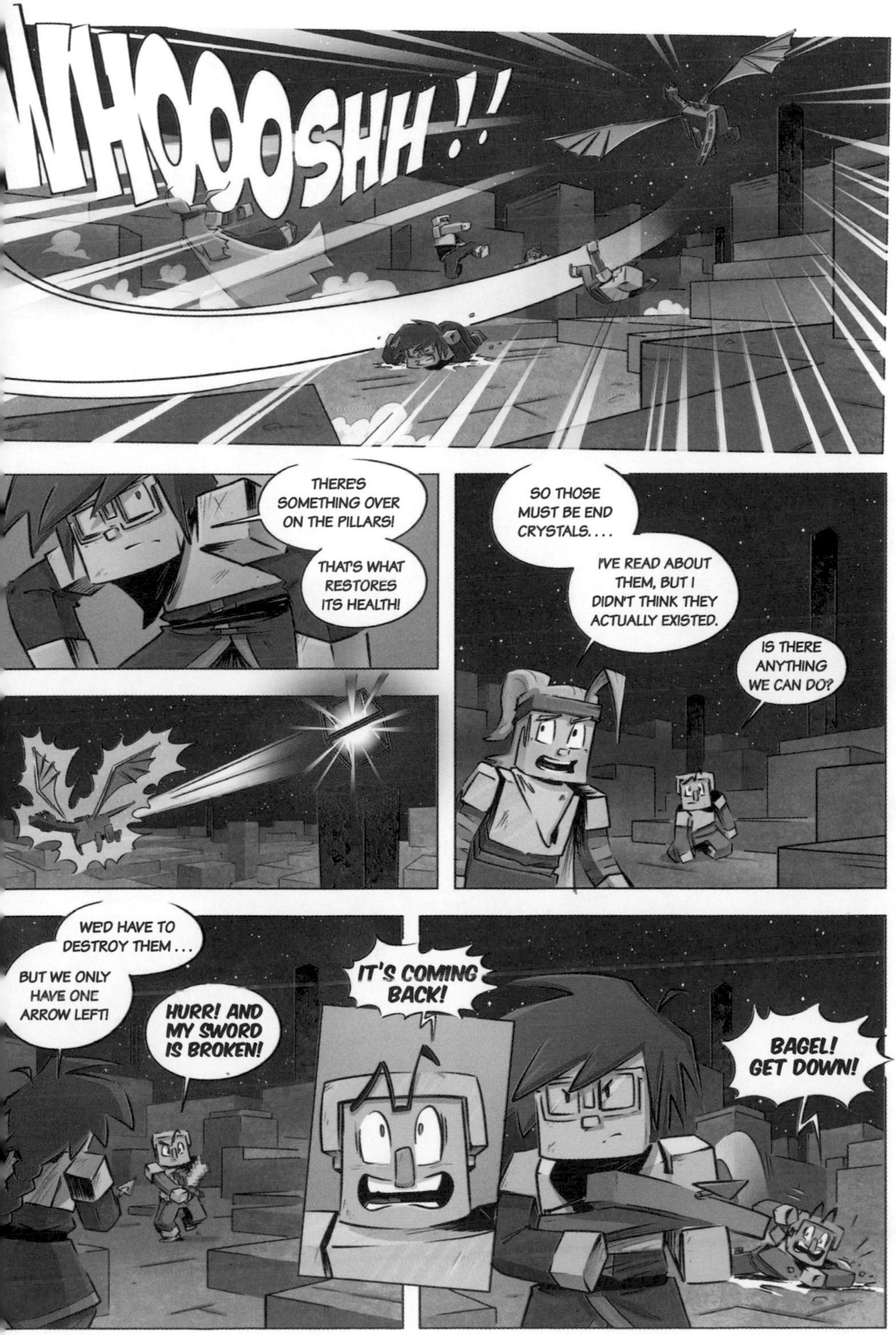
WHOOOOSHH!!
THERE'S SOMETHING OVER ON THE PILLARS!
THAT'S WHAT RESTORES ITS HEALTH!
SO THOSE MUST BE END CRYSTALS. . . .
I'VE READ ABOUT THEM, BUT I DIDN'T THINK THEY ACTUALLY EXISTED.
IS THERE ANYTHING WE CAN DO?
WE'D HAVE TO DESTROY THEM . . .
BUT WE ONLY HAVE ONE ARROW LEFT!
HURR! AND MY SWORD IS BROKEN!
IT'S COMING BACK!
BAGEL! GET DOWN!

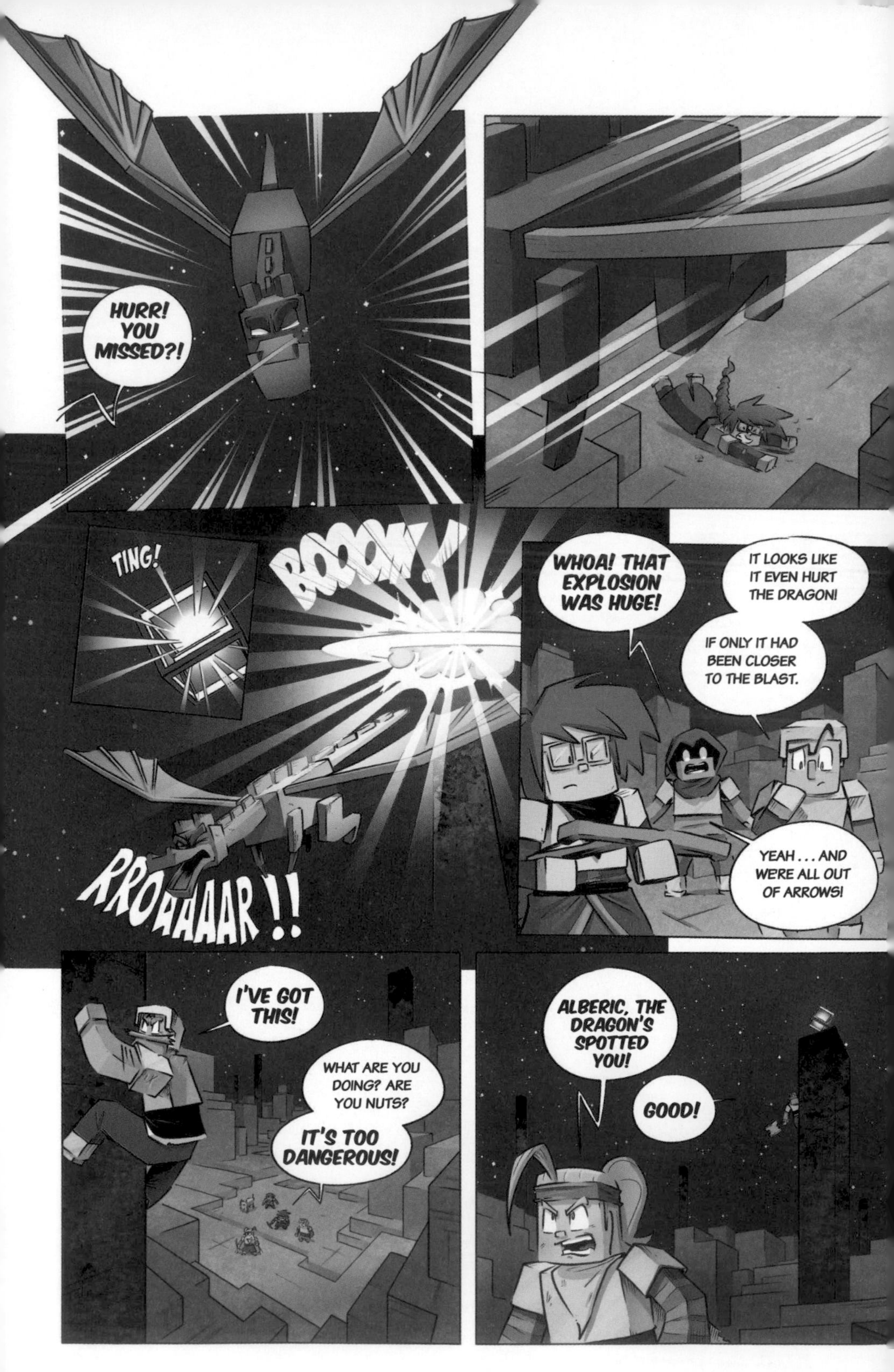
HURR! YOU MISSED?!
TING!
BOOOM!!
RROAAAAR!!
WHOA! THAT EXPLOSION WAS HUGE!
IT LOOKS LIKE IT EVEN HURT THE DRAGON!
IF ONLY IT HAD BEEN CLOSER TO THE BLAST.
YEAH . . . AND WE'RE ALL OUT OF ARROWS!
I'VE GOT THIS!
WHAT ARE YOU DOING? ARE YOU NUTS?
IT'S TOO DANGEROUS!
ALBERIC, THE DRAGON'S SPOTTED YOU!
GOOD!

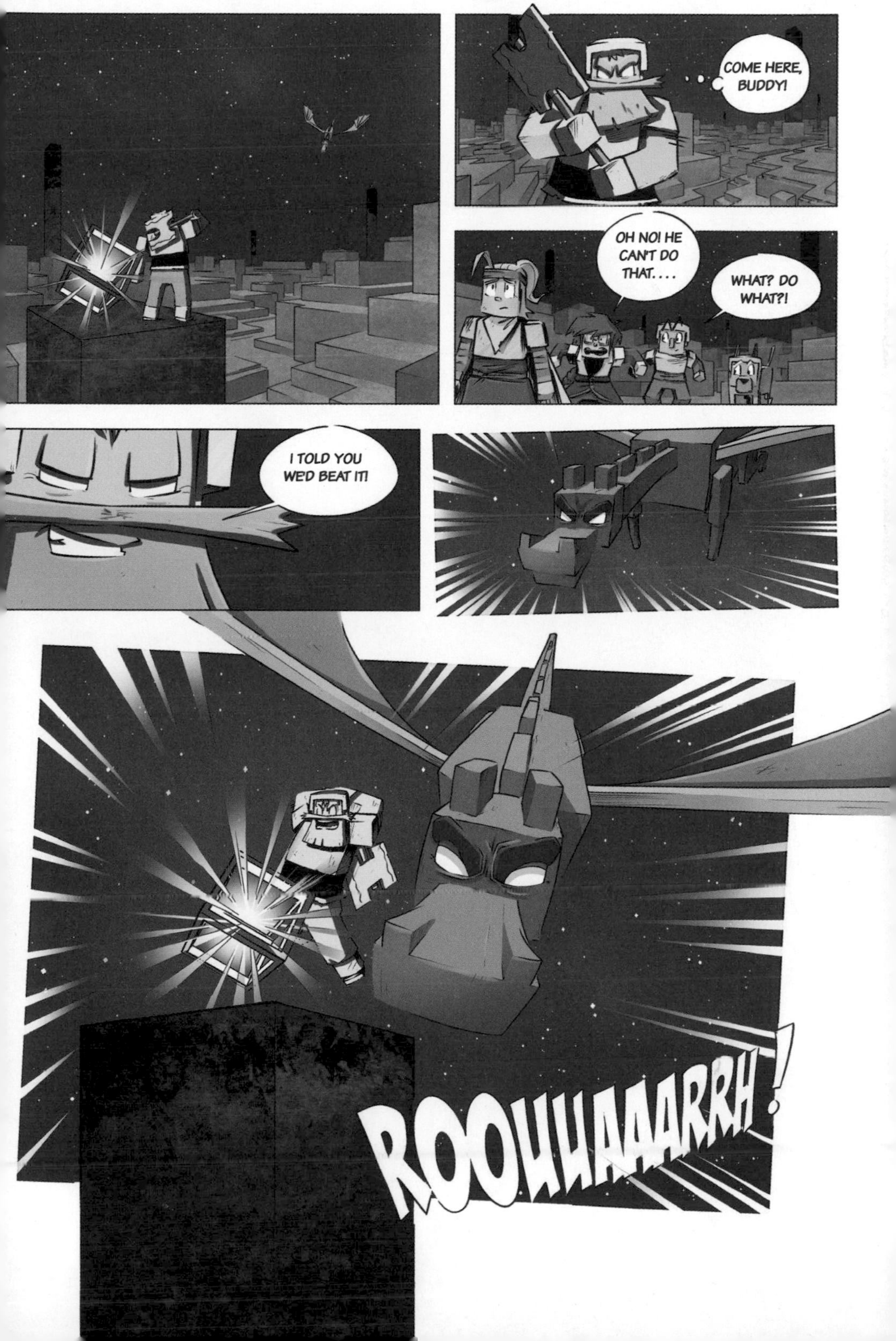
COME HERE, BUDDY!
OH NO! HE CAN'T DO THAT. . . .
WHAT? DO WHAT?!
I TOLD YOU WE'D BEAT IT!
ROOUUAAARRH!

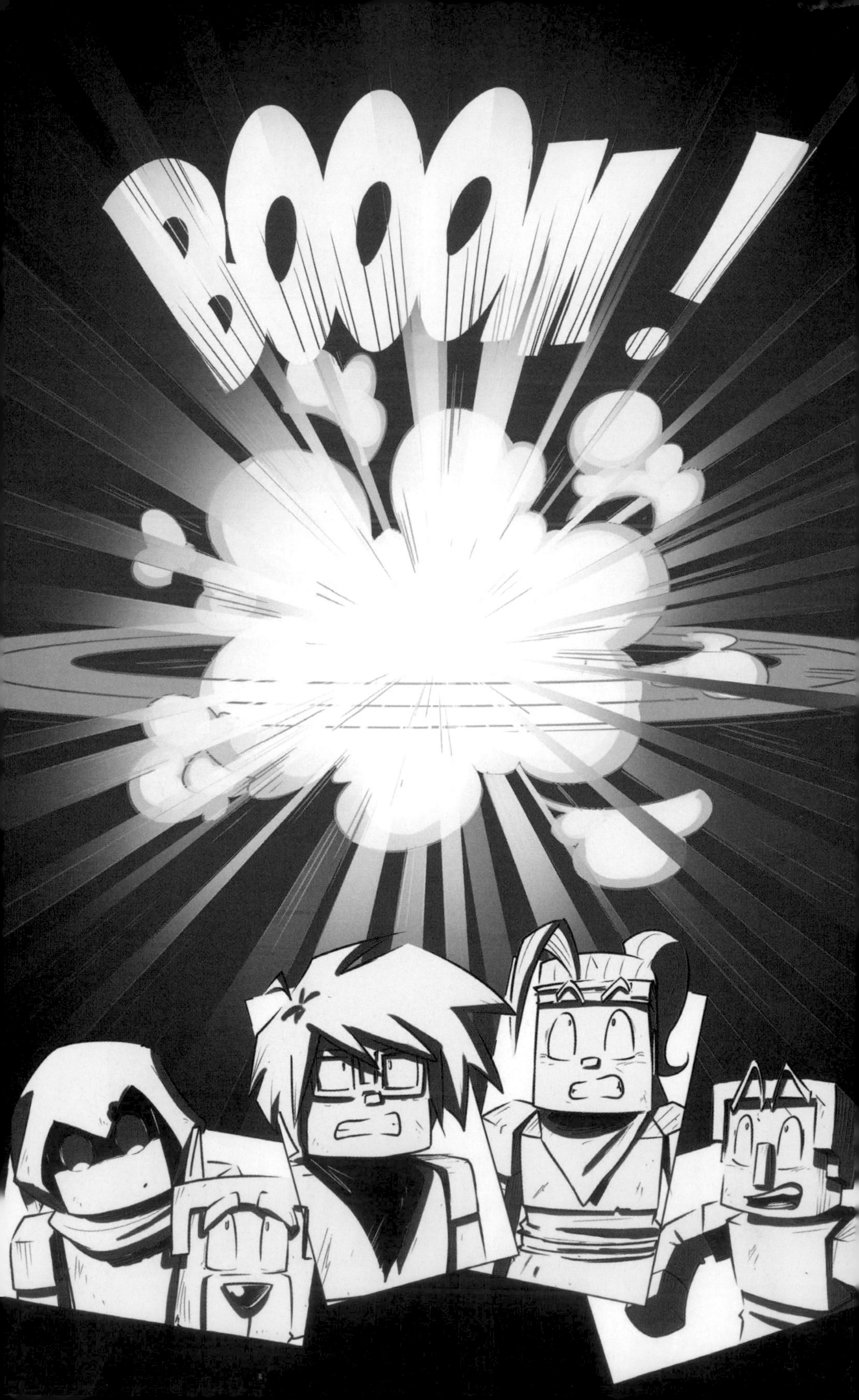
BOOOM!

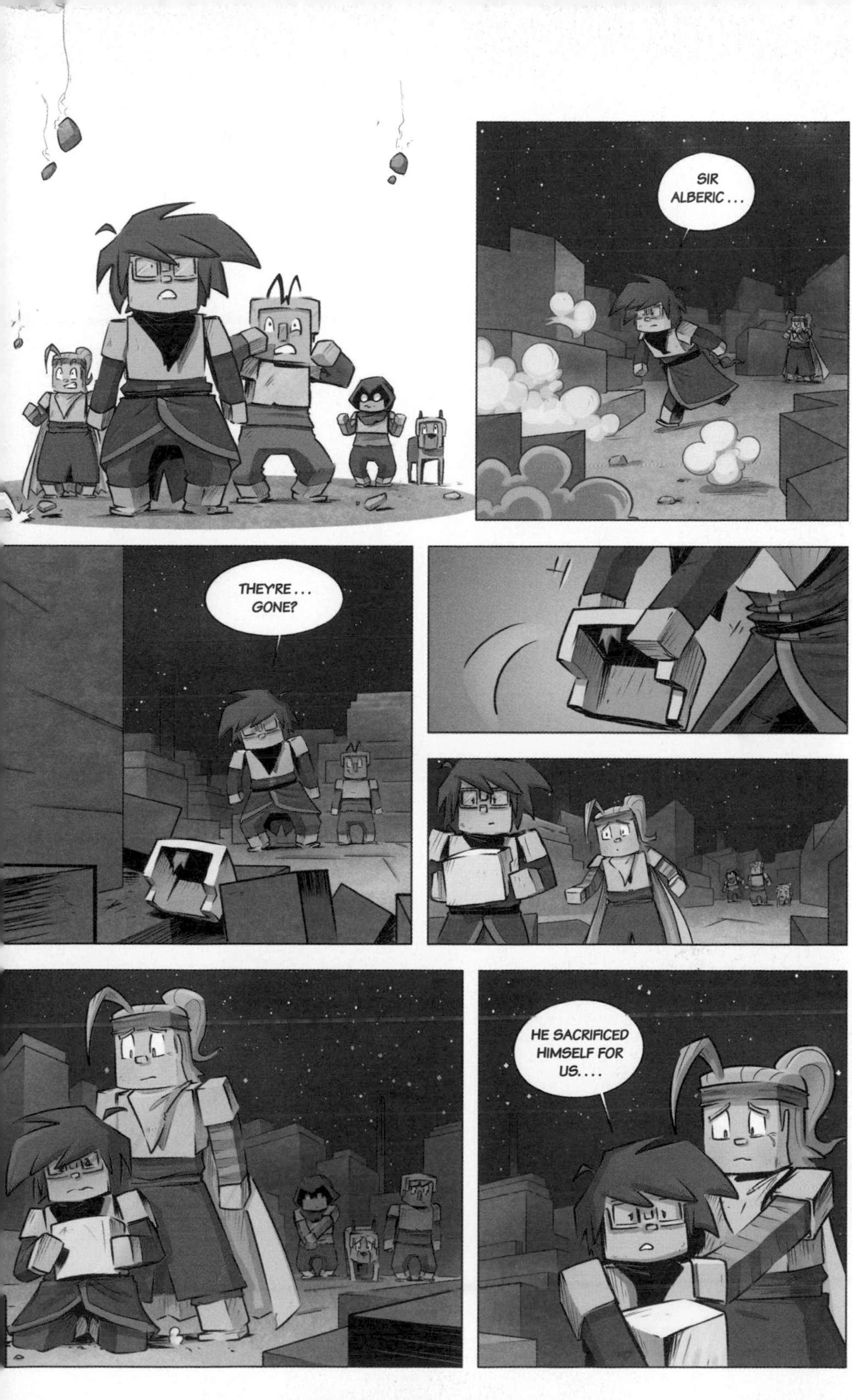
SIR ALBERIC . . .
THEY'RE . . . GONE?
HE SACRIFICED HIMSELF FOR US. . . .

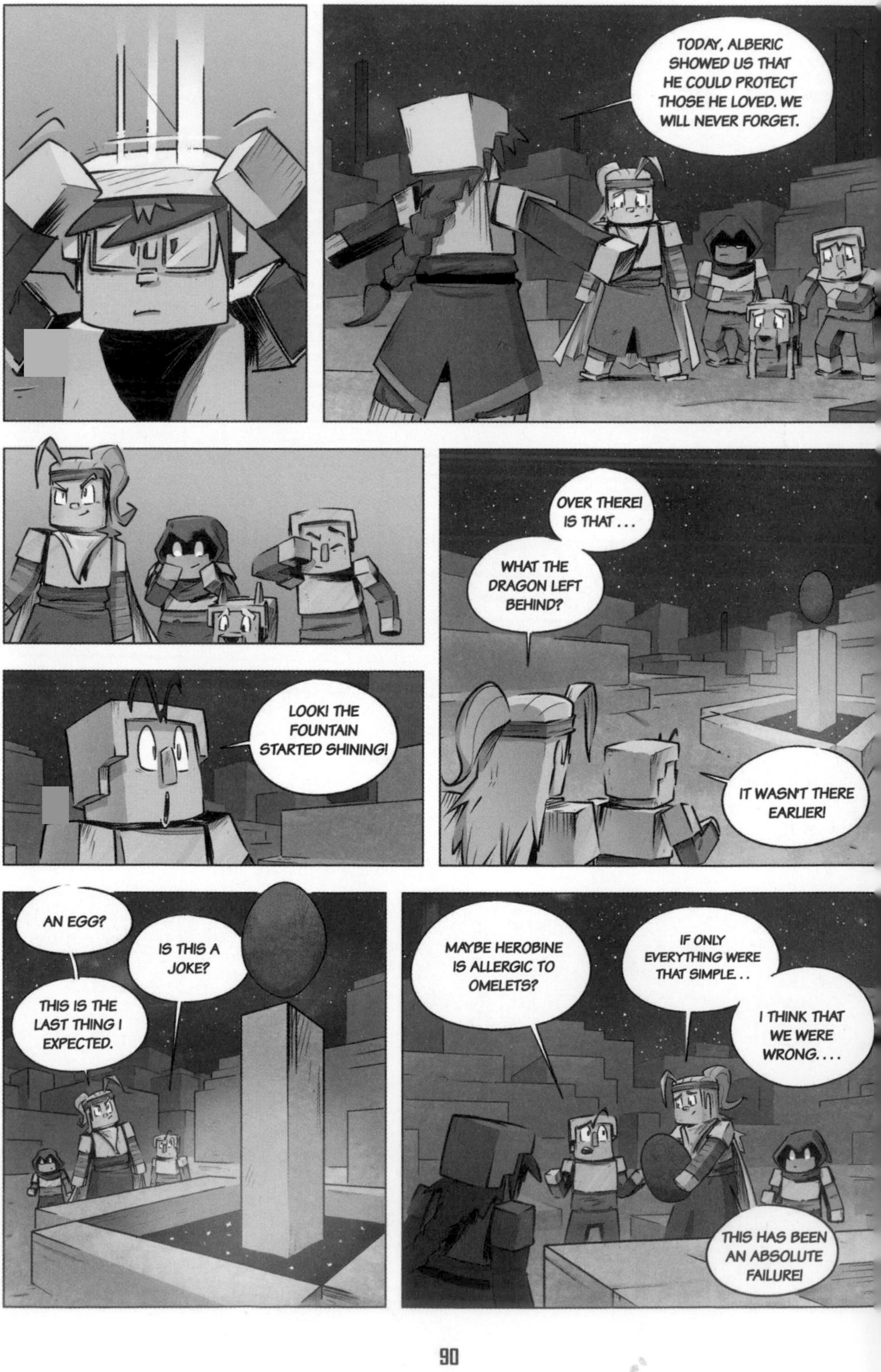
TODAY, ALBERIC SHOWED US THAT HE COULD PROTECT THOSE HE LOVED. WE WILL NEVER FORGET.
OVER THERE! IS THAT . . .
WHAT THE DRAGON LEFT BEHIND?
LOOK! THE FOUNTAIN STARTED SHINING!
IT WASN'T THERE EARLIER!
AN EGG?
IS THIS A JOKE?
THIS IS THE LAST THING I EXPECTED.
MAYBE HEROBINE IS ALLERGIC TO OMELETS?
IF ONLY EVERYTHING WERE THAT SIMPLE. . .
I THINK THAT WE WERE WRONG. . . .
THIS HAS BEEN AN ABSOLUTE FAILURE!

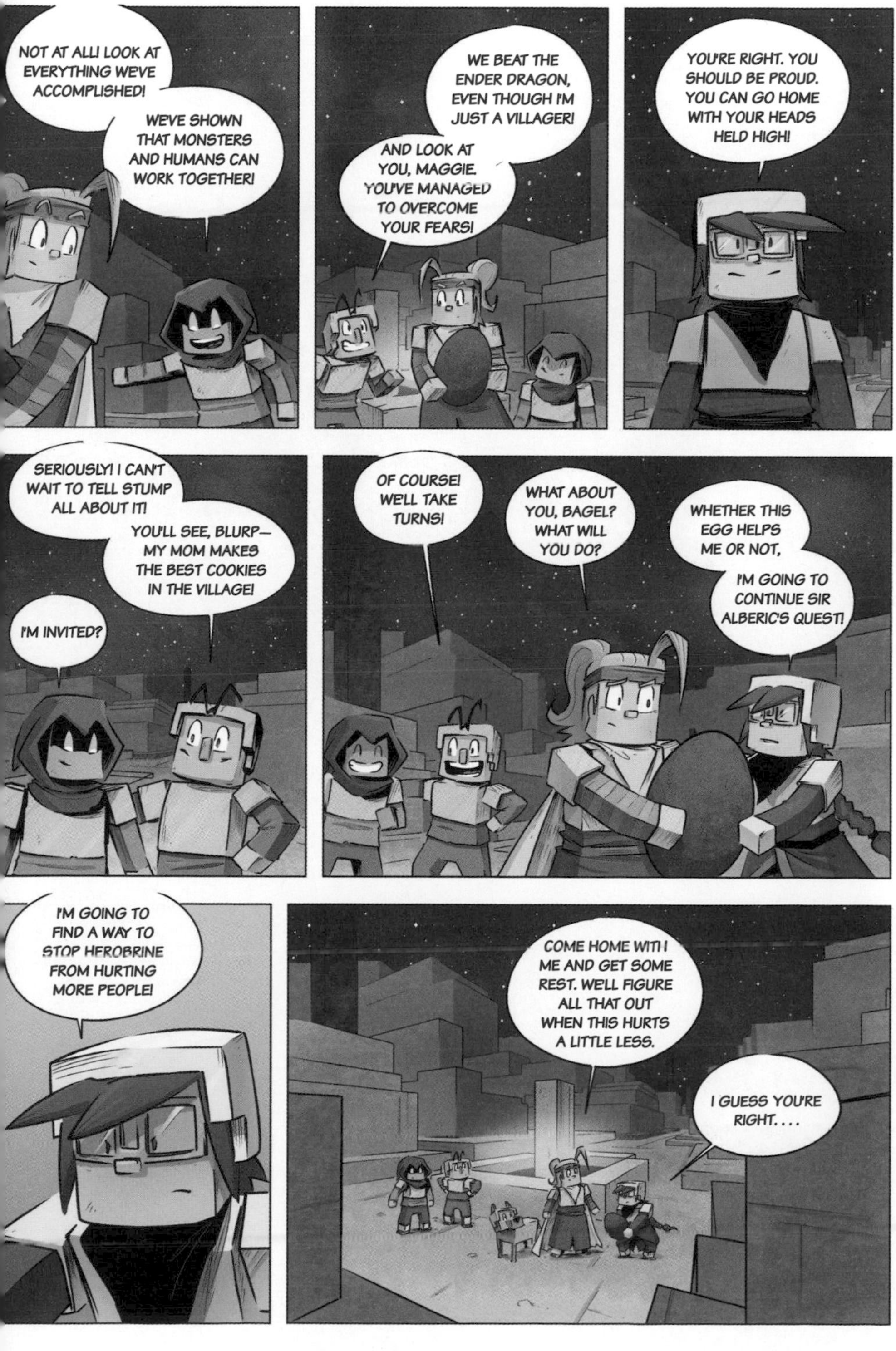
NOT AT ALL! LOOK AT EVERYTHING WE'VE ACCOMPLISHED!
WE'VE SHOWN THAT MONSTERS AND HUMANS CAN WORK TOGETHER!
WE BEAT THE ENDER DRAGON, EVEN THOUGH I'M JUST A VILLAGER!
AND LOOK AT YOU, MAGGIE. YOU'VE MANAGED TO OVERCOME YOUR FEARS!
YOU'RE RIGHT. YOU SHOULD BE PROUD. YOU CAN GO HOME WITH YOUR HEADS HELD HIGH!
SERIOUSLY! I CAN'T WAIT TO TELL STUMP ALL ABOUT IT!
YOU'LL SEE, BLURP— MY MOM MAKES THE BEST COOKIES IN THE VILLAGE!
I'M INVITED?
OF COURSE! WE'LL TAKE TURNS!
WHAT ABOUT YOU, BAGEL? WHAT WILL YOU DO?
WHETHER THIS EGG HELPS ME OR NOT,
I'M GOING TO CONTINUE SIR ALBERIC'S QUEST!
I'M GOING TO FIND A WAY TO STOP HEROBRINE FROM HURTING MORE PEOPLE!
COME HOME WITH ME AND GET SOME REST. WE'LL FIGURE ALL THAT OUT WHEN THIS HURTS A LITTLE LESS.
I GUESS YOU'RE RIGHT. . . .

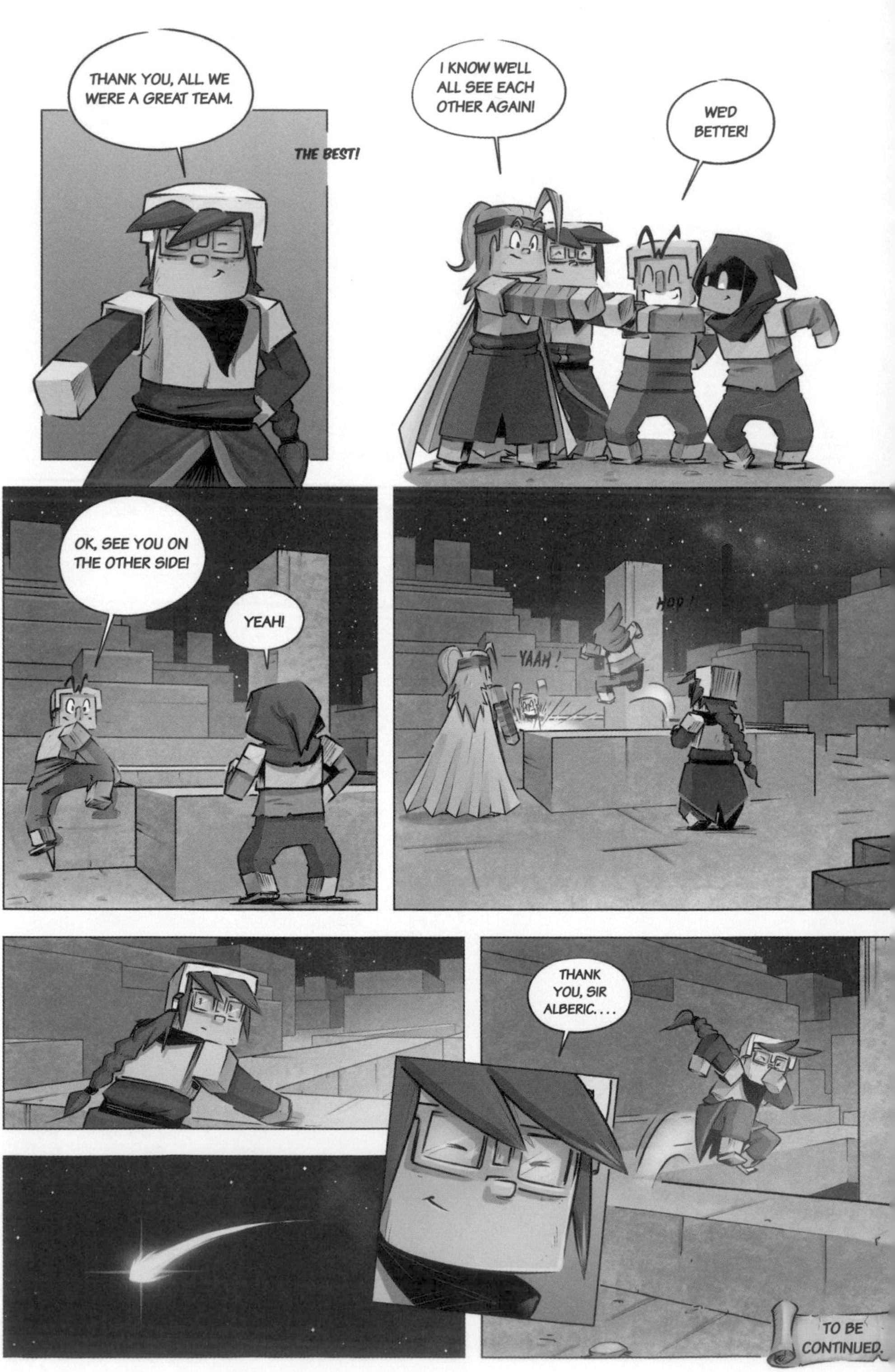
THANK YOU, ALL. WE WERE A GREAT TEAM.
THE BEST!
I KNOW WE'LL ALL SEE EACH OTHER AGAIN!
WE'D BETTER!
OK, SEE YOU ON THE OTHER SIDE!
YEAH!
YAAH!
HOP!
THANK YOU, SIR ALBERIC. . . .
TO BE CONTINUED.

ABOUT THE AUTHORS

PIRATE SOURCIL is a comic book author known for his blog and his comic series *Le Joueur du grenier*, published by Hugo BD. He is also a fan of geek literature and passionate about the world of gaming.

After studying carpentry, **JEZ** turned to drawing and graphic design and decided to make a career out of it.

ODONE is a French illustrator and specializes in adding color to many comic books.

DIARY OF AN 8-BIT WARRIOR

DIARY OF AN 8-BIT VILLAGER WARRIOR

Runt, the villager who wants to be a warrior (like Steve)

CUBE KID
ILLUSTRATED BY SABOTEN
AN UNOFFICIAL MINECRAFT ADVENTURE

DIARY OF AN 8-BIT WARRIOR
FROM SEEDS TO SWORDS

The continuing adventures of Runt, the villager turned warrior

CUBE KID
ILLUSTRATED BY SABOTEN
AN UNOFFICIAL MINECRAFT ADVENTURE

DIARY OF AN 8-BIT WARRIOR
CRAFTING ALLIANCES

Adventures continues for Runt, the village warrior

CUBE KID
ILLUSTRATED BY SABOTEN
AN UNOFFICIAL MINECRAFT ADVENTURE

DIARY OF AN 8-BIT WARRIOR
PATH OF THE DIAMOND

CUBE KID
ILLUSTRATED BY SABOTEN
AN UNOFFICIAL MINECRAFT ADVENTURE

DIARY OF AN 8-BIT WARRIOR
QUEST MODE

CUBE KID
ILLUSTRATED BY SABOTEN
AN UNOFFICIAL MINECRAFT ADVENTURE

DIARY OF AN 8-BIT WARRIOR
FORGING DESTINY

CUBE KID
ILLUSTRATED BY SABOTEN
AN UNOFFICIAL MINECRAFT ADVENTURE

AND MEET EEEBS, THE MOST NOOBIEST CAT IN THE OVERWORLD!

TALES OF AN 8-BIT KITTEN
LOST IN THE NETHER

Follow the adventures of Eeebs, the noobiest cat in all of Minecraft.

CUBE KID
ILLUSTRATED BY RICHARD "SABOT" SABOTEN
AN UNOFFICIAL MINECRAFT ADVENTURE

TALES OF AN 8-BIT KITTEN
A CALL TO ARMS

See what happens next to Eeebs, the most disobedient cat in all of Minecraft.

CUBE KID
ILLUSTRATED BY RICHARD "SABOT" SABOTEN
AN UNOFFICIAL MINECRAFT ADVENTURE

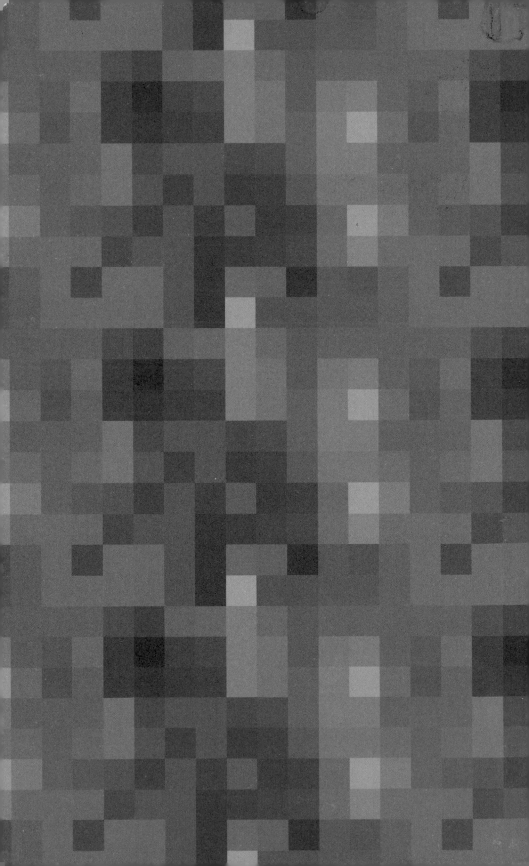